SMOKE ON
THE WATER

Rae Stewart

Book layout © 2016 BookDesignTemplates.com
Cover design by Simon Avery at idobookcovers.com © 2023
Smoke on the Water/Rae Stewart. - 1st ed.
ISBN 9798376794111

It's out there.

ABOUT THE AUTHOR

Rae Stewart worked as a reporter for ITN, GMTV, Sky News and Scottish Television for more than twenty years before becoming a communications consultant in 2009. He lives in London with his family.

You can follow Rae on Twitter @MrRaeStewart

Other novels by Rae Stewart

THE VIBE
BORN TO BE WILD
BAD MOON RISING
IF YOU WANT BLOOD
WELCOME TO THE JUNGLE
MORE THAN A FEELING
PROBLEM CHILD
PURPLE HAZE

Contents

CHAPTER ONE

Sound the alarm

Deep Purple killed Mike Jennings.

Although maybe that's a bit unfair. After all, it wasn't a bunch of '70s rockers with bad hair and greasy jeans who slammed a ball hammer into his temple, stuck big stones in his pockets and dumped him in one of the deepest bodies of water in western Europe.

But still.

If Mike Jennings hadn't been listening to 'Smoke on the Water' on his headphones, turned way up to 11, he might have noticed the alarm. And if he'd noticed the alarm, he might have been able to stop everything escalating so quickly. Things might have ended very differently.

But he didn't notice. And it escalated. Which ended up with him sitting on the bottom of Loch Ness being very dead.

So, maybe Deep Purple should bear at least some of the responsibility here.

The frigging alarm. He was supposed to listen out for it, instead of being deeply engrossed in a throbbing bass line, crunchy guitars, and a particularly fascinating digital display of soil analysis from the loch bed.

Anyway, it's more likely he'd have heard the alarm if he hadn't set it to 'mute' about an hour earlier. It was habit. Mainly because it always scared the hell out of him when it went off late at night while he was working. It went off far more often than it should, and it was always for boring reasons.

So, as he sat gazing at his computer screen in the large, empty laboratory, reviewing the day's results, alarm muted, halfway through his third can of particularly zesty craft IPA, he was oblivious.

Oblivious to the alarm, and oblivious to the tall man in a dark waxed coat who'd slipped through the lab door and was creeping up behind his chair, arms outstretched.

Just as Mike was about to copy over some crucial figures into an open document, the intruder's fingers stretched towards his neck. Inches away, closer and closer. Close enough that the intruder could see the fine hairs on the back of Mike's neck. The hands hesitated for a moment, fingers flexing, then darted out and snatched his headphones off.

"Haaaaaaaaah!" yelled a voice in Mike's ear.

Mike yelled back, almost spilling off his seat before getting a grip on his shattered wits, leaping up and trying to punch his attacker in the guts.

"You really are a dozy melt, aren't you," his attacker said, dodging the punch and laughing. "I could have been anybody."

"Not funny, Jules," Mike said, pointing a finger in the other man's face. "Not funny at all. Probably soiled myself. Again."

Dr. Julian Conway sniggered and flopped down on a swivel chair, sliding it up to Mike's desk. He'd been out at the local pub while Mike went through the results from the latest bore holes they'd drilled in the loch bed. He peered at the computer screen.

"Anything interesting so far?"

"Seriously, Jules, it's completely out of order. You could give me a stroke one of these days."

"I'm not really that kind of boss," Jules said. "More a hearty handshake kind of guy." He started tapping at Mike's keyboard. "Anyway, what've you got for us?"

"Nothing major. Couple of anomalies in the third set," Mike said, still struggling to get his breathing under control. "Not sure if it means anything yet."

"May as well call it a night, then," Jules said, pushing long hair out of his face. "Although there is one more thing."

He reached out very deliberately, hovering his finger above the F2 button on Mike's keyboard. He grinned up at Mike. As his finger plunged down, the whole lab filled with an excruciating wail.

"Jesus!" Mike shouted, grabbing at his ears.

The alarm. Or, more specifically, the un-muted alarm. The one he was supposed to listen out for.

Mike pushed past Jules and thumped his finger down on the mute button again, his heart hammering.

"Saw the warning light flashing in the corridor," Jules said, sitting back and putting his hands behind his head. "You're not supposed to turn the sound off. You know that."

"Yeah, I know, I know, but it does my head in. There's always something getting into the holding tank. Salmon, seal, whatever. Pisses me off. Complete waste of time."

"Fine, but you know who pays our wages. And he wants the alarm on."

"He's never going to know, is he? We haven't told him the last three times it's gone off, so why would we bother now? You know there's nothing out there, I know there's nothing out there, so why should we bother with this stupid charade?"

"Oh, for God's sake. Just because, alright? Don't keep making everything into a battle between you and 'the Man', okay? Anyway, we're going to have to check it out."

Mike edged Jules out of the way, grabbed his mouse, minimized a couple of pages then clicked the icon allowing him access to the building's CCTV system. Nine boxes appeared on his screen, all of them grainy and murky.

"Can't really see much with just the security lights on," he huffed, looking at Jules.

"Brilliant. Well?"

"Well, one of us has got to go down there."

"I outrank you."

"I've been working harder than you."

"I've got my best shoes on."

"They're shitty old Converses! Not exactly...those posh shoes, whatever they're called. Anyway, I'm tired."

"And I'm drunk. It's dangerous for me to go down all those stairs."

"Oh, for God's sake." Mike grabbed a coat from the back of his chair and headed out of the lab, then down a long white corridor to a security door at the end. He swiped his card on the reader, pushing through the door when it clicked unlocked. Then down four flights of clanging metal stairs to the basement, which housed the huge internal holding tank containing thousands of gallons of fresh loch water.

The tank was linked to an external harbour butted onto the building, jutting out into the loch. Movement sensors on automatic underwater gates allowed creatures of significant size to swim into the harbour, and then into the internal tank, but they couldn't get back out again unless let out by staff.

The alarm in the lab went off every time the automatic gates were triggered, and Mike was fed up with it. In the past month he'd had to spend ages guiding two seals back out of the tank, as well as trying to catch numerous salmon in long-handled nets. He was fed up with eating them too. There were only so many ways to make salmon interesting. Anyway, he was a serious scientist, not a fish wrangler.

Two and a half minutes later, Mike's desk-phone started ringing. Jules leant over and looked at the ID screen. An internal call. He snatched up the handset.

"Sceptics R Us, how may I help you?" he said in a sing-song voice.

"Get down here," Mike said, his voice tight, strained. "There's......just get down here. Right now. You're not going to believe this."

He slammed the phone onto its cradle and rushed back to the tank to have another wide-eyed look.

Jules sped down there in a couple of minutes, worried at the weirdness in Mike's voice.

Now both of them stood at the side of the water tank staring in, their mouths moving but words failing to form. Their eyes were stuck, unable to move away from what they were looking at. Something that just shouldn't be there.

"You know what this means, don't you?" Jules said eventually, his voice quiet and shaky. He reached his arm around Mike's shoulders. "I think we're about to be famous. Properly stupidly famous. Buckle up, Mikey boy – your name's about to appear in the newspapers."

Well, yes. But that's not always a good thing.

CHAPTER TWO

Welcome to Loch Ness

It's funny how tales grow in the telling. It all seemed quite simple at first. A local news website based in Inverness reported that two scientists were suspected to have drowned after their empty research boat was found drifting on Loch Ness in poor weather conditions.

But by the time the national newspapers wrote it up a day later, the focus of the story had changed somewhat. Or, as one particularly excitable tabloid put it:

HAS NESSIE KILLED?

To which the answer was almost certainly 'no'.

But that didn't stop similar headlines blaring out at Zander Burns as he grabbed a selection of newspapers at Inverness airport soon after landing on the early flight from Luton.

He'd dashed north as fast as he could, despatched by his boss, the Vice-Chancellor of Addington University. As the PR man for the university which employed the missing scientists, Zander's instructions were straightforward - get to Loch Ness and liaise with the authorities and the media. And, most importantly, limit any damage to Addington's reputation.

The potential battering of the university's image was set out in stark terms by the Vice-Chancellor on the phone the previous evening. The key point was that the police said privately there was evidence both men were drunk. And the scientists were essentially representing the university – they'd made a big deal of their loan to the vast NessieWorld theme park being built on the shores of Loch Ness. So, the idea that they died on an ill-judged, late night, drunken boat ride didn't exactly smack of academic professionalism. And that could make the university look bad. It was Zander's job to make sure it didn't.

He scanned the stories as his taxi swerved him around the edge of Inverness and down the loch shore to the village of Drumnadrochit. He hardly noticed the spectacular scenery passing by his window, the purple heather blooming on the hills in early Spring sunshine. His mind was utterly focused on the task ahead.

One tabloid summed up the approach many of the newspapers had taken.

Two Nessie-hunters who vowed to catch the monster are believed to have become its first ever victims.

Research boffins Julian Conway and Michael Jennings disappeared after taking their boat out onto the mist-covered loch late on Monday evening.

Their abandoned craft was found drifting by a local fisherman yesterday morning. Local Nessie experts now fear the monster has killed for the first time.

"It wouldn't surprise me if Nessie has done for these lads," said one local man who asked not to be named. "She's bound to be fed up with all these folk trying to find her, sticking probes and sonars and whatnot into the loch. Maybe Nessie's fighting back."

Local police will only say that the scientists are missing, presumed dead. But sources close to the investigation say there are big questions about the men's disappearance.

It's believed they were involved in secret research at the multi-billion-pound NessieWorld theme park, due to open this summer. Local speculation suggests they were trying to find proof of the Loch Ness monster's existence – perhaps even trying to catch Nessie herself as a centrepiece for the new theme park.

NessieWorld's controversial owner, the former MP and strip-club baron Frank Fisher, was unavailable for comment at his luxury villa overlooking Loch Ness last night.

The theme park has been beset by a number of delays and disputes. Following this latest tragic incident, local people are now questioning whether the whole project is cursed.

Zander threw the paper down on the seat next to him. Utter garbage. The men weren't hunting a monster - they were analysing soil samples. They were DNA experts, but it had nothing to do with finding mythical beasts. Yes, okay, they were prepared – indeed, encouraged - to ham it up a bit for the media when the theme park had first approached the university to get some scientists on board. The university knew it was being used, but it was a two-way thing. NessieWorld got some white-coated respectability attached to it, and the university got a big injection of much needed research money – and a higher profile. Everyone was happy.

Except no-one's happy now. Two men are missing, probably dead.

They were decent men, Jules and Mike. Zander was responsible for giving them media training when the link-up between the university and the theme park was announced. How to dodge tricky questions about finding the monster without completely trashing the idea that one existed, that sort of thing. Playing the game.

Decent, ordinary blokes – for scientists. Good company. He'd taken them out to celebrate after all the media interviews a couple of years ago. An excellent night. So although he didn't know them that well, it was well enough to feel sick at their likely deaths.

He dragged his overnight bag from the taxi. The Drumnadrochit Arms was a small but sturdy Victorian mansion set in the middle of the village. As he was about to go in, he noticed an old woman shuffling out into what was a relatively busy road.

Zander dropped his bag and rushed over, waving at an oncoming car to slow down. He reached for the woman's arm.

"Can I just help you a bit there, my love?" he said, bending down towards her, smiling.

"Hands off, pervert!" the woman said, snatching her arm back and continuing to cross. "I know all about your type. Sex, sex, sex, that's all you think about. Well, these bones don't come cheap, so you can forget all about jumping them."

She shuffled to the other side, leaving Zander in the middle of the road with his arms out, mouth open, baffled.

A toot from a slowing car jerked him back to life, and he retreated back to the pavement. The old woman, now safely on the pavement on the other side of the road, blocked the way of a middle-aged couple in matching blue plastic macs and pointed over towards Zander.

"Watch that one," she said. "One of those sex addicts. Can't help themselves. Rutting away like there's no tomorrow. Look at him – he can barely stand. Exhausted from pestering clean, God-fearing folk like myself for all sorts of dirtiness."

Zander ducked into the hotel as the couple stared over at him, shaking their heads.

He felt a bit disorientated as he dumped his bag beside the small reception desk, trying to work out what he'd done wrong.

"I see you've met Bessie, then?" said the receptionist.

Zander looked up at her. She had cool, grey eyes, very pale skin, black hair cut short at the sides. Rings pierced her nose and left ear. Crisp, white shirt, tartan waistcoat and skirt. She frowned and cocked her head, making clear she expected an answer.

"I saw you out the window," she said, in case that helped.

"Oh, the old lady?" Zander said. "I was just trying to help her across the road. It seemed a bit dangerous for her to be doing it by herself."

"And did she accuse you of a specific sex crime, or was it a more general sex thing?"

"More general. Definitely more general. Not that I was actually...." Zander trailed off, not sure where he was going with this.

"It's okay, it just means she likes you," the receptionist said. "If she accuses you of something specific, that's where the trouble starts. The police and all that. Letters to the Queen. Anyway, how can I help?"

"I've got a reservation. Burns. Zander Burns."

The receptionist raised a finely drawn eyebrow at him. He reminded her a bit of that posh bloke on TV who lived on that island on the west coast, then rowed naked across the Atlantic. Although not on the same programme. Tall, healthy-looking, blondish hair. She tried not to picture him nude with an oar in his hand.

"Zander?"

"Yes. The booking might be under Addington University."

The receptionist's face fell immediately. She looked down, suddenly fascinated by the keyboard she was tapping at.

"Ah, yes – here it is. So, you're here because of the ....?" She paused, looking up.

"The accident, yes."

She shook her head.

"It's awful - such a shame. They were pretty much regulars in the bar here. Really nice guys, both of them. Did you know them?"

"Well," Zander said slowly, "I'm kind of hoping I still do. That they're still alive."

"Of course," the receptionist said quickly. "Sorry, I didn't mean to give the impression that....it's just, what people are saying around here."

"It's fine – I know it doesn't look good. But I have to hope. And where there's hope... But to answer your question, yes, I do know them. And you're absolutely right - good guys."

"Sorry. Again," she said, cheeks slightly flushed, looking down at her hands. "Christ, I'm really not very good at this front-of-house stuff - I'm just filling in today. Here's your key. You're on the second floor." She nodded towards double doors to the side of the reception desk. "Breakfast is through there, seven thirty until ten during the week."

Then she made a quick escape through a door at the back of reception marked 'Staff Only', letting the door thump closed behind her. Zander was left to guess which room he was in from the worn number on the plastic key fob in his hand.

The first thing he did when he eventually got into his tired chintz and tartan room was check in with his boss, the university's Vice-Chancellor, Richard Gladwell.

"All a bit messy, frankly," Gladwell said once Zander got him on the line. "Absolute tragedy about these poor boys – Julian's work in particular was a great credit to the university. World-leading stuff. But to get pissed up and go for a joy ride in the research boat in the middle of the night? What on earth were they thinking? It's really not how you expect two of your top scientific researchers to behave, especially on something as high profile as this. It's really not how we want to be seen."

"Quite. Who's with the families?"

"Oliver's handling all of that side of things. He'll be in touch.

Oh, and we've arranged for you to meet the local police later this morning, and then you're down to see the man who owns the theme park, this Frank Fisher character. I suspect you know all about him. Anyway, it's worth knowing that I've had a chat with the Chancellor and we both agree that it would be best if the university's name and our involvement in this whole theme park endeavour wasn't mentioned in the press from now on. I mean, it's not really necessary to drag us into all of this, is it? A tragic accident, after all."

"That's going to be difficult. Jules and Mike are officially our staff, just on secondment to NessieWorld. And it's hardly a secret that we're involved in all of this – there's plenty of material for journalists to re-heat if they want."

"Yes, but the Chancellor feels that their employment status isn't really relevant in the context of the circumstances surrounding the accident. Yes, low profile is the way to go, I think. Not that I need to tell you any of this – you're the public relations expert, after all."

Gladwell chuckled at his own joke. Although it wasn't a joke. More like an order. Zander got the message, although it bugged him like hell.

"I'll do what I can," he said, trying to sound positive. He took down the details about his meetings, then rang off.

He checked his watch. Nearly time to meet the local cops. He swiped through texts and emails on his phone. Four journalists looking for comments. He'd hold them off until he'd had time to talk to the police and get a bit more background. And work out how to persuade them not to mention the university.

But first, a bit of light browsing to remind himself about the bizarre life and career of the man he was due to see later – Frankie 'The Big Fish' Fisher, the self-styled saviour of Scottish tourism.

CHAPTER THREE

The Big Fish

Councillor Gordon Mackay had only seen a barracuda once in real life before. Snorkelling in the Maldives. Him rather than the barracuda.

He clearly remembered the moment he first saw it - perfectly still, just hanging in the water, a long bullet of hard, silver muscle, checking him out. The cold, staring eyes. The jutting jaw. The open mouth revealing rows of small, vicious teeth.

He remembered the way he felt too. The terrifying rush as he wondered whether he was going to be attacked. Shortness of breath, sickness in his belly.

Good holiday, though. Expensive. A silver wedding celebration with Moira. Paid for, ironically enough, by the man sitting across the desk from him. The man who, right now, reminded him of that barracuda. But with a redder face. And a more dangerous bite, potentially.

And he felt the same way as he did on that holiday - the scary bit just before the barracuda got bored and swam away. But Frankie Fisher didn't look like he was going anywhere. And to be fair, they were in Fisher's office, so he probably wasn't.

The silence dragged on. Fisher staring, perfectly still. Councillor Mackay beginning to squirm, sweat leaking out of his pink, shiny head.

When Fisher eventually spoke, he did so in a slow, controlled, calm way. It wasn't like him.

"Gordon. I'm not entirely sure I follow you. There simply cannot be a problem with the operating licence at this late stage. It is impossible. Quite impossible." Fisher shook his head. "It's all been sorted. *You* sorted it. You're the Chair of the Licensing Committee – unless there's been some overnight coup on Inverness City Council that I haven't heard about. It's in your gift. And you sorted it."

"Aye, I know, Frankie. But it's the Convenor. He's decided to call it in for another look. You know what he's like – he loves throwing his weight around, and he's never been a fan of this whole theme park idea. And he's been starting to get a lot of pressure from the hotels and restaurants further north. They think you're going to suck business away from them. They've only just got their act together, acting like a block, a cartel. There's a lot of votes in there, a lot of influence."

"Influence?" Fisher sat back in his big leather chair. "Oh, I suppose that's alright, then. Although, these people with influence – are they going to provide five thousand new jobs for local people? Another ten thousand in the supply chain? Are they?"

Fisher's voice was beginning to rise now, speeding up to his natural fast pace. Getting louder too. Louder, faster, angrier. Normal Frankie Fisher mode.

"Are they going to put millions and millions and millions of pounds into the local economy every year? Are they going to pull in so many people to this miserable cultural wasteland that you won't know what to do with all the cash you've got spilling out your pockets? Are they? Because you know what, Gordon? I don't think they will. I think they'll do what they've always done, providing shitty service in their shitty hovels and serving shitty food to a bunch of low-spending shitheads who'll never come back because they feel ripped off.

"That's what I'm trying to change, you know that. And NessieWorld will make a lot of people very wealthy around here. Who's bringing in that money? Me. No-one else. Not some shitty-arsed B&B owner in Auchterfuck who's married to his sister and hasn't changed the sheets in ten years. It's me. Frankie fucking Fisher esquire. All of it's down to me. And you were the one with the big, swinging dick, telling me you could sort out all the official shite. This is not the time to be going all limp on me, Gordon."

Councillor Mackay swallowed with some difficulty. Fisher always seemed to have that effect on him.

"It's out of my hands, Frankie. I've tried – there's nothing more I can do. Look, if it makes any difference, I can bend a few ears, maybe see if we can make it all go away in the next month or so."

"Too late. Far too late. We're supposed to be soft-launching early summer. I can't have my entire licence to operate hanging in the balance while I'm literally spunking millions of quid into this."

"Well, as I say," Mackay said again, crossing his arms, "there's not much I can do about it."

Frank Fisher went quiet again, the barracuda look back on his face.

"Does our friendship mean nothing to you, Gordon? The last four or five years, we've been pretty tight, wouldn't you say?" Fisher clasped his hands together, squeezing them for emphasis, the effort making a vein pop out on his red forehead. Mackay worried that he was about to burst.

"Well, yes, of course it does, Frankie. You've been very good to us since you came up here, don't think I'll forget that."

"I *have* been good, haven't I? The cars – both you and Moira. The big house in Nairn – you'd have struggled to get a mortgage for that, wouldn't you? The holidays, the golf club fees, your eldest's university fees....do you want me to go on?"

"No, no, you've made your point," said Mackay, holding up his hands. "You've been more than generous, I know that, the whole family appreciates it."

"Oh, don't worry about that," Fisher said, his sharp teeth stretching out into a wide grin. "That's all nothing. It's just...money. It's what friends are for. What good's a friend if they can't do their other friends a favour now and then?"

"Yes, I see where you're going with this, Frankie, but I've done a lot for you. I have. I built up support in the council, in the local press, I spoke up for you when others wouldn't, unblocked it when it was blocked, forced through planning permissions and road diversions and power access and God knows what. I've done my bit – you know I have. I've taken all of this as far as I can. Come on, it was always going to be difficult, something this controversial. This business with the two scientists isn't helping."

Fisher took a long, slow breath and sat back in his chair.

"Maybe you're right," he said. He looked up at the ceiling, around the walls, out the window, seeming to consider it. "Maybe you're right. Maybe it was always going to end up in a dead end like this. Maybe I just thought too big. That's the problem with being a visionary, it's difficult for the little people to see what it is you're aiming for. The stars, Gordon. That's what it's all about. The thrill of success, the glamour. And we had a bit of that glamour, didn't we? At those parties. The *special* parties," he said, smiling, leaning forward to emphasise 'special'. "What was the name of that wee glamourpuss you were into at that last party at the house? Champers, or something?"

"Chardonnay," said Mackay quietly, his face beginning to flush.

"Chardonnay! That was it! Now she was an absolute cracker if you don't mind me saying. Money can't buy a body like that. Well, it can, but you know what I mean. Anyway, it's a pity we won't be having any more of those parties, not if this all gets delayed again. That'll be me done."

"Oh, I'm sure you'll rise again, Frankie," Mackay said, putting on a smile, but a nervous one. "Anyway, those parties were getting a bit too much for a man of my age, if you know what I mean."

"Oh, I do, Gordon, I do. Never mind. Off you go, don't worry about me."

Gordon Mackay remained stuck to his seat for a few moments, surprised. He hadn't expected the conversation to be so easy, for Frankie Fisher to be so reasonable. Eventually he peeled himself off the leather tub chair and reached out his hand for Fisher to shake.

"Sorry about this, Frankie. You do understand, though, don't you?"

"Absolutely. No hard feelings - it's just business. Actually, before you go, I've got a wee present for you," Fisher said, rummaging in his desk drawer.

"You and your presents. You're far too generous," said Mackay, hoping for a watch. Rolex or Omega would be nice.

"Here it is," said Fisher, grinning, holding out a flat, black plastic rectangle. "It's a memento. Of the good times we've had together."

He flipped open the plastic case, took out a DVD and slipped it into the player beneath the large TV on his office wall. A couple of flicks at his remote and the screen came alive.

It's a bedroom. There's a man on all fours on a big bed, wearing only a Scotland football top. A naked woman in a Margaret Thatcher wig and mask is kneeling behind him. And going at him with an enormous black dildo.

"That's some picture quality, wouldn't you say, Gordon? I mean, it's low light, but these new cameras can pick up everything these days. Look – you can even see the sweat on your forehead there. Not surprised, given the size of that monster old

Chardonnay's bunging up your dung funnel. Makes *me* sweat just looking at it."

"Frankie....I...." Mackay didn't know what to say. Even if he did, he wasn't sure he would be able to say it.

"Of course, silly me," said Fisher. "I forgot to put the sound on. You get excellent sound quality through this wireless system I've got. Just have a listen to this."

At a touch of a button the whole room is filled with a rhythmic grunting, more animal than human. Then the odd word, or fragment of a word, at each thrust. Fisher turned up the volume.

'Soo.....soo.....soo....ness...ness...buh....buh.....buh....can...can ....can....dal....dal.....dal...gleeesh! Eeesh! Eeesh!'

Fisher flicked off the sound, ejected the DVD.

"Is that what I think it is, what you're saying there?" he said.

Mackay nodded once, head down, looking at the carpet. "Scotland World Cup squad. Argentina, 1978."

Fisher laughed long and loud.

"Seriously? You're getting beasted up the keester by some Maggie-looking hoor, and you're reeling off the names of the men who brought unending shame upon our great though potentially overconfident country? I mean, what the actual juddering fuck is that all about? Is it to make you blow your load or stop you from doing it? Actually, I don't want to know - forget I asked. Either way, you're a sick puppy, Gordon Mackay. One sick, deviant puppy. Can you imagine *that* on the front page of the Inverness Courier? Might even make the BBC News. Or Channel 5 more likely. Don't worry if you lose that one, by the way," he said, sliding the DVD into Mackay's suit jacket pocket, "I've got plenty more where that came from. Like, if you want to hand out copies to Moira and the kids, relatives, your colleagues on the council, people you see at church, that sort of thing. Although I could just send them direct, save you the bother."

He guided a shaking Mackay towards the office door.

"Yes, great parties," said Fisher. "Happy days."

As he opened the door, Fisher leant in close to Mackay. His voice low and slow. The purple vein in his forehead pumping.

"Get it. Fucking. Sorted."

And with that, he slapped Mackay on the back and slammed the door behind him. He swaggered over to the drinks trolley at the back of his office, poured a big splash of malt whisky into a crystal tumbler, and carried it over to the picture window. From there he could see down the hill towards Drumnadrochit, over the top of Urquhart Castle, and right over to the theme park site on the other shore. His empire. His legacy.

NessieWorld will be the legacy which makes his name – which clears his name. Forget all that crap that people say behind his back about being a disgraced MP or a small-time hood or a bit of a porn-hound. NessieWorld will wipe all of that from the slate. He will be remembered for far bigger and better things. He will be respected. Finally.

He caught sight of his reflection in the window, the sharp glint of determination in his eye. He slowly lifted his glass in a swell of pride and toasted himself.

Lots to do before then, of course.

Work, work, work. There's always something. Cowardly councillors, awkward scientists. Always something to stamp on. He needs a big gulp.

CHAPTER FOUR

The sun always shines on TV

The police officer seemed to be breathing. Appeared to be made of flesh. Even the hair was quite convincing.

But Zander Burns was sure he was dealing with a robot. Some bizarre Highland version of the Terminator. Except they crushed you with dull words and blank stares rather than massive guns and hands which turned into swords.

"You do realise I'm actually trying to help, don't you?" Zander said, well past the end of his tether. "I'm not trying to trick you into revealing some big secret. I'm just after your working assumption. The papers said you thought Jules and Mike had drowned, and I'm not an idiot – that's pretty much what it looks like to me too."

"We do not recognise that statement, and it wasn't officially sanctioned by Police Scotland. Look, Mr Burns. We have a job to do, a process to go through, and we will do what we can to find your colleagues. What we cannot and will not do is leap to a conclusion without any evidence to justify it. I know you're looking for certainty one way or another, but Police Scotland is not in a position at this present time to give you that. This is a missing persons inquiry, and that is how we will proceed until evidence emerges to the contrary."

A total waste of time. As he got into his cab outside the bland, modern police station in the middle of a bleak industrial estate, Zander reviewed the whole sorry situation.

Yes, it was a bit embarrassing for the university. It had been a risk to their credibility in the first place, letting a couple of their most respected scientists be based at a theme park, of all things. Having to go along with the 'well, we're not here to look for monsters but if we turn up any proof during the course of our work' nonsense.

But it was Zander who'd pushed to make it all happen, despite the risk. For a start, the money on offer from NessieWorld was too good to turn down. It wasn't every day people turned up at the university's door with a bucketload of cash. It wasn't the most high-profile university, which is why Zander was always looking for ways to build its recognition factor, attract students and backers. Placing positive stories, briefing the right newspapers, getting involved in projects to show the university in a positive light.

And now two of his colleagues were probably dead. They wouldn't even have been there if Zander hadn't been so persuasive in selling the potential PR benefits of the stunt to the university's Board.

So, yes, the circumstances were a bit embarrassing for the university, as the Vice-Chancellor had made so very clear. But that was nothing compared to the tragedy for anyone who knew Jules and Mike.

And it meant some of this was on him, maybe all of it. He had a duty to both men as well as the university. This wasn't just about protecting the university's reputation, whatever the Vice-Chancellor said.

As his cab neared the theme park site, Zander began to realise for the first time how big an enterprise it was. The place was vast.

He'd read his briefing material, scanned articles online, but nothing had prepared him for the incredible reality of it all.

NessieWorld stood on the southern shores of Loch Ness at the Inverness end, just next to the small village of Dores. Nearly one thousand acres of fun for all the family. Or it would be in a few months. It clearly wasn't quite ready yet. But he could see it all rising up past the perimeter fencing – the towers, the rides and rollercoasters – the biggest theme park in the UK. It stood out starkly against the low hills and the dark loch, a monster-size funfair grafted onto wild countryside.

Zander's cab passed trucks and vans heading away from the site, and he was caught in a mini traffic jam trying to get into a grand entrance with more of the same type of vehicles. Plumbing, electrics, construction. The place was absolutely buzzing with workers rushing to get it ready.

"Here to see Mr. Fisher," Zander said to the security guard, and he and his cab driver were directed to the main admin block in a Victorian version of a castle, all pointed turrets, crow stepped gables and a steep slate roof.

He was shown into a large wood-panelled room with stag antlers hanging on the walls, a crackling fire in a tall stone fireplace, and – sitting in a high-backed brown leather chair - an angry-looking overweight middle-aged man with a red face, slicked back dyed black hair, and startlingly blue eyes. Zander recognised him from the photos.

"Mr. Fisher, thank you for seeing me," he said, holding out his hand. "I'm Zander Burns from Addington University."

"Zander?" Fisher said, accepting the handshake but not getting up. "What kind of a name's that? What's wrong with Tom or John or Steve, for Christ's sake?" Fisher grinned, making it clear that he was joking.

"Oh, I'm sure my parents had their reasons," Zander said, feeling a bit uncomfortable. Yes, people sometimes had questions about his name but never put quite as forwardly as this. "Anyway," he said, "I'm just here as liaison for the university, dealing with the police, the media, that sort of thing. Here to help in any way I can."

"Of course, of course," Fisher said. "Terrible tragedy. Two

young men like that. Didn't know them personally - it's not quite my area, this science stuff - but I'm sure they were lovely fellas."

"Well, I'm holding out hope that they're still lovely fellas, and that they're sleeping off a major hangover in some barn somewhere. But it's not looking good."

"No, it's not, is it," Fisher said, frowning. "It's good that we can have a chat, though, because I'm sure you've got the same outlook as me. As much as this is a terrible tragedy, we wouldn't want it to have an impact on the park itself, if you see what I'm saying. It wasn't as a result of anything to do with NessieWorld, and it's in no-one's interests to go down that route. I see some of the papers have been a bit snidey about it all, saying the park's cursed and all that shite. Fucking typical press, trying to make a drama out of a molehill, so it's down to the likes of you and me to set it straight. Terrible tragedy - nothing to do with the park. That's what we should be saying. We'll be opening on time and there's no reason for anyone to doubt that."

Zander decided to be non-committal.

"Thanks," he said. "I'll bear that in mind. First things first, though, it would be good to see where Jules and Mike were working. While the police are treating this as a missing persons inquiry, I want to gather as much information as possible to help find them."

Fisher paused for a moment, thinking about it.

"Yes, I don't see why not," he said eventually. "Hold on there a second."

He got up, shuffled over to the heavy wooden door, stuck his head out and shouted.

"Anne-Marie! Anne-Marie! Where the fuck are you?"

A woman in her late 30s decked out in glamour model chic tottered around a corner with a notepad and pen.

"Aye, what is it?" she said, chewing on a big wad of gum.

"Get hold of Mary. Say she's to take us to Nessie Cove, see the labs. And tell Banjo and Easter to come along too."

"Aye, ok. When?"

"When d'you think? Now!"

"Alright, keep your hair on, just checking."

Anne-Marie gave Fisher a sour look, then turned away. Fisher focused his attention back to Zander.

"They'll be here in a minute. Could do with your help on something first. The TV people are here, wanting to do an interview with me. They're up on the roof, getting some shots of the park. You come up too, make sure I get everything right."

Without waiting for a reply, let alone agreement, Fisher marched out of the room and started up a broad staircase covered in a thick tartan carpet.

The view from the roof was spectacular. Over to the right, the loch itself, steely grey on an overcast day, like a giant broadsword laid down in the landscape. To the left, the heather clad hills rising in purple waves. And in front, the mini city of rides and slides, roads and restaurants that Zander had glimpsed before.

Workers moving around the paths, landscapers planting trees and laying turf, dancers practicing sequences on a central square, painters on scaffolding disguising the fake walls with castle-shaded paint.

"About two miles from end to end," Fisher said, moving beside Zander to take in his baby. "Quite something, isn't it? Been a dream of mine since I was a youngster. Used to come up here from Glasgow on holidays. Beautiful place and all that, but bugger all to do once you'd had a wander round Urquhart Castle and maybe bought a plastic dinosaur from one of the tatty tourist shops. All this potential, but no actual proper fun. No reason for people to hang about.

"All that history – the ancient tales of a water horse, a kelpie. Then the sightings from the 1930s onward. The photos, the films, the sonar experiments. It's world famous.

"But these Highlanders – honestly. Did they know what to do about it? They've got this potential cash monster sitting here, but not a clue what to do. There's about half a million people visit Loch Ness every year - did you know that? Half a million. But what have they got to spend their money on? Pretty much fuck all. Yes, there's Urquhart Castle, but all the money from that goes into the government's pockets. And it's just a fucking ruin anyway. Where's the fun in that? Then there's a couple of amateur 'exhibitions', one of which basically says there's no fucking monster. Who wants to hear that? Who wants to come all this way to have their imagination stamped on?

"So, then I come along. I've got my dreams. I want to give people something to look forward to. Okay, they probably won't actually see a real monster, but they can have the *idea* of one, the possibility that there's something strange and magical out there," he said, sweeping his arm out across the loch. "And that's what it's about. Putting a bit of magic in people's hearts. They've got enough to be miserable about in their boring, ordinary lives, so why shouldn't we give them a bit of escapism? People love this stuff. They don't want a bunch of glum-faced Presbyterians telling them 'it's not real, it doesn't exist, now finish your tea and fuck off back to work'.

"Because what's Loch Ness without the monster? It's just a deep, dark, freezing pit of water. People don't want the truth. They want what I can give them - dreams. I'm putting magic into their dreary lives. And you can't put a price on that. Although I'm aiming for about a grand per family, actually. Maybe two if they go for the hotel package. I mean, even magic has overheads.

"But these Highlanders, they're little people with little minds and little horizons. They're happy with the crumbs the tourists leave for them. But I'm thinking big. The little people will always try to do down people like me – men with vision. But they don't know Frankie Fisher. Frankie Fisher is not the kind of man to let the little people stop him. This will put Loch Ness on the map. Nothing and no one is going to stop that. Right, let's get these TV bastards done and dusted. Remember, it's tragic, but nothing to do with us. The park will go on."

A reporter and camera crew are set up on the far side of the roof, angled to take in the loch and the theme park as a backdrop to Fisher's interview. After introductions, they pressed 'record'.

"So, Frank Fisher, obviously a terrible tragedy," the reporter said.

"Yes, our hearts are with the families. Lovely boys, both of them. Top professionals, the very best. They really believed in this place, and I feel the best way to honour their memory is to open this world class venue on time this summer, offering families an absolutely unique entertainment experience. It's what those two men would've wanted."

"It sounds like you've given up hope that they'll be found alive."

"Anyone who knows Loch Ness, anyone who knows how bad the weather was the other night, anyone who knows about the strange things that happen out on that water – it's not something that can give you hope."

"So... are you saying Nessie might have something to do with the men's deaths?"

"Look, who knows what happened out on the water. The dead of night, thick mist. All we can say for certain is that two fine young men appear to have lost their lives. And if I know those two, before those icy waters squeezed the last breath out of them, they would have said, 'best of luck, Frank. Carry on and make NessieWorld the big success it deserves to be. Don't let us down'. And I won't let them down - I can promise you that."

"Can you tell us more about their work and why they were out on the loch at night?"

"That is a bit of a mystery. They weren't on the NessieWorld clock, as it were. Maybe they were just bored. Not much to do around here, after all. But as for their work, I'm not the expert. You'd be better off talking to this man," Fisher said, motioning to Zander off camera. "He's from the university the men came from. He'll fill you in."

Zander had been watching the interview with a mix of distaste and grudging respect. As a PR man, he had to admit that Fisher was a decent performer, a good talker, adept at getting his message across. But his crass salesmanship was too much.

Now felt like he'd been pinched on the arm. He wasn't prepped for an interview. Wasn't expecting to do one.

"Thank you," the reporter said to Fisher, then turned to Zander. "Sorry, I didn't catch your name, sir."

"Zander Burns. Zander with a 'z'. Addington University."

"So, Mr. Burns, can you shed any light on what the men were doing out on the loch late at night?"

"Not really, no. As Mr. Fisher has said, they were off duty at the time when they went missing."

"Could their decision to go out on the loch late at night have something to do with their work?"

"Again, it's difficult to see how. Their work was – is – about what's called metagenomics, collecting and measuring environmental DNA samples from soil and sometimes water, analysing it, categorising it. These samples are more easily gathered during the daytime – there's no reason why they'd have done it at night."

"Can you explain a bit more about their work? The rumour

is that they were searching for proof of the Loch Ness Monster herself."

Zander paused, remembering Fisher's plea. Also remembering the reputation of the university and his colleagues.

"Metagenomics and environmental DNA work is absolutely cutting edge. It's what Addington University is becoming known for, and both Jules and Mike were a big part in making that happen." He gave himself a mental kick for talking about them in the past tense. "Loch Ness is a perfect place to carry out this kind of work, identifying hundreds, maybe even thousands of organisms that live or have lived in the loch, mapping their DNA sequences. I just want to go on record to thank Mr Fisher for funding the research, because it could go a long way to improving people's lives by helping to develop things such as new antibiotics."

Zander could see the reporter's eyes cloud over with boredom halfway through his answer. It wasn't what they were after.

"And what about the speculation locally that Nessie might be responsible for the men's deaths?"

"At the moment, my colleagues are missing. I hope that's all it is. If anyone's seen them or has any information about where they might be, I'd urge them to contact the police in Inverness. We just want them safely back in the lab, carrying out this vitally important work."

The reporter thanked him, nodded to the camera operator to switch off, and they started dismantling their equipment.

Zander and Fisher made for the stairs, Fisher out in front, hurrying down.

When they got outside, a woman in a beige uniform was waiting for them beside a golf buggy done up in NessieWorld branding.

"This is Mary," Fisher said, waving at the woman. "My operations chief. She'll be able to give you the tour of the labs and all that. Not quite my area."

Mary nodded a curt greeting at Zander and got into the front of the buggy.

"Oh, and this is Banjo," said Fisher, gesturing to a wiry, weaselly looking man with longish greasy hair, standing beside a black pick-up truck. "He deals with security."

Banjo gave a strange grin, showing crooked tombstone teeth with several gaps. A huge hulk of a figure struggled out of the truck and stood behind Banjo, towering over him.

"And Easter," said Fisher. "He works with him. Honestly, look at that massive head of his. Looks just like one of those Easter Island statues, doesn't he? Probably why they call him that. Don't actually know – never asked. Maybe it's his actual fucking name. Strange thing, names. Knew a man called 'Innocent' once. Turned out he wasn't, though. Anyway, this lot will take you where you want to go. Anything you need, just ask them. I've got some other stuff to deal with."

With that, Fisher scurried back towards his office with a half wave behind him, leaving Zander with no option but to get in the golf buggy behind Mary. Before going in the main door, Fisher stopped, turned and stared at Banjo and Easter. He didn't look best pleased. He pointed to his eyes with two fingers, then pointed at Zander. Banjo nodded once, and both men climbed into the pick-up.

Orders received and understood.

CHAPTER FIVE

Nigel's making plans

To be fair to him, Nigel Bellingham did sometimes wonder whether he was madder than a big box of really bonkers frogs.

He wasn't alone in thinking that. Although maybe other people thought it more often than he did.

After all, he'd given up a decent career in a nice part of England to squat on the shores of Loch Ness for the past twenty-five years.

He had XTC to thank for that. As with many other Nigels of his era he was gently teased about his name at school due to XTC's late 70s hit 'Making Plans for Nigel'. But it was the sentiment behind the song – that poor Nigel's mundane life was already planned out for him in excruciating detail by other people – that stayed with him.

He didn't want a boring life. He didn't want to be able to predict every single boring stage in that boring life. He wanted adventure.

But all that foreign food, though. And unreliable transport systems. Elastic attitudes to hygiene. Maybe a smaller adventure was in order.

So, he saved up what little money he could, packed in his job as a trainee quantity surveyor, and left his confused and concerned parents and their Home Counties cul-de-sac. He headed for the Highlands of Scotland and the only story that had ever properly fired his imagination since a family holiday when he was 10 – the prospect of an unknown animal, possibly even a trapped relic of the dinosaur age, living amongst us.

He'd only meant to stay for a year. That was the plan - get

the best ever photo of Nessie, achieve worldwide fame and un-told riches, and then....well, he'd figure that bit out when he got to it.

But a year stretched to two. And then four. Then more. He couldn't remember when he stopped saying 'just one more sea-son' and started thinking about it as home.

Two and a half decades in a semi-tent, semi-shack, on the stony shore of Loch Ness near Urquhart Castle. Through bitter winters, wet springs and autumns, and midge-infested sum-mers. Just him, his hovel and a gas cooker, scraping a living by selling arty prints of his photographs.

Photographs of the loch at its moody best. But with one common feature. None of them featured a shot of the monster. Not one.

Of course, he knew all the best spots to go to increase his chances of spotting Nessie. The locals would tell him about strange things they'd seen, even if they weren't about to admit it in public. He knew everything there was to know about the Loch Ness Monster, was regarded as a local expert. But had he actually seen the damn thing? No. Not yet.

The locals seemed to accept him after about ten years or so, putting aside his Englishness and his vagrant life. Come winter, with the tourists gone, he'd find a villager no longer had need of a jumper or a coat or some boots and had left them in a bag outside his hut. Or someone might have over-bought food and needed to give some away, or there'd be odd jobs that came his way even though his skills were limited. And on his rare visits to the pub, he might sometimes discover his pint had been re-filled when he wasn't looking.

Some might call it charity. Others called it community.

Nigel was sitting in a much-repaired picnic chair on his small, stony cove beside Urquhart Castle, looking out over the calm loch, the water like black glass. His long-lensed camera sat in front of him on a tripod, as ever, just in case. He picked up a handful of pebbles and flicked them out on the surface, watching the ripples spread out in perfect circles.

Yes, people had seen some strange things out there and had told him about their experiences. It's what kept him going, kept him believing that he'd get the big money shot someday. But he could do with some money now. The photo sales were going down every year, now that everyone had a professional-level camera at the end of a stick and the means to show the world their photographic genius immediately. They didn't seem to need or want his carefully composed landscapes.

A bit more money. Just to make life a little easier.

And maybe there was someone who'd be interested in parting with a bit of money to keep Nigel quiet about something strange. Something he might have seen on the loch a couple of nights ago.

How much was it worth? A hundred? A couple of hundred? A thousand?

He chucked a stone as far out into the loch as he could. It cut through the surface with a sharp plop. He watched the ripples again. Getting ever wider. Actions have echoes, repeating again and again. Do the ripples from the stones carry on forever?

Maybe he can throw a rock into someone's plans, get a regular ripple of cash every week, month, year, whatever.

But only if he protects himself. How do you get a message to someone about making a deal and keep your back covered? How do you show that you've got something to trade, that you're worth doing a deal with?

Nigel pushed himself up out of his chair, stretched his limbs, then went over to the small mirror hung on a nail at the side of his shack, the spot where he'd have a cold shave sometimes if he felt like it.

He squinted at the mirror. A middle-aged man with a weathered face and long, grey dreadlocks stared back at him. Should he shave? He ran his hand over a stubbly chin, three or four days' growth rasping against his palm. No, it was fine.

He looked up the hill towards the castle car park, up by the main road. Yes, the TV satellite truck was still there. He'd checked it out earlier, wondering what it was, and found out they were due to do a live broadcast for that evening's news with an update on the missing men. Not that there was much to update about. Not yet anyway.

It only took him a few minutes to reach the truck. A pot-bellied man in thick glasses was leaning against the bonnet, smoking. A large satellite dish on the top of the vehicle pointed up to the sky at 30 degrees.

"You with the TV?" Nigel said. The man nodded. "Got some information for you."

Without taking the cigarette from his mouth the man walked around the side of the truck and banged on a sliding door. When it slid open, he jerked his thumb back at Nigel.

"Someone wants a word," he said.

"About what?" said a young man in a smart suit sitting inside the truck, hemmed in by technical equipment and small TV screens.

"Didn't say," the man said, then left to continue his fag break.

The young man looked over at Nigel, not quite managing to keep annoyance off his face. If he'd had a pound for all the time-wasters who'd badgered him to be on TV…. And this one – well, he looked as mad as a box of frogs.

"How can I help?"

"You a reporter? For the TV?" Nigel said, getting close. The reporter crossed his arms, on the defensive.

"Yes. Sky News."

"You doing a story about the men who went missing? The scientists?"

"Yes, we are. Why?"

"Then you're going to want to talk to me."

"Why would I do that?"

Nigel grinned.

"Because I know some serious shit."

CHAPTER SIX

Nessie's Lair

Puking a bucket of lemonade onto a woman's head from a height of ten feet is not what's generally regarded as a five-star review.

Alton Towers, aged 13. Zander Burns had been on a ride with multiple loops and lurches after a very fizzy lunch. Feeling the urgent need to chuck, he looked for a bin but couldn't find one. Remembering what he did when he was sick on a ferry the year before, he retched over a railing. But this time, instead of his spew landing in the sea, it drenched a woman with multiple tattoos and black-rooted blonde hair having a furtive cigarette on the walkway underneath.

Amazingly, her cigarette stayed alight. The rest of her was soaked in a sticky teenage vomit cocktail. Oddly enough, she didn't take much comfort from her Superking's survival.

It was the last time Zander could remember being in a theme park. And the last time he'd wanted to be in one. Theme parks, it must be said, just weren't his thing. The noise, the screaming, the queues. The fizzy vomit shooting out of his nostrils. Not his thing at all.

But seeing NessieWorld up close, even he was impressed.

At ground level the site seemed even bigger to Zander. As the buggy passed some of the rides, he was wowed by the sheer scale of some of them. He noticed many had little to do with Nessie or Loch Ness. More like a general tour of mythical monsters. Nessie and Chums, perhaps.

There was Yeti Mountain, with a vertical drop rollercoaster. Highland Fling, a giant circular swing which rose up above the whole park. Zombie Train - with, Zander counted, fifteen roller-coaster loops. The Curse of Ben Nevis, Bigfoot Lodge, Chupacabra Howl, the Mummy's Tomb. Fake mountains, fake castles, fake waterfalls, fake monsters, but all done on a sensational scale.

Some of the rides moved slowly, going through testing. Others had workers still constructing sections of track. Groups of young people ran through drills with a clip-boarded instructor, the women in very short tartan dresses, the men in too-tight tartan dungarees. They were all surprisingly good-looking and toned. As the buggy passed one group, Zander could hear Eastern European voices.

"We've been recruiting from all over the world," Mary said over her shoulder. "The training's been going on for the last month, making sure they're ready for the summer."

"So, not just jobs for locals then," said Zander, leaning forward to make himself heard above all the activity around him.

"Lots of jobs for everybody. A lot of the locals are in behind-the-scenes roles, technicians and such. But Mr Fisher wants the public face to be very classy, very high quality. Hence the.....supermodels, whatever." Mary almost mutters it, and it makes Zander think. She doesn't have a local accent either, but – pleasant and healthy-looking as she was - neither could she be mistaken for a catwalk model. Maybe there was some resentment at the number and type of staff coming in.

"You didn't fancy one of these uniforms, then?"

"Good God, no! In this climate? No, it's hardly my game. I'm strictly logistics. I like to see a plan, and make sure people are doing what they're supposed to be doing. I'm not into all that shop window stuff."

They swerved round a mini roundabout, neatly avoiding a marching band stuffed full of bagpipers warming up, squeezing their pipe bags to wake up the wails.

"That's where we're heading for," said Mary, pointing towards a large, domed structure down at the water's edge. "The lab's in there, along with the control centre and the aquarium."

They parked right outside the glass front doors, the entrance designed to look like the open mouth of a huge beast. This, according to the ten-foot sign above the door, was Nessie's Lair – including an aquarium promising shark walks, rays, moray eels, piranhas, and daily shows with orcas, dolphins, walruses.

Inside, they walked through glass-walled corridors with empty fish tanks on either side, then Mary swiped her card on a 'Staff Only' maintenance door, and they moved through a hot tunnel with pipes overhead and aircon units trying to keep everything at the right temperature. Banjo and Easter were always lurking a few steps behind.

The tunnel joined others, there were stairs to climb, numerous turns, and Zander soon felt lost and disoriented. Luckily Mary seemed to know the way. She stopped at one door, turned to him with an expectant look on her face.

"Are you ready for this?"

He wasn't sure what he was supposed to be ready for but nodded anyway.

Mary swiped again and opened the door onto a gangway. Zander followed her, and instinct and shock forced him to take a step back. They were perched high above a cavernous auditorium, with rows and rows of seats forming three quarters of a circle around a giant pool of water. Like an indoor version of SeaWorld, with room for thousands of people to watch whatever aquatic entertainment the park put on. One end of the structure opened out into the loch, with two big gates holding back the water.

"Quite something, isn't it?"

Zander nodded, feeling a little queasy at the height.

"This is probably the star attraction," said Mary. "The shows will be here, four or five times a day. Dolphins, orcas – I know some people are not sure about having orcas do shows like this, but...." She shrugged. "Lots of people want to see them. We haven't got them here, yet. I think Mr Fisher's still negotiating with some place in China. He's been buying up lots of species from aquariums and shows around the world. Just a matter of getting them into the country and in here. Most of the stock will come in about a month before we open."

"What are the gates for?" said Zander, pointing to them.

"Ah," said Mary, a half smile creeping on to her face. "That's Mr Fisher's big plan. That's so that Nessie can get in."

"I beg your pardon?"

"Yup, that's the plan. There are sensors in the loch outside the gates which triggers them to open if anything big enough comes near them. What we're telling the world is that if Nessie comes to have a look, the gates open, she comes in, the gates close, and we've got her. And can show her to the world. For a price. It's Mr Fisher's big thing."

"Yes, but.." Zander searched for a way to say it delicately. "What if, by some chance – and I'm talking hypothetically, here – what if Nessie doesn't actually turn up?"

"What?" Mary feigned surprise, that same half smile still on her face. "You mean a hypothetical monster might hypothetically not turn up to be quietly captured? We should wash your mouth out with soap for saying such a thing. If only the merch shops were open, we could get some Nessie shower gel." She winked over at Banjo and Easter. Banjo sneered back.

"Well, in the absence of a monster to show people, there are the orcas, seals and the rest. But as Mr Fisher says, it's the idea of it that matters. The ambition. What sort of Nessie theme park would we be if we didn't want to actually have Nessie as the centrepiece? You've got to dream, haven't you?"

With that, Mary turned and strode along the gantry, which stretched right around the vast, fake cave thirty metres above the pool below.

Through a door at the end, and into a breeze block corridor, then swiped through double doors into a large office with a high ceiling, rows of workstations and computers, big screens on the wall at one end. Men and women in white coats, tapping on their computers, bringing up data on the big monitors on the wall in front of them.

"This is the control centre," Mary said. "All the rides, the power, the support systems – it's all done from here. If there's a problem anywhere, this lot will know about it first. Here," she said, pointing over at two desks at the side of the room. "This is where your people were based. They also had a small lab through that door to do their tests on the samples. The police have already been in for a look."

Zander went over and sat at one of the desks. He wasn't sure what he was supposed to look for, if anything. Nothing personal on the desks themselves. He opened a desk drawer. A mess of papers, paperclips, stickies, marker pens, a half-finished pack of mints, a chipped enamel Star Wars keyring. He tried the other drawers. More of the same. Finally, he fired up the computer, logging in with the details he'd been given by his IT department.

Lots of files under subheadings, all organised by date. Spreadsheets, Word doc write-ups of findings. All very dense and scientific. He opened up the file with the latest date and clicked on the spreadsheet. A message flashed up on the screen.

"You did not close this programme correctly. We have identified the last document you worked on and have saved it in a temporary file for you. If you wish to save this file, please click here."

A preview of the file was shown on the left-hand side of the screen. All just numbers to Zander. He looked at the timestamp. File saved 02.33 on the 5th of the month. The day after, or rather the morning after, the men went missing.

"Have you seen this?" he said to Mary. She looked over his shoulder and shrugged.

"Not really my department," she said. "Banjo – you know anything about this?"

He seemed to think about it for a second, scratching at his greasy head before coming over for a look at the computer screen.

"What am I supposed to be looking at?" he said, a bit aggressively for Zander's liking. He realised that he didn't actually know what 'security' function Banjo played in the organisation.

"The time stamp – here," Zander said, pointing to the figures on the screen. "If he switched off his computer at half two in the morning, then it was after that they went missing. The police said to me they thought it was between ten and eleven, based on the time Jules left the pub. Which means they haven't looked at this computer, which isn't brilliant. This puts it in a whole different timeframe. Don't know if it changes anything, but it means they were here much later than we all thought."

"So? Just gave them more time to get pissed. Probably why they thought it was smart to take the boat out. Completely off their heads." Banjo turned to Easter and grinned a crooked grin.

"Could we just...." Zander held up his hands but stopped himself from expressing his anger any further, remembering that he was a guest. "They were colleagues of mine, friends."

Banjo moved back to stand beside Easter, his face creased in an angry frown.

"Anyway," he said. "Doesn't change anything. We know they left here, went through that door over there, went down the stairs to the dock, took the boat out. Door records prove it.

Swipe cards."

"Between ten and eleven? Or after half two?"

Banjo didn't say anything for a moment, just stared at Zander with flat eyes.

"About eleven," he said eventually. "Yeah, sure that's what the log said. Just before eleven."

Fine, thought Zander. There must be another explanation for the time stamp. Probably didn't matter in the long run. The men were still missing, whatever time they left the building.

"I suppose I should see the boat," he said, although he was just doing it for form's sake so he could report back that he'd done it.

Banjo and Easter led the way this time, with Zander and Mary following Easter's lumbering bulk along a bare corridor. They swiped through a security door and then down a long flight of metal stairs with three landings to break up the descent. At the bottom, in a double height, triple width corridor Zander saw a sign on large double doors reading 'Holding tanks – strictly no admittance'.

"Any point looking in there?" he said.

"No," Banjo said quickly. "All that area's been completely searched."

"I didn't mean search it," Zander said, a bit thrown. Why would he want to search it? "I meant just have a look. While were down here. It's a pretty impressive place."

"You don't have clearance to go through there. Very high security in that part of the building. Highly valuable beasts are going to be in there. Anyway, we've got to get on."

Banjo marched off towards a door towards the other end of the corridor which gave access into the show auditorium. They were nearly level with the loch, beside the giant cave entrance. There was small pier to the right of the opening where the boat was moored. 'The Kelpie', a 30-foot, older style motor launch.

He was led along the wooden pier to the side of the boat.

"Go in if you like," Banjo said, but made no move of his own to board the boat.

Zander climbed across and down into the well at the rear of the boat. There wasn't much to see. He stuck his head under the canopy covering the steering wheel and electrics, then opened the hatch leading on to three short steps into the body of the boat. A cramped sitting area with more electrical equipment, and a small table covered in empty lager cans. There were some in a waste bin too, along with an empty bottle of whisky of a brand unknown to Zander.

"Cops left it like it was," Banjo said, right at his shoulder, startling him. He could smell the thin man's sour breath. "A right session they must have had."

Zander nodded. He'd seen enough.

There was nothing more to say. Nothing more to do. It was pretty clear. His colleagues were gone, and they weren't coming back.

CHAPTER SEVEN

Secrets and messages

One of those days. The sort of day when you need a drink or two, with food as an optional extra.

Back at the hotel Zander stuck his head into the room marked 'Lounge Bar'. High backed tartan chairs, cheap prints of stags, lochs and hills on the walls.

And completely empty. He thought about it for a second. Not quite what he was after. If he was going to drink alone, he'd prefer to do it in the company of other people.

He pressed the 'Please Ring for Attention' button on the reception counter. After a few minutes, attention turned up, the same woman who'd checked him in. Tartan skirt and waistcoat, black hair, grey eyes, quizzical look.

"Can I help?"

"Yes," Zander said. "Where can you get a decent drink around here? Apart from in there," he pointed towards the lounge bar. "No offence."

"A *decent* drink?" She seemed to think for a second. "Your best bet's probably the train station in Inverness."

"Really? And that's got a good bar in it, has it?"

"No, it's got a crap bar in it. But you can get a train from there to Edinburgh. There's a good bar round the back of Waverley station. Probably the nearest place for a *decent* drink."

"Edinburgh? But that's.....ah, I get it. That's very helpful – thank you. But let's just say I felt in more urgent need of a drink than that. So, somewhere nearer. And which doesn't feel," he pointed to the lounge bar again, "as overwhelmingly sad as that."

"There's the Dores Inn on the other side of the loch. That's got some tables outside, views of the loch. Quite popular with the tourist trade. About twenty minutes in a taxi. If you can find one."

"Okay, let me put it a different way. Where would *you* choose to drink? Not that I'm being forward, I don't mean it like that," he added.

"Like what?"

"In an inappropriate, creepy, flirty kind of way. I'm just genuinely interested. You're young, probably quite stylish when you haven't got all those clothes on. When you've got *other* clothes on, *other* clothes, not *no* clothes. I didn't mean....it was the tartan uniform, I meant."

"What uniform? These *are* my normal clothes."

Zander tried to think of a way out of the hole he'd dug, but the sides seemed pretty steep.

"I'm sorry," he said, holding his hands up. "It's been quite a day. I'm going to stop speaking now. But if you could point me in the direction of a local bar with local people, I'd be much obliged."

"Well, if you don't mind a bit of sawdust and spit, there's always the Drum. Local people seem to like it."

"And where can I find it?"

"Go outside, turn right, go along to Glenkirk Crescent, turn right again, along there for a bit, then cut through the path beside the garages, a slight left, another right, and that's you."

"Thank you. Appreciate it."

Feeling tired, embarrassed and slightly depressed, Zander left the hotel and followed the instructions as best he could. He got the Glenkirk Crescent bit, but he wasn't sure how long he was supposed to follow it. He retraced his steps and saw an overgrown path between two houses with some garages behind.

He cut down there, followed a clearer tarmac path beside the garages, walked between another couple of cottages, and there it was before him.

The Drum. A low rise, flat-roofed 70's style extension stuck on the back of a much grander building. A building that was clearly the Drumnadrochit Arms, where he was staying.

He pushed through the swing door into the pub and walked into another world. It was busy, even this early in the evening. A mix of old men in tweed, younger men in overalls, some young dark-clothed kids in the corner, a family or two. Country and Western music drifted out of some hidden speaker, providing an accompaniment to the silent pictures on the old TV fixed up by the ceiling in one corner of the room. On the walls, pinned up photos of smiling people in different stages of drunkenness, fliers for ceilidhs and landscaping, a framed rugby shirt, newspaper features on local football and shinty teams, and an old, nut-brown caman – the fearsome shinty stick – fixed above the bar.

And standing behind the bar, in the one example of tartan in the whole place, was the receptionist from the hotel. Smiling at him. After a fashion.

"Just out of interest," he said to her as he leaned on the pine bar. "Could I have got here by walking through the hotel?"

"Absolutely. But I thought you'd prefer the scenic route."

"You are a very strange individual."

"I'm Catriona," she said, holding out her hand. "We should probably introduce ourselves formally if I'm going to continue using you for sport."

"Yes, that seems reasonable," Zander said, taking her hand. "And I'm Zander."

"With a 'z'. Yes, I remember that very clearly, don't worry about that."

"And if you don't mind me asking, why are you using me for

'sport'?"

"Because it's fun. And because," she said, looking away from him, examining a beer pump for a second, "you're obviously quite down about what happened. Thought you could do with some cheering up." She looked back up at him. The grey eyes weren't so cold this time.

"In a slightly unconventional way."

"Convention's not really my strong point."

"And customer service is?"

Catriona frowned at Zander for a second, then laughed.

"No. I'm rubbish at it. This is just a holiday job, helping out my dad. It's his place, the hotel. Well, it was - he just manages it now. Owned by the great Mr Fisher. The theme park man."

"Yes, I met him today. Interesting character."

Zander examined the beers on draft, noticing with surprise that they were all from different small craft breweries. In the fridge behind the bar, it was the same story. Cans and bottles of obscure brands outnumbered the famous labels. He chose something from the Black Isle Brewery, a deeply golden ale frothing up nicely in his glass.

"On the house," Catriona said. "The least I can do. Actually, your friends were very fond of that, Jules and Mike. Quite into their craft beer."

"I remember," Zander nodded. "Very particular about what they drank. It was a bit of a mission as far as they were concerned, I think. Life's too short to drink crap beer."

The words made him sad again, so he raised his glass to the men silently and took a long pull at it.

"Any more news about them?"

"No, nothing. But I think everyone's pretty much of the same view. I mean, the police won't say anything officially at the moment but it's pretty clear they think they both went over the side somehow." Zander shook his head. "But what I don't understand is what they were doing out in the boat in the first place. There was no reason for it. The boat's for collecting water samples, and you don't do that at night. It just doesn't make any sense to me."

Catriona looked around the bar and spotted a middle-aged man with a beard and checked shirt.

"Shuggie," she said, raising her voice to cut through the hubbub. "Shuggie, over here a minute."

Shuggie made his way to the bar, leaning on the bar-top beside Zander, nodding to him as he did so.

"You were in the bar the other night when Jules was here, weren't you?" Catriona said. "Did he say anything to you about needing to take the boat out?"

"Not a word. No reason he would. Only an idiot would take a boat out on a night like that."

Catriona shot him a sharp look.

"This is Mr. Burns," she said, gesturing towards Zander. "He's Jules's colleague from the university."

"Sorry," said Shuggie, standing up straighter. "No offence, like. I just meant it wasn't a good night for being out on the loch. The mist and that. I don't know how much they knew about boats, but you wouldn't go out in those kind of conditions without a good reason."

"And did he mention anything at all that might have been a reason?" Zander said. "Did he seem ok? Anything unusual?"

Shuggie considered it for a few moments.

"Like I say, it was just normal chat. Talking about the footy, talking about some gig coming up in Inverness. Nothing about taking the boat out. Last thing he said to me was that he was heading over to the lab to get Mike, bring him back for last orders."

"Really? Wasn't he a bit pissed?"

"Yeah, but not *pissed* pissed. I mean, definitely pissed but not so pissed he couldn't drive a Landy round the loch to the lab. Mist isn't too bad on the roads usually, just hangs about on the water."

"And he was planning to come back here? Both of them?"

"What he said. They stay in the village, so Mike would have to get back here somehow anyway."

"But something changed their minds."

"Aye. Probably never know now. Anyway, I hope it's not going to cause any problems for the park. Lot of people replying on that place."

"Shuggie," Catriona said, butting in. "There's more important things than a theme park."

"Alright for you to say. Your dad's set up now since he sold this place. Some of us need the money that's going to come in once we get this tourist boom Mr. Fisher keeps going on about. And you'll benefit as much as we do."

"You're not a fan of NessieWorld, then?" Zander said to Catriona.

"Sure, it's generating jobs, with more to come. I just think it's a bit tacky. The Highlands are famous for their beauty. For nature, wilderness, for peace and quiet. Not for millions of screaming kids eating junk food in some fake Highland village. It'll change the place, and not for the better."

"And is that what a lot of people around here think?" said Zander.

"If you asked most people in here, you'd find it was about 90% in favour," said Shuggie, prodding the bar with a thick finger. "You can't survive on the scraps we get from tourism right now, and there's just not enough jobs elsewhere. Frankie Fisher promised to use local suppliers when he can, and he's been true to his word. We're already seeing the benefit. And

Drumnadrochit will see the benefit even more once the place is up and running. Folk need places to stay. They can't all afford to pay for rooms at that hotel he's building."

"Castle Fisher?" Catriona said, her mouth curling at the side, one eyebrow raised. "Sounds really classy. Hot and cold running haggis in every room"

"Really?" said Zander.

"No. Not really."

"Anyway," said Shuggie, "you'll not find many who'll slag off Mr. Fisher for what he's doing for us." Then he raised his voice and pointed at the two old men in tweeds and flat caps sitting quietly at a nearby table. "Apart from those old bastards over there."

The two men looked up at Shuggie. One of them, tall and thin, with a neat white moustache. The other man smaller, rounder, red-faced.

"Hang on, hang on," Zander said at Shuggie, annoyed. "That's not on. I know this is your local, but it's totally not on to speak to people like that. Completely out of order."

"Why?" said the taller old man, speaking up with a firm, strong voice. "We're old."

"And we're bastards," said the smaller man. "When roused."

"Okay," said Zander, slightly confused. "Anyway, so you're not keen on the theme park business?"

"Correct," the tall man said. "It is a folly. The jobs available to locals are not sustainable. The number of staff needing to be brought in is causing housing problems in Inverness, it will drain custom from other tourist attractions, crowding them out. I'm not against moderate development, but this is completely out of proportion, and it's being shoved through by a dodgy, fly-by-night pornographer who has no connection with - or understanding of - Highland life. I could go on."

"And you both feel the same way?"

"Well, not quite. Hector is more of what you might call an animal rights activist. His interests are more about the general influx of tourists around the loch rather than the specific development."

"Want them to piss off," Hector said. "Leave Nessie alone."

"Hector pickets the tourists at Urquhart Castle," Catriona said, leaning over the bar, smiling towards Hector. "All very polite, it's got to be said. Just stands there with his sign."

"What does it say?" Zander asked.

Hector stared at him for a moment.

"Leave Nessie Alone."

"Ah. I see. So you already told me that. I didn't realise. And do you mean it? I mean, do you believe in Nessie?"

Whatever answer might have come disappears under a chorus of calls from other punters asking for the TV to be turned up. The late evening news, and the loch was on.

Catriona flicked the remote at the screen as a presenter introduced a report about the latest on the scientists' disappearance.

There was nothing Zander didn't already know. Pretty shots of the loch and the half-built theme park were covered by a voiceover explaining the basic facts. Then a short soundbite from a police spokesman, then Frank Fisher appeared. Some cheered, some booed. They'd used Fisher's answer about it being a tragedy and the need to honour the men's work by carrying on. Zander dreaded seeing himself pop up any second, but it didn't happen. Maybe he'd been too boring to use.

The report ended, and the pub started babbling. But then a couple of people shushed the others. There was more.

The presenter said there was some breaking news about the incident, and that they could speak live to their reporter Matt James, who was at Urquhart Castle.

"What do you have for us, Matthew?"

Matt James, with his salon-quality hairdo framed by Urquhart Castle and the loch, took a deep breath and started speaking quickly.

"As you heard in my report, the police are treating this as a missing persons inquiry, but I can exclusively reveal that there's some new information which might suggest foul play is involved. With me now," he said as the camera pulled back for a wider shot, "is local Nessie expert Nigel Bellingham, who's made a career out of studying the loch and the legend of the monster. Nigel, what can you tell us?"

The pub got noisy with mutterings of 'It's Nigel! Look at him! Someone's given him a comb! Can you believe our Nigel's on the telly' and other similar comments until people were shushed again so they could hear what Nigel had to say.

"Well, yeah," Nigel said, swallowing hard. "The thing to remember is I've been here a long time, yeah? Like twenty-five years long. I know this loch, I know there's things go on out there, people tell me things. And sometimes people see something, and they don't know what it is, think it's something else, want it to be something else. Sometimes there's no explanation, yeah? You see what I'm getting at?"

"Not entirely," the reporter said, trying to keep a polite tone. "What did *you* see out on the loch two nights ago?"

"Well, this is not about me. I'm irrelevant. See what I'm saying? In the grand scheme. Point is, police are saying there was a boat out that night. Fair enough. But what I'm saying is, what if there was another boat out there? What if somebody saw something like that, another boat - that could change things. Changes the whole narrative. And what would that other boat have been doing? You see what I'm saying? Maybe someone wouldn't want that boat to be seen, wouldn't want the narrative changed."

"Look I'm sorry to press you on this, but did you or did you not see another boat out there near the boat with the scientists on it?" LIKE YOU BLOODY TOLD ME YOU DID! he wanted to scream at Nigel but managed to restrain himself.

"Like I said, it's not about me. But people tell me things, things they see, always have. I'm a keeper of secrets around here. Secrets people don't want spread around. I'm good at keeping secrets. And maybe someone out there thinks a second boat should be kept a secret, I don't know, not my call."

Nigel stopped talking, smiled, relatively pleased with himself. Subtle message fired off into the ether thanks to the miracle of satellite technology.

"Thank you, Nigel Bellingham. And that's it from me, live at Loch Ness. Now back to the studio."

The picture changed to the studio presenter, who started to talk about a scandal at a hospital in Leicester. The pub crowd broke into loud chatter, some laughing at Nigel's performance, deer in the headlights, rambling, not his finest hour. Never mind, they'd stand him a pint next time he was in, just for the entertainment value alone.

Up at Urquhart Castle, reporter Matt James had a face like an angry baby. His finely coiffed hair would have torn itself out if it could've. He yanked the earpiece from his ear and turned on Nigel.

"What in the name of Christ was all that? You specifically told me you'd seen another boat out there, that there were two boats together out in the loch that night. That's the only reason I put you on! You've completely wasted everyone's time, and I'm going to get it right in the neck from my editor in about..." his phone started ringing "now, actually. So, thanks a whole big bunch for fucking up my week. Go on - do one!"

With that, the reporter turned away and started grovelling into his phone. Nigel stood still for a second, and then ambled over to the camera operator who was busy unplugging cables.

"He said there was fifty quid in it for me," Nigel said, his hand out.

"Not my problem, mate. You'll need to take it up with him."

Nigel looked back over to the reporter, who was pacing up and down with his phone stuck on his ear, his head hunched over, listening more than talking. Maybe not the best time to approach him.

Never mind. What's fifty quid when it comes down to it? Should be a much bigger payday if the message has hit the target accurately. Nigel drifted away from the satellite truck and into the deepening gloom of the evening, back down the hill towards his shack.

High on the hill above Drumnadrochit, in a Costa-style villa with a huge TV in a huge lounge with huge white leather sofas, Frankie Fisher picked up his TV remote and froze the news.

"Doll! Doll! Where are you? Doll!"

He dragged his pot-belly off one of the sofas, shuffled through the thick shagpile towards the door, and stuck his head out.

"Doll! Anne-Marie! Where the fuck are you?"

Anne-Marie tottered out of the kitchen, wooden stirring spoon in her hand, looking annoyed.

"What?"

"Where's Banjo and Easter?"

"How the fuck am I supposed to know? They're your heavies. Nothing to do with me."

"Well can you get hold of them for me? Please. Need to see them urgently."

"I'm in the middle of doing your tea! Why don't you call them?"

"Chain of command. It shouldn't be me calling them. That's

your job. My Executive Assistant."

"Executive Assistant my arse. Cook, slave, skivvy, whatever."

"You forgot sex goddess."

Anne-Marie raised the spoon but dropped it again just as quick. She smiled a little, despite herself.

"Fine. I'll get them. But if the mince burns, that's your fault. And you'll eat it whether you like it or not."

She disappeared back into the kitchen, and Fisher retreated to the lounge again. He replayed the interview while he waited for the men to arrive. This was not good.

"Boss?" Banjo said, sticking his head into the lounge. Fisher waved him in, and Easter followed, ducking slightly to get in the door.

"Watch this," Fisher said, and the three of them stood in front of the TV watching Nigel's strange interview.

"So what do you think he meant by that?" Fisher said, pausing the TV again once it was over.

Banjo bit at his lip. He wasn't nervous - he just wanted to taste the blood.

"I think he's talking shite," he said. "He knows nothing."

"Are you sure about that?" Fisher said, fidgeting. "Are you absolutely, totally, 100% carat gold sure about that?" His face was getting redder. "Because I'll let you in to a teensy, weensy secret. I'm not entirely confident that he's talking shite. That sounded to me very much like the opposite of shite – undigested food, whatever. That sounded to me like he knows something, that he's seen something, or knows someone who has. Either way, there's a message there. A big fucking foghorn about keeping a secret. And who the fuck you think that's aimed at? So what I want to happen now is for you two fuckheads to go out, find him, and find out what he knows. What he knows and what he wants."

"What if he doesn't play ball, boss?"

"Then you have my permission to give him a wee scare."

CHAPTER EIGHT

Field studies

You never really know what earth tastes like until it's been crammed into your mouth.

You might think you do. You might think it tastes kind of...earthy. You might think it has that 'loamy' quality people go on about when they describe the smell of damp earth, although if you don't know what a loam smells like it's not much help.

But no. As Nigel Bellingham found out, it tasted like blood. Although that might have been due to the blood pumping out from the jagged gap where his tooth used to be before a sharp stone knocked it out. And blood from where his lip had burst. And there might have been some blood sneaking into his mouth from his busted nose too.

The whole 'earth tastes like blood' controversy wasn't at the front of his mind, though. What he was more concerned about was finding a way to stop two psychos dragging him through a field behind a tractor. Again.

It hadn't been so bad at first, as being dragged through a field goes. But then they'd gagged him because of the noise he was making, trapping the blood and soil in his mouth, making him choke and struggle for breath. And then they'd bound his hands behind his back to stop him going for his gag.

And then dragged him through a field by his feet, his body turning and twisting through the stony furrows, mud and rocks and roots ripping and grabbing at him, his burst nose hoovering up mud when his body turned face down.

It wasn't exactly the way he'd expected the evening to pan out.

It had seemed so promising at first. The message had clearly got through. The arrival of a pick-up truck, the offer of a chat somewhere quiet, the drive up to fields high above the loch. So far so according to plan.

But when he held back on what he knew, judging that to be his main card and not wanting to play it too soon, that's when it had all got a bit Wicker Man.

"Do you like water skiing?" the smaller of the two men had said to him, the weaselly one.

"I'm not sure," Nigel had said back to him, a bit uncertain, wondering where all this was going to go.

"Tell you what," the weaselly one had said. "Let's have a go at it. Just for a laugh. See if it helps you remember a bit more. Exercise is good for that sort of thing."

"Not sure I'm with you. Water skiing? At this time of night?"

"Well, we don't actually have any skis. Or water for that matter, not up here. We'll need to...what's the word? Improvise."

Which is when the big man grabbed him - crushed him, really - dragged him over to a tractor, tied a rope tight around his ankles, and the agony began.

It must have been around fifty metres the first time, although it felt longer. Then the weasel man had got out, told him to stop shouting, insisted that he spill what he knew, and when he wouldn't, he gagged him and tied his hands.

And although the second time was longer and worse, at least it seemed to be over.

The tractor had stopped. Easter stayed in the driving seat while Banjo jumped down into the field, cursing the mess it was making of his boots and jeans. Still, all in a day's work.

He bent down next to Nigel, brushed soil away from his eyes, and pulled the gag off.

"Any danger of some sense getting into that thick head of yours?" Banjo said at him, although Nigel couldn't hear him properly with a ringing in one ear and mud in the other. His heart was hammering so hard he thought it might burst out his chest. Instead, he struggled to pull himself up to sitting position then retched up over Banjo's boots.

"Ach, ya dirty...!" Banjo finished his curse by thudding his sick-covered foot into Nigel's stomach.

"Right! No more pissing around!" Banjo said, getting close to Nigel's face again. "What. The fuck. Did you see? Tell us, and all this can stop. Simple as."

Nigel wheezed and gasped, the pain in his stomach battling the pain in his chest, arms, head.

"Your boss," he said, coughing it out. "I need to talk to your boss."

"In that case we've got ourselves a wee problem, haven't we? Because my boss doesn't want to talk to you. Doesn't want you saying anything to anyone. But before you don't say anything, we want to know what it is you won't be saying. You get me?"

Nigel Bellingham thought he got him, but the terror and pain was making his head a bit fuzzy.

Banjo wasn't happy with the delay in getting an answer, so he booted him in the stomach again, shoved the gag back around his mouth and jumped up into the tractor cab with Easter.

"Take him around again," he said as Easter sparked the engine into life. They set off down the field, building up speed. Faster and faster than before. Near the bottom, Easter threw the steering wheel around to take the tractor in a sharp turn before it came to the fence. The tractor banked as they took the corner, the speed cutting as they turned, then almost stopping as Easter pointed it back up the hill. They set off upwards, but something stopped the tractor going further, as if it was being held back.

Banjo looked over his shoulder into the gloom but couldn't make out anything.

"Bastard's probably grabbed hold of something," he said. "Give it some major fucking revs. He'll let go soon enough."

Easter stamped his foot down on the accelerator pedal. The resistance continued. He revved even harder, the engine screaming at him. The tractor leapt forward, throwing the men back in their seats, and then they were riding up the field again, back towards the top.

"Right," Banjo said when they got there, motioning Easter to stop. "You have a go at him this time. Fucking sick of being the nice guy."

Easter nodded his huge block of a head, unfurled himself from behind the steering wheel and climbed out of the tractor.

Banjo lit a pre-rolled roll-up he had in his jacket pocket, spitting out a few loose strands of tobacco. On his second deep inhale, he became aware of Easter standing near his side of the tractor.

"That was quick," Banjo said, surprised. "What's he saying?"

Easter mumbled something in a deep rumble.

"What? Speak up, man."

"He's not saying nothing."

"Well what the fuck you doing standing here, then? Get back and make him say something! Or do I have to do everything around here?"

Another mumble from Easter, looking down at the ground.

"What? I can't hear you."

"He can't say anything."

"Why not?"

"Can't find his mouth."

"What the fuck are you talking about? Where do you normally find people's mouths?"

Easter shrugged. "On their heads."

"Well, then. Problem solved."

"Can't find his head."

"What do you mean you can't find it? It's on the top of his shoul.....oh fuck!"

Banjo leapt down from the tractor in a panic and rushed around to the back, following the rope in the dim light. The rope led to a pair of ankles. Which were attached to legs, a torso, a chest, arms, shoulders. And that's where it got a bit messy.

"Where the fuck's his head gone?" Banjo said, looking up at Easter.

Easter struggled to find the words, ended up shrugging again.

"Well, fucking find it!"

The two men set off at pace, checking either side of the tractor tracks in the mud. When they reached the bottom of the field, the reason for their hold up earlier became much clearer.

The problem was some rusty farm equipment by the side of the fence, including the remnants of a wide multi-bladed plough. Attached to it, stuck between two of the blades, was the raggedy-necked head of Nigel Bellingham. He didn't look happy.

And, to be fair, neither did Banjo and Easter.

An hour later, the barracuda was back. The stillness. The hanging jaw and sharp teeth.

Then Frank Fisher circled Banjo and Easter, who were standing in the middle of his home office. He moved around them slowly, with small, deliberate steps, tapping a 4-iron golf club on the end of his shoe, staring at the men the whole time. There was a smooth flow to his movements, almost an elegance, despite the tension in his facial muscles and in the room.

He completed the full circle, standing right in front of Banjo, their faces an inch apart.

Silence. Stillness. Tension.

"Boo!" Fisher said. Banjo flinched. Then Fisher dropped his voice, almost to a whisper. "You see? That's a wee scare."

"Sorry, boss," Banjo said, fidgeting.

"When you scare someone, the point is, you make them grateful, eager for the absence of scariness. You understand that?"

"Definitely. As I say, boss..."

"So, when someone's had a scare, they might behave a bit better. To make sure the scariness stays away."

"Totally, boss, it's just...."

Fisher swung his golf club fast, just missing Banjo and Easter's heads before he smashed it down into a vase of flowers that Anne-Marie had placed on a side table that afternoon. Glass, tulips and gerberas spattered everywhere. He raised the club back up again instantly.

"So why...!"

crash

"...the fuck...!"

crunch

"....am I...!"

splinter

"...hearing...!"

thump

"...this...!"

shatter

"SHITE!"

Fisher heaved in deep breaths, his face purple, his eyes bulging.

He threw the golf club into the wreckage of the side table, stumbled to his desk and collapsed into the black leather swivel chair.

"What the fuck did I do?" he said to the ceiling. "I must have done something really fucking bad in a past life to be punished like this, being landed with a pair of useless cunts like you two."

He leant forward, staring at each man in turn.

"Is it not bad enough that the cops are sniffing around about those scientist bastards? I'm trying to calm things down here, get everything under control, isolate threats. You were supposed to talk to him. Find out what he knew. Find out what he wanted. Not tear his fucking head off."

"An accident, though, boss," Banjo said, taking a step forward towards the desk, hands out pleading. "It was just a bit of torture gone wrong. It was working, he was just about to spill everything."

"Well he spilled something, didn't he. All over the fucking field. Anyway, right now we don't know what he knew, don't know what he's told anyone or who he's told it to. A lot of loose ends. I could do without this kind of stress, quite frankly. So how have you got rid of the body?"

Banjo and Easter looked at each other, unsure who should say it. Banjo nodded at the bigger man.

"Outside in the pick-up," said Easter.

"Outside? Outside here? My house? You brought a mutilated bastard to my house? What the fuck were you.....out! Out now! Take it as far away as you can, right up into the fucking hills, bury it as deep as you can, bury it so deep the only way anyone will find him is if some fucking dingo digs him up in a shallow grave in Bastardsville, Australia. Now!"

Both men started for the door, but Fisher's voice stopped them dead.

"Wait! Tell me you've got the head as well. You haven't left it sticking on a fucking pole in the middle of Drumnadochit or some shite like that?"

"No, boss. It's in the back with the rest of him."

"Right, then. Off you fuck. And don't come back until everything's totally cleaned up. I'm talking abso-fucking-lutely spotless."

The men disappeared out of the door as fast as they could. Fisher grabbed a bottle from his drinks cupboard. As he heard the growl of the pick-up's engine, he poured a substantial slug of whisky into a tartan coffee cup, looked at the mess he'd made, and gave a long, deep sigh.

"Fuck-a-doodle-fuck."

CHAPTER NINE

The man from Glasgow

Frank Fisher was not one of nature's worriers. He'd always been fuelled by a strong cocktail of confidence and optimism, always thought he'd come out on top. Even when he didn't, he'd find a positive way to spin it, convince himself that he'd won.

But he was worried. And he didn't like the feeling.

There was so much at stake this time. He'd bet everything on NessieWorld, because the potential rewards were so great. Not just the money, but the status too.

Victory was near. The game was in its final few minutes - he couldn't afford anything to go wrong now. What had Sir Alex Ferguson called it? Sweaty arse time, something like that.

Everything had been going so well. Mainly. Most of the humps in the project were behind him – all the hassle with the permits, the land use, moving a B road, planning permission. All of that was exhausting to deal with, but it was done. And yes, there'd been some delays, but everything was on track for the summer, more or less.

But suddenly now, a few complications. The scientists, the licensing problem, the headless tramp-looking guy. And now, his star ride – Nessie's Revenge.

He could feel a thin line of sweat sliding down his back and slipping into his arse crack. In a metaphorical sense.

Not how he wanted to start the day.

Fisher was in his home office getting ready to go down to the site. He'd had a call about problems with Nessie's Revenge, the most spectacular ride of all, the one which would make the park's name.

Apparently, he needed to see it for himself before they tried to sort it, so his team said. Although he couldn't think why - he wasn't exactly a trained mechanical engineer.

He heard an engine, and saw through the window that a dark car, a big Audi or BMW or something like it, was crawling up his drive.

Who the fuck was this, and why the fuck were they turning up unannounced? He was going to call for Banjo but remembered he'd given him the morning off, or a couple of hours anyway, after the late-night funeral.

"Doll! Doll!"

The music from the lounge next door cut out, and Anne-Marie came to the door in her gym kit, lurid tight leggings and a cut-off top.

"See who that is, whoever that bastard is coming up the drive," Fisher said. "Tell them to fuck off – I'm not in. Unless they're important, of course. We're talking royalty and upwards. Otherwise, they should book an appointment. I don't like folk just turning up."

A couple of minutes later Anne-Marie came back into his office, closing the door behind her.

"Think you'd better see him. Says he's from Glasgow."

"Who cares where the fuck he's from? He can't just bowl up here expecting an audience."

"No, he's from *Glasgow* Glasgow."

"Oh. Right. *That* Glasgow." Glasgow, their shorthand for the criminal empire of his sometime boss and major investor Tommy Gallagher. *That* Glasgow. "Who is he?"

"Never seen him before. Says his name's Liam something."

"Liam something. It's just as well I don't actually pay you to be my PA. If I did, I'm pretty sure I could get a refund."

"Ha bloody ha. Anyway, he's waiting downstairs. Want me

to bring him up?"

"I suppose. Not happy about Glasgow visiting unannounced, though. Check him out with your mate down there. Roxanne, whatever her name is. Text me when you find out."

Anne-Marie left, then came back with a youngish man, maybe mid-twenties, with short, neat hair and a black suit.

"Here he is," Anne-Marie said, showing him in. "Can I get you anything? Tea, coffee, something stronger?"

"Just water will be fine," the young man said, speaking to Anne-Marie but keeping his eyes on Fisher.

"What about you? Mr Fisher," Anne-Marie said.

Fisher seemed distracted and didn't reply straight away. He was wondering why this young man was looking at him without any fear or reticence. He had one of those thousand-yard stares he'd heard about, the type that snipers have. Dead eyes.

"Come in, come in," he said. "Liam, is it? Have a seat. No, Anne-Marie, nothing for me. I've got that meeting I've got to go to in a minute, I'll get something there."

Liam sat down in a chair in front of the desk and put his hands in his lap.

"First of all, Mr. Fisher," he said. "I wanted to thank you for seeing me at short notice. It is an absolute pleasure to meet you finally. I've heard a lot about you."

"Well, I haven't heard a thing about you. So..." Fisher let it tail off, giving one of his predatory smiles.

"Of course. Forgive me. I'm Liam Keane, and I work in Mr. Gallagher's executive fleet hire division."

Fisher inwardly shuddered at the name 'Gallagher'. There weren't many people he'd admit to being scared of, but the biggest, baddest, richest and most psychopathically violent of Glasgow's gang leaders was one of them.

"As what? A driver?"

"Financial adviser," Liam said, smiling despite the provocation. "Growth, investment, procurement, that kind of thing."

"Ok. And you were just passing and thought you'd drop in?" Was this streak of piss in short trousers about to try a protection racket job on him? Did he know who the fuck he was playing with?

"Call it investor relations if you like, Mr. Fisher. As I'm sure you're well aware, some of Mr. Gallagher's companies, and those of his associates, are due to make significant investments in your enterprise in the next few days, and as such they are keen to ensure that the investment remains a wise and reliable one."

"And this has all been agreed and worked through over a long time," Fisher said. "Longer than you know. Probably started when you were still at school. Look, son, it's very nice of you to pop by and all that, but I've got a business to run here. Things to do, so if there's nothing else...." Fisher started getting up from his seat.

"You make an excellent point, Mr. Fisher. You have indeed got a business to run, and I certainly don't want to get in the way of that. And people associated with Mr. Gallagher are keen that nothing gets in the way of that either. But it's fair to say that there are concerns."

"Concerns? What concerns? Nobody's got any reason to be concerned about anything. Everything's absolutely fucking tickety-boo. Build's nearly complete, staffing and training's underway, marketing's gearing up. Once the final investment's cleared, we're good to go."

Fisher's mobile pinged with a text. He flicked his eyes down at it, saw it was from Anne-Marie. A short message.

Legit says R. Rising star.

He looked back at Keane, who started speaking once he was

sure he had Fisher's full attention.

"But are we, Mr. Fisher? There are some people in Glasgow who are, shall we say, uncomfortable with how things stand at the moment. And these are people who don't like feeling uncomfortable, particularly if they are on the verge of making substantial investments. It's not good to have nervous investors, especially if you're the one making them nervous."

Fisher snorted a laugh.

"That's very good. Have you used that before, that line? It's very good. Very smart. Probably from some 'How to Get On In Business' book, am I right? 'How to Pretend You've Got a Big Swinging Dick When You've Actually Done Fuck All', that kind of thing. Think I saw that one in WH Smiths at the airport. Look," he said, leaning on his knuckles on the desk-top, staring hard at the young Liam Keane. "We will open on time, on budget, as agreed, as planned. End of. No nervousness at this end."

"But there do seem to be some unfortunate headlines at this end, don't there. The missing scientists. Anything we should know about that?"

"Just some accident. Got pissed, fell overboard, fuck all to do with me. Yes, it's unfortunate, but it's not my job to babysit some test-tube freaks to make sure they don't top themselves. It's a one-day wonder. Okay, maybe two days. Blowing over already. The 'papers'll move onto something else soon enough. Anyway, I've been using it to get some publicity for the park. No point wasting a good opportunity like that. I can always buy myself some new scientists. Nothing to worry about."

Keane regarded Fisher very coolly, letting a quiet stillness come over the room.

"And the problem with the operating licence?"

How the actual living fuck did he know about that?

"Not sure I'm with you. What about the licence?"

"We hear there's a blockage."

"Don't know where you're hearing that, but I can assure you there's no problem with the licence."

"In that case, why is the Council Convenor – a Councillor Thomson, I believe – why is he calling in the licence decision to have another look? Because that is what might be termed an existential problem for your theme park, isn't it? No licence, no big launch, no income. And that's exactly the sort of thing which makes potential investors worried."

Seriously – how did some jumped up flashy wideboy bastard from Glasgow hear about the inner workings of a Highland Council? It wasn't public knowledge. This was all behind the scenes. And he did *not* like the sudden appearance of the word 'potential' attached to the money he needed.

"Oh, *that*. I wouldn't worry about *that*. There was some talk about that maybe a month ago, but my people on the Council were quick to stamp on it. Just some power-mad bastard looking for a little pay day. He's been sorted. It's all locked down tight now."

"So you've got the licence?"

"In the bag."

"And I can take that back to Glasgow, can I? A 100% assurance from you that there is no problem with the operating licence, and that everything is going to plan?"

"You want me to repeat myself? Think I already said that."

"Just for clarity, Mr. Fisher. The people we're talking about like to be reassured, and they like to know who is taking ultimate responsibility for that reassurance."

"Listen, sonny. I don't know you from Adam, but I know your boss and your boss's boss, and *his* boss, and on and on. I've been doing this shite longer than you've been breathing, so although I'm delighted you're taking such a keen interest in my operation here, it really doesn't have the slightest fucking thing to do with you. I know Tommy Gallagher, and Tommy Gallagher knows that when you back Frank Fisher, then Frank Fisher is going to deliver. One hundred and fifty fucking percent. Happened so many times before that I'd need an extra brain just to remember them all. So take what the fuck you want back to Glasgow, but take it quickly because I've got shitloads of grown-up stuff to do today. Anne-Marie!"

The door opened almost immediately.

"Yes?"

"Mr. Keane is leaving. Escort him to the door, would you, doll? He's a young man in a hurry."

As they watched the sleek black car drive away, Anne-Marie looked at Fisher and saw that he was pumped up from the meeting. The young man had clearly got him going.

"A bit rude," she said.

"Wasn't he just? Coming up here unannounced, trying to shout the odds about my business. *My* business. Don't know who the fuck he thinks he is."

"No, I mean *you* were rude."

"Of course I was. You can't have little shits like that squaring up to you as if they're some hotshot. I've been in this game far too long to let someone like that get the drop on me. They're like dogs, these youngsters. Mad fucking dogs. You can see it in their eyes. You've got to show them that you're a bigger dog than they are. Send him off with his tail between his legs."

"Just saying. Roxanne says he's on the way up, that Tommy Gallagher thinks highly of him. One for the future. She's got her ear to the ground. Not like you up here."

"The fuck that s'posed to mean?"

"You're not as plugged in as you were, being up here so long. You know what it's like – people rise and fall. And if Tommy Gallagher's sending up someone like him, maybe it's trouble."

"Trouble." Fisher huffed at the thought, then went through to the lounge to get a drink. A bit early, but the fizzing in his veins demanded it. Anne-Marie followed him in, flicking the sound up on the TV, an episode of her favourite soap replacing the dancercise channel.

"There's no trouble," Fisher said as Anne-Marie settled on the sofa. "He was just a little nothing. Believe me, if Glasgow thought there was any trouble, they'd have sent the Jimmies. If Jimmy Donohue and Jimmy Nuts walk into your house, you know you've probably fucked up big style somewhere down the line. And that you'd better sort it sharpish unless you want to walk like a cowboy and talk like choirboy for the rest of your life."

Fisher took a big gulp of his whisky.

"But that little wannabe? No danger. Anyway, fuck it, let's have a tune. The blood's up. Got some jones in my bones. Alexa! Play some classic fucking 80s music!"

"Classic 80s from Spotify" said the soothing voice through the surround sound speakers, and the first notes of the Human League's 'Don't You Want Me, Baby?' filled the room.

"Now *that* is a fucking *tune*!" Fisher said, starting to shimmy around the room, grinning. And then as the first verse was about to come up he decided to make it a special karaoke session, dancing up to Anne-Marie and pointing at her.

"You was working as a HOOR in a titty bar! When I fucked you!"

"Fuck off," she said, trying to watch her soap through the music.

"True, though, isn't it," he said, stopping singing but still trotting around the lounge in quick little steps, shaking his thing to the music. "I hadn't spotted you in the club, you'd still be grinding your bahookie into some loser accountant's clammy crotch for a tenner a go. Instead of living in palatial luxury beyond your wildest dreams."

Anne-Marie tried to carry on watching the TV, but Fisher was in front of her now, wiggling his hips and fiddling with the buttons on his waistband. As the music swelled to the chorus, he raised both his arms wide, let his trousers slip to the floor and belted out:

"*I just want a BJ! I just want one now-ow-ow-ow! I just want a BJ! I just...*"

"Oh, for fuck's sake, give it me, then," Anne-Marie said, motioning him forward. "Anything to stop that bloody racket."

She grabbed his member and got to work on it, then put her hands on Fisher's hips to move him slightly to the side so that she could still see the TV.

Living the dream.

CHAPTER TEN

The big ride

They were just waiting for the bodies to wash up.

Although they hadn't actually said it in such brutal terms, that was the message Zander took away from his latest meeting with the police. The 'search' wasn't exactly going full-throttle – a couple of cops taking a tour of the loch every so often, looking at the shoreline, particularly the bits least visited by walkers. It was just a waiting game now.

And that was that. The police were about to confirm to the media that they now believed the two men were dead, and that the search was being called off.

Zander had agreed a quote on behalf of the university to go into the police press release, then phoned the Vice-Chancellor so that he could explain the situation to the families.

Zander was glad he didn't have to make the call to the families himself. Although they were expecting the worst, it was always devastating to have it confirmed – to crush out that last tiny glimmer of hope. He'd been on too many door-knocks back when he was a journalist, trying to speak to the recently bereaved. Sometimes having the door slammed in his face, sometimes invited in for tea and biscuits and the eventual, inevitable breakdown. There to document private pain, to observe, intrude. No, he was glad he didn't have to do that anymore.

There was nothing left to do except hang around for a few hours in case any remaining TV crews wanted a statement on-camera. There was a flight to Luton in the late evening, and he intended to be on it.

He gazed out of his hotel window at the lead-coloured loch. More than two hundred metres deep in some places. A long way down. A lot of cold, dark water. For a second, he had a flash of the two men down there somewhere, dead and drifting in the murk, but he shook it from his mind before it could chill him to the bone.

Could anything else be down there? Was there even the remotest possibility that there was some sort of creature that had evaded every attempt to find it over the best part of a century? The romantic in him liked to think so – there was some sense to what Frank Fisher had said, about the thought of it being more important than the reality.

But ultimately it was ludicrous. There wasn't even one tiny bit of scientific evidence to support the existence of anything unusual in Loch Ness. Even the most famous photographs had eventually been revealed as fakes.

Good luck to them if they wanted to make some money from the myth, but he wouldn't be joining the tourist crowds any time soon.

Time to pack. Time to go.

"So what am I supposed to be looking at?" Fisher said, standing with a small team beside the metal skeleton of Nessie's Revenge, the ride he was sure would make the place world famous.

"It's best that we show you, Mr. Fisher. Is that okay?" said one of the site engineers in high-viz vest and hard hat.

"As long as you tell me what I'm supposed to be looking at when you show me," Fisher said, as if to a child. A child he clearly didn't like very much.

"Sure. It's the animatronic monster, out in the water."

The engineer spoke into a walkie talkie, and the ride hummed and cranked into life.

It was like many other big rides. Punters sat with their legs dangling free while the ride took them through loops and turns and drops and twists. What made it different was that towards the end of the ride they would plunge towards the loch itself, then straighten up with the customers' feet seeming to almost skim the surface of the water. Then, in a finale dreamt up by Fisher himself, a huge animatronic monster head, half dinosaur, half dragon, would burst up out of the loch with open jaws, as if trying to bite the riders. They would, of course, slide easily through the huge mouth as it twisted at the last moment, escaping with a final jolt of screaming terror.

He wanted his ride to be the biggest, the best, the most terrifying ever – the ride that would have them queuing until Christmas. Engineers and designers had worked on it for two years, and this was the final testing phase before going live. It had taken long and tedious negotiations with health and safety wonks to get it all signed off.

Frankie Fisher did not want to hear that there was a problem. But that's why the team wanted to show him. They knew that if he was just told about it, he would probably blank it out and hope for the best. Seeing was believing.

The 8-person cart, empty of punters, sped through the track as they all watched. Swooping and swirling, going though sidewinders, hairpin turns and sudden drops. As it swept down towards the loch, the cart started jerking, and Fisher watched as the green monster head pushed up through the water, half opened its jagged mouth, then stopped. The cart stopped too, stranded halfway up the incline heading towards the beast.

"So, there it is, Mr Fisher," the engineer said. "We've been trying and trying, but there's a problem with the animatronics. It jams before it can twist, and that then makes the safety brake kick in and stops the ride."

"And how do you fix it?"

"That's the problem, Mr. Fisher - we're not sure we can. We've been through it with the designers again and again. There's no technical reason why it shouldn't work, although it's maybe got something to do with the complexity of the movement. This hasn't been done before. There's quite a lot for the monster's head to do, quite a bit of movement, and so it either could be something mechanical or it's some glitch in the programming. But either way, we've come to the conclusion," he said, casting around at the others standing in a rough circle behind him, "that a big decision needs to be made. And you're the only one who can make it."

"And that is?"

"Lose the monster. The ride works absolutely fine without it, smooth as you like. But as soon as we connect the monster head to the system, we get this. We could spend another six months trying to fix it, which is no use to anybody. Making the decision now to bin the monster could save a lot of grief in the long run."

They waited as Fisher walked down to the water's edge and looked at the stuck monster head. The lead engineer followed him, joined by Mary, his operations chief.

"No," Fisher said after a minute. "This is the heart of the whole park, the only ride which is all about Nessie. You can't have it without the monster. It doesn't work."

"But what if we just had the monster sitting there all the time, not moving?" the engineer said. "So, it's there, but there's not the problem of having to coordinate all the movements with the actual ride itself."

Fisher shook his head. He didn't need to think about it. This was his baby, the part of the park he felt most connected to and he wasn't about to give up just because it was difficult.

"You ever seen a Great White breach?" Fisher said. "A great

big throbber made of shark muscle, thrusting right up out of the water? Terrifying. It's something to see, it really is. There's videos on YouTube – you should take a look. And that's what I'm trying to get at here. Without Nessie, this is just a ride. A pretty good ride, probably scary enough, but no different from a hundred others. The difference is Nessie, the big surprise, rising up out of nowhere to take a bite at you. It's proper terror. You can imagine people genuinely shitting themselves. It'll be all anyone talks about. 'The day I had so much fun at a theme park that I crammed my pants with major bum slugs'. Why would I want to take that away from them? No. The monster stays. And it moves. I don't care how much it costs – this has got to be ready for opening day."

The engineer sighed, took off his hardhat, wiped his sweaty hair.

"I completely understand why you want it, Mr. Fisher. We know how important this is to you. But we simply don't know if we can fix it. We've tried everything we can think of."

"Did you hear that stuff I was saying a few seconds ago?" Fisher said, staring at the engineer, who nodded. "That was me closing the conversation. I wasn't actually inviting or expecting a continuation of our fascinating little chat. So, spend what you need, find the people that you need - the people who *can* fix it - and do it quickly. See? Problem sorted. Right!" he said, rubbing his hands together and turning to Mary. "Are those toilets over there fully operational yet? Because just thinking of that ride's got my adrenalin going. Need to drop the boys off at the pool, if you get my drift."

"Our wild nightlife too much for you, is that it?" Catriona said as Zander handed over his key, making him laugh.

"No, that was the high point, actually," he said, smiling. "It cheered me up. The Drum is going straight into my top 10 best bars in the world list."

"I take it you don't get out much."

"Not really, no."

"Anyway, I hope everything works out. And that the families get some closure."

"Me too. Although I don't know if you ever get over something like that. Both relatively young guys, parents still alive. It's awful."

"It all just seems so....weird," Catriona said.

"What do you mean?"

"Well, there's no answers. What were they doing out there, why did they suddenly need to go out in the boat? They just don't strike me as the types to get all silly and take a boat out in the middle of the night. They were nice enough, but they were serious men. Serious about their work, serious about their beer, serious about science. It just seems so out of character. And now with Nigel disappearing."

"Disappearing?"

"Ok, maybe not disappearing, but no-one's seen him since he was on the news. A couple of people have been looking for him, came here asking about him, but there's no sign. And he's always around – he's got nowhere to go – so that's weird too."

Zander's taxi pulled up outside the front door. He picked up his bag and smiled.

"Not everything has a neat answer, I suppose," he said. "Anyway, must be going. It was a real pleasure to meet you. Genuinely. Even with all the weirdness."

"I'll walk out with you. Need a fag break anyway."

Catriona walked out from behind reception, grabbing a packet of cigarettes from a drawer.

Outside, orange ripples of cloud framed a setting sun as Zander looked up to the hills above Drumnadrochit, taking in the wild beauty of the place for the last time.

"Thanks for everything, Catriona. I appreciate it," he said, wondering about lost opportunities as the taxi driver swung his bag into the boot.

"Back down to the deep south with your fancy bars and fancy cocktails and fancy beers," she said, lighting up. "Although you can get them here too, of course."

"Yes," said Zander smiling. Then stopped.

"What was that you said earlier?" he said. "Serious men, serious about their beer."

"Yes. Well, they were. You know that. Almost obsessive, but in a nice way."

"That's right. Wouldn't drink anything unless it was hand-crafted by some tiny collective who strained it through old Van Halen t-shirts, that kind of thing. But what was on the boat?"

"What do you mean?"

"They were on the boat, supposedly drunk. That's the police assumption. I saw the evidence myself, all these cans."

"So?"

"Cans of lager. A dozen or more, on the table, in the bin. Cheap supermarket lager. Not what you'd call 'craft' by any stretch of the imagination. Cooking lager. Not the sort of stuff they'd drink, not in a million years."

"Meaning what?"

"Meaning," Zander said, opening the boot and grabbing his bag, "that I'm not going anywhere. Someone else was on the boat."

CHAPTER ELEVEN

The bothering

He hadn't been a journalist for several years, but that didn't stop Zander Burns being a nosy, contrary bastard at times.

There was a reason so many journalists became PR people. Not just because they understood the media and what made a story, but because the journalistic qualities of inquisitiveness and tenacity were crucial for dealing with threats to their employers' reputation.

Because to stop an issue becoming a story in the first place sometimes meant forcing their employer to deal with it before it blew up. Which meant digging away at internal problems, asking the questions nobody wanted asked.

And, he realised now, he hadn't been asking the right questions. Admittedly, he hadn't been expecting to ask any questions at all. His role, very simply, was to act as a reassuring mouthpiece for the university.

But he had several problems with the situation. And he'd been assuming that others – in the police, for instance – were asking the right questions, poking sticks into dark corners to flush out the truth.

Was there a bigger truth beyond two pissed men taking a boat for a joyride and ending up drowned? Probably not, as it seemed so obvious.

So why were so many things bothering him?

The timings on Mike's computer, which showed it had been shut down hours after Jules had arrived at the site.

The evidence of their drunkenness being cans of booze

they'd have flung away in disgust.

The fact that it was all so out of character for them to do something wild and reckless like taking a boat out onto the loch in poor visibility.

And then that weird bloke Nigel on the news. What was all that about? And where was he?

Okay, it wasn't the Kennedy assassination – he wasn't claiming there was some huge conspiracy going on. But there were more than a few odd things going on, and he was beginning to wonder if he was the only one – apart from Catriona – who wanted answers.

Zander dropped a quick email to his boss to say he was staying on to tidy up a few loose ends – nothing specific mentioned – and that he'd call tomorrow with an update.

Fifteen minutes' walk took Zander to the roadside carpark high above Urquhart Castle, an absurdly picturesque ruin hanging onto the edge of Loch Ness. Hector was standing beside the path down to the castle in tweed jacket and flat cap, with a homemade placard on a stick.

LEAVE NESSIE ALONE! it said in big, bright red letters. Then 'Please' written underneath in smaller script, as if jammed in as an afterthought.

A couple of tourists were getting selfies with Hector, so Zander simply nodded hello as he passed, Hector giving a curt nod in reply.

Down the zigzag path through neat lawns towards the castle, then cutting off halfway to take a worn track through the grass towards the wooded field at the side. An informal style crossed the fence next to a sign saying 'Nessie Hunter Nigel B welcomes you! Professional Photos for sale!'

Once over, Zander could see Nigel's shack, just where Catriona said it would be – a bizarre shed on a scrap of land next to the stony shoreline. The bottom half was made up of irregular planks of wood and pieces of board held together with ropes. The top half, mainly canvas but with a rusted corrugated iron sheet covering half of the roof, held up by four poles.

A regular-looking front door with nine small glass panels faced the loch. Zander knocked, then called out.

"Hello? I'm looking for Nigel."

No reply. He looked around, knocked again. There was a window of sorts to the side, but it seemed to be just layers of scruffy cellophane. There was no chance of seeing through it.

He tried the handle. The door opened with only a slight shove.

"Hello?" Zander gave it a beat, then ducked down through the low doorway and moved inside.

The place was a masterclass in efficiency. One room, with a narrow bed across the end, some shelves above, a small square table and one chair, a camping gas stove with canisters underneath, and the walls lined with what looked like offcuts of thick carpet. One small chest of drawers, with some items of clothing hanging on hooks above it. Everything had a place; it was neat, clean and organised. On the shelves above the bed, box files with dates on the spines going back years, history books on Loch Ness, the Highlands, folklore and photography.

And beside the bed, next to a sturdy wooden box with a lock on it, was a tripod with an expensive-looking long-lensed camera attached to it, a Canon. Zander was no expert, but he thought it must be worth a grand or more. And it was just sitting there in an unlocked shack.

Looking around, there was nothing to suggest Nigel had left in a hurry - or to suggest anything at all, really. Nothing suspicious. Just as if Nigel had stepped outside for a moment and would be back any second.

But the camera bothered Zander. Maybe people still left

their doors unlocked in the Highlands, maybe they were more trusting. He had no clue if that was the case. But it didn't feel right just leaving it there, especially when Nigel hadn't been seen for a while.

He knew he was crossing a big black line, but he took out a business card from his wallet, scribbled 'have taken camera for safekeeping. I'm at Drumnadrochit Arms hotel. Call me please', then left it on the table as he scooped up the camera and tripod, then got out fast, feeling oddly spooked by the whole thing.

Back in his room he began to regret it. It had seemed sensible at the time, but he'd just technically stolen a valuable piece of property. For good, honourable reasons, perhaps – but judges probably heard that all the time.

Oh, well – in for a penny.

He lay back on his bed, studied the controls for a few moments, then switched on the camera. A large screen on the back flashed up a glorious shot of the loch on a sunny day, just a few white clouds blemishing a deep blue sky. He toggled through a few more pictures. Daytime shots – a gnarled tree down by the shoreline with flat black water behind it, purple hills rising up behind a red-roofed white cottage, artful shots of driftwood sticking out of the loch. Moodier shots of dark clouds looming over choppy waters, which Zander thought would look cool in black and white. He remembered that Catriona had said something about Nigel making money off tourists by selling prints of the loch.

The last frames he looked at were less impressive. He could make out Urquhart Castle lit up at night, but it was blurred, as if a grey film covered it all. There were perhaps a dozen shots like that, kind of atmospheric but they didn't really do it for Zander. The last four shots on the camera were completely grey – nothing to see at all. He thumbed through the earlier shots again, then a red battery symbol flashed on the screen for a few seconds before the camera went dead.

Zander wanted to know if there was anything else worth seeing on the memory card, so he slipped it out of the camera and stuck it in his shirt pocket.

When he got downstairs there was an older man on reception - Catriona's father, Zander guessed. Tall and balding, with a face that looked permanently disappointed and sorry.

"Have you got anything that I could look at a memory card on, please, a laptop or..."

The man was shaking his head before Zander was even halfway through the question.

"No, nothing like that," he said. "Sorry."

"Oh. Ok. Is Catriona around by any chance?"

"In the bar, I'd expect," the man said. His eyes narrowed ever so slightly. "Why?"

"No reason. Just wondering."

"You go out the front," the man said, "take a left, then go along..."

"Okay with you if I take the short cut?" Zander said, smiling at him. "Through there, is it?" He pointed to a door to the right of the reception desk and started walking towards it.

"Of course. Be my guest."

The Drum was quiet, just a few tables occupied. The TV showed a rolling news channel but the sound was down, with music coming from the wall-hinged speakers instead. Something 80s, Zander was pretty sure. Catriona was behind the bar sitting on a stool reading a book, a battered copy of an old novel. She glanced up.

"Hi," she said. "Any luck?"

"Wasn't in. Couldn't really tell if he'd been there recently. Everything looked fine, apart from the place not being locked. His camera was in there, so I brought it back here. To look after it for him."

"You broke into his house and stole his stuff?"

"No. Just kind of strolled in slowly. And stole his stuff." He eyed the beers on draft. "Could I have a Black Isle Blonde, please?"

"Keep your eyes off my thighs, you dirty minded beast," said old Bessie, wobbling on a stool down the other end of the bar. "I might be a blonde but there's nothing cheap or easy about me. I am out of your league, sonny."

Zander nodded politely at the resolutely grey-haired Bessie as Catriona poured his pint, smirking.

"Anyway," he said to her as she set the glass in front of him. "I've got the memory card from his camera, but I need something to look at it on. Maybe there's something on it which explains what on earth he was banging on about on TV."

"Ask Donald and Hector, they might be able to help."

Zander raised his eyebrows.

"Seriously?"

"Seriously."

He took his pint over to their table and asked if he could join them, sat down, then told them about the memory card.

"That sounds right up Hector's street," Donald said. "He's quite the whizz with computers and technology and all that malarky."

Zander pictured Hector tapping away at some ancient Amstrad with two fingers, struggling to get to grips with putting attachments onto emails.

"Have a look?" Hector said, holding out his hand.

Zander took out the memory card and gave it to him, not expecting much. Hector looked at the small black square for a few seconds, then looked at Donald.

"Extreme Pro. 64 gig. 4K too. Decent. Need my HP," he said.

"Now, clearly," Donald said, "I don't actually understand what he just said. But I think I get the general gist. He's got a device of some description which may allow you to view said memory thingmy. I think." He looked back at Hector for confirmation. Hector nodded once.

"What is it you're looking for anyway?" Donald said.

"Not entirely sure, really. Anything which throws light on what Nigel was saying before he disappeared."

"And you came about this memory card how exactly?"

"It was in his camera."

"And how did you find that?"

"I took it from his hovel. Hut. House."

"So, what you're saying – to a retired but still fairly well-connected member of Her Majesty's constabulary – is that *this*," Donald said, nodding at the memory card Hector still held in his hand, "is stolen goods?"

"Borrowed goods. Borrowed temporarily goods. Giving it back as soon as I can goods."

"Oh, that's absolutely fine, then." Donald rolled his eyes. "Anyway, it's good that Hector's handling it rather than me. He's the one with form, as it were."

"In what way?"

"Hector Menzies is, or rather *was* before his retirement, one of the finest burglars ever to come out of the Highlands. Never caught him. Never found out it was him before we were retired and past it. He could get in anywhere, even places with really high-tech security. *Especially* places with really high-tech security. The Tartan Panther, we used to call him at headquarters."

"Why?"

Donald shrugged.

"We just thought it sounded really cool."

"What about the high-tech, stuff. How did you get past all that?" Zander said to Hector.

"Hacker," Hector said.

"Funny thing was," Donald said. "He never seemed to take anything, nothing substantial or valuable anyway, not from what we could make out. Just made it obvious he'd been there. A safe left open but untouched, expensive pictures rearranged, secret files printed off, that kind of thing. And he'd always leave a little scrap of tartan. Like a calling card."

"So why did you do it, if you didn't take anything?" Zander said to Hector.

"Pens."

"What?"

"Took pens."

"Yes, I meant to say," Donald said. "He always seemed to take pens. Bics, Parkers, whatever was lying about."

"Like a trophy, you mean?" Zander asked Hector.

"No. Just needed pens."

"Ok. So apart from the pens, why did you do it?"

Hector shrugged.

"Kicks. Bored."

Zander bought them drinks by way of thanks after Hector agreed – mainly at Donald's prompting – to examine the card for anything unusual and report back. In the meantime, Donald would put a word in with the police in Inverness about Nigel's vanishing act. There was no-one else to speak up for him, after all.

After a meagre dinner of sandwiches and crisps, Zander went back to his room to give more thought to selling it all to the university. How exactly was he going to explain this strange need to stay on?

He saw the mess as soon as he opened the door. Not a big mess, but one he certainly hadn't made himself. The mattress half off the bed, his carry-on case emptied, the bedside table drawers open. It must've been a quick job, because there wasn't much to steal. Except Nigel's camera. Which was gone.

CHAPTER TWELVE

Means, motive, opportunity

The hotel manager was useless. Nope, didn't see anybody, nothing unusual. Didn't even seem interested in taking it further until Zander insisted.

The constable sent by HQ in Inverness was equal to the manager's uselessness. A low bar to crawl under, but he hunkered down and managed it anyway.

After a thorough check it was obvious to Zander that the only thing missing was the camera. Which made it all a little complicated, seeing as he didn't own it and wasn't entirely clear of the exact model, age, specification, cost. Possibly due to it being stolen goods, although he glossed over that slightly, claiming he'd borrowed it from a friend. A friend he hadn't actually met and who was currently missing, he neglected to add.

Because at the back of his mind were three options. There had to be a strong chance that Nigel had come back home, seen the note on Zander's card, been pissed off that his camera was gone and come charging up to the hotel to grab it back. Rifling through his room was out of order, but could he really blame him for wanting to get his stuff back?

The second option was that a hotel guest or member of staff had stolen it, which is perhaps why the manager - Catriona's father - was keen to play it down.

Another option was that someone with criminal tendencies had been to Nigel's hut, seen the card and decided to take a big risk by going to the hotel and stealing it. Which seemed pretty unlikely.

The young policeman noted down a few details, took Zander's mobile number, and said they'd be in touch if they heard anything.

"Very sorry," the manager said to him once the policeman had gone. "We do warn guests not to keep valuables in their room."

"It was there for about an hour and a half," Zander said. "You'd think it'd be pretty safe in a locked room in a small hotel in a small village in the Highlands. It's not exactly New York in the 80s, is it."

Zander left the manager muttering and went out of the hotel for a walk to cool his head. Almost as soon as he was out the door, a black and white blur leapt on him.

"Jesus!" He jumped back.

"Down, Shep!" said Donald. "Don't worry, he's just being friendly. Mind you, I also say that to folk he ends up biting. Not sure I'm entirely au fait with his motivations."

Shep sat down and looked up at Zander, tongue hanging out. It almost looked like it was smiling.

"Just taking Shep out for a post-pub constitutional. Doesn't like being cooped up in the house while I'm hitting the bright lights. Join us if you like."

Zander fell in with them as they walked through the village, cutting off towards a low hill. He told Donald about the camera and the uselessness of the manager.

"Oh, he's not a bad man," Donald said. "Been through a lot, has Bruce. Losing the hotel was kind of the final straw. Not the man he was. Probably only Catriona that keeps him going, and we don't see all that much of her these days."

"Why not?"

"Student in Edinburgh. Back here in the holidays and the odd weekend. Think she makes excuses to come up, keep an eye on the old man. A good girl, a kind girl. Takes after her mother, God rest her soul."

"Oh. I didn't realise."

"Well, it's a long time ago now. Cancer. Bastard disease. She was just a wee one at the time, Catriona. Bloody cruel thing to happen to a child. Evil, really." He shook his head.

They kept walking, a deep orange glow lighting up the clouds to the west as the late Highland sun finally gave up for the day.

"You mentioned you're ex police."

"I did, yes. Forgive me, I haven't properly introduced myself. Detective Inspector Donald MacDonald, Highland Constabulary, retired, but at your service."

He clicked his heels and bowed his tweed-bunneted head.

"Might need to get you out of retirement," Zander said. "I'm not getting very far with the police officers who are actually supposed to be working." He ran through the questions he'd been asking himself.

"That does seem to have a bit of a whiff about it," Donald said eventually. "Although anything with Frank Fisher's name attached to it is bound to stink a bit."

"I'm not sure what I'm supposed to do about it. I mean, is any of it connected or is it all just random nonsense? And then this business with Nigel's camera. If there are any connections, I'm struggling to see what they are."

"Maybe you need to look at it a different way," Donald said, guiding Zander down a path across a wide village green. "Let's assume for a second that your colleagues are, unfortunately, deceased. And let us also assume, for the sake of exploring it, that it wasn't an accident. Is there anyone who would benefit from them being out of the picture?"

"No. I mean, their work is important but it's not something you'd kill for. There's competition between universities, and the pharma companies are interested in what's going on, but I can't see how that translates into Jules and Mike being targeted in any way."

"Is it possible they found out something in the course of their research that others - such as these pharmaceutical companies, for example - wouldn't want anyone else to know about? A lot of big money involved in these companies, after all."

"I mean, it's possible – theoretically," Zander said. "But again, I can't see a pharma company setting up a hit over something like this. Or maybe I'm being naïve. Maybe they're topping people all of the time to prevent them finding a cure for the cold."

He kicked at a stone, sending it skiting along the path, Shed trying to race after it until pulled back in by Donald.

"Means, motive, opportunity," said Donald. "The basis for identifying a suspect – if a crime's been committed, that is, and we're not sure it has in this case. Motive, for me, is the most important element. If you really want to go down this road, I'd suggest you start mapping out the people around your scientists, then start examining what circumstances might give any of them a motive. Start right at the centre, with the two men themselves. Crime of passion, maybe? Then move out the way, like ripples. Their family, their employers," he said, raising his eyebrows at Zander, "friends, rivals. You get the gist. Then potential motives. Different scenarios, however fanciful. Then start narrowing it down. As the great Sherlock Holmes famously said, once you eliminate the impossible, then whatever's left is .... shite on a bicycle."

"Did he say that?"

"No, it's Shep. Having an evening dump, and I've forgotten to bring out the jobbie bags again." Shep was squatting by the side of the pavement, curling out a major turd. "Don't have anything suitable on you, do you? A shopping bag? Burlap sack?"

"Not specifically on me, no."

Once Shep had finished, Donald stood there wondering what to do. He slid his shoe towards the pile of steaming faeces, considering nudging it towards the grass verge, but pulled back before he touched it.

"I'm sure it'll be fine," he said. "Nobody's going to be walking along here at this time in the evening. It'll probably get eaten by foxes overnight, they'll eat anything. Anyway, let's get out of here before the dogshit police turn up. Just in case."

They turned, faced along the road towards the village in the fading dusk, and started to walk back. Zander let the thoughts drift through his head. Means, motive, opportunity. So who had the motive?

After longer than seemed necessary, Easter had found a suitable cable for charging the camera. Now, after just twenty minutes, a green light glowed on its side.

"Well, it is ready then? Come on," Fisher said to him, making rushing, flapping motions with his hands.

Easter unplugged the camera, handed it to Banjo, who took it over to where Fisher was sitting at his desk.

"Right, let's see if the bastard managed to see anything," Fisher said, grabbing the camera out of Banjo's hands and pressing the 'on' button.

The camera made a digital tinkling sound as it powered on, then the message flashed up on the small viewing screen.

'No memory card'.

Fisher gripped the camera tighter, his knuckles turning white. Then he raised the camera up as if he was about to smash it down onto his desk, but he stopped himself, lowering it gently.

His face boiled red, the vein standing out on his temple.

"Any problem, boss?" Banjo said, getting ready to step back from the desk quickly.

"Problem? Yes, there's a fucking problem. Yes in-fucking-deedy. The problem is, why the fuck do I actually pay you good fucking money instead of just keeping you in a fucking cage and throwing you scraps of meat every so often? Why do I hope that other than your legendary ability to be mentally violent towards people, you might be able to carry out the simplest fucking task? Why, in short, am I looking at a camera without any pictures on it?"

Banjo came forward, took a quick look at the camera and stood back again.

"Says there's no memory card, boss."

"I know there's no....." He stopped, put the camera to the side, laid his hands flat on the desk, then let his forehead sink down towards them. Then, with a deep intake of breath, he shot upright in his chair.

"Find it. Just fucking find it. We don't know what that cunt had, what he knew, who he'd told. And now, very possibly, that *other* cunt *does* know. So you need to find out, but subtly. Subtle is the word. Do you know what subtle means?"

"Is it....?" Banjo said, then paused.

"Find out without creating a holocaust of body parts. Be smart, get the information, and don't pull anyone's arms off if at all possible, pretty please and thank you. Now fuck the fuck out of here to the other side of fuck, and don't come back until you've got some information I can work with."

The men left sharpish. Fisher stood up, going over to his big window and looking out at the amber light fading over the hills.

But he didn't see the beauty of it all. He was looking inwards.

"Mr. Zander fucking Burns," he said to himself. "You are beginning to get right on my tits."

Hector Menzies wondered where he would go tonight. To the top of the Empire State Building? To the boardroom at Facebook? Or maybe to the Italian Prime Minister's bedroom?

Choices, choices, choices.

For instance, the other night he had a very pleasant stroll around the Sistine Chapel. Couldn't see the ceiling, of course, the cameras weren't pointing up there. But the corridors were very nice.

Maybe he could visit the past instead. Look at some of the recorded CCTV footage from local places, see if it threw up anything interesting. Aye, now there's a thought.

Hector sat back from the bank of computer monitors set up across the vast desk in his spare bedroom. It was nice to get out and about, even if it was virtually. A little digital dander. Have a little peek, and leave no trace. Good to have a hobby.

But there was something he should do first. He'd promised to have a look at the memory card for that young man. See if there was anything of interest.

Hector took the memory card from his pocket and slipped it into a reader plugged into one of his computers. He fired up an advanced photographic app and started examining the pictures. There were hundreds. For an hour he looked through the landscapes and loch views, magnifying them to see if any people, boats or vehicles captured by Nigel had any potential significance. Also, whether there was anything which could even vaguely be described as mysterious – a shadow in the water, ripples, wakes. He made a few notes in pencil on a pad by his side, jotting down the image numbers and anything worth returning to for a closer look. He paid particular attention to the most recent pictures, the night-time ones of Urquhart Castle which appeared to be blurred in some way.

It was obvious to Hector, but he checked the date stamp in the card's metadata anyway. Yes, as he thought. Taken a few nights ago, the night the scientists went missing. Not blurred – it was mist. Nigel was trying for some arty, moody shots of the castle lit up through the mist, but it hadn't quite worked. He'd seen the photos Nigel sold and this didn't stand a chance compared to some of the more picturesque shots on the card.

For the sake of it, he ran the pictures through a basic programme which cleaned them up, removing the noise from the pixels. At first there was nothing. And then he noticed the faint appearance of a line on the left-hand side of the frame. He ran the picture through more elaborate tests and filters, trying to bring out a clearer image.

It took a while, but eventually he sat back to give himself a wider look at what the programme had come up with.

It was faint. If you didn't know, you'd miss it. But yes, there was definitely something there.

Hector smiled.

"Bingo."

CHAPTER THIRTEEN

Out of bounds

The monster was enormous. Ten metres high, with thick, hairy arms reaching out, ready to crush anything in its way. It loomed over Zander as he stared up at its red-tipped teeth and deep-set dark eyes.

"Are you sure that's what a Yeti's supposed to look like?" he said to Mary, the operations chief, who was standing beside him. They were waiting for a crane to lower the model monster in front of the Yeti Mountain ride with its gut-churning vertical drop.

"If you want anatomical and historical accuracy, you've probably come to the wrong place," Mary said with a half-smile. "It's about the idea of it all. Have you not heard Mr. Fisher's speech about it? It's about the image. You'd know all about that, you're one of those people that hands out the Kool-Aid, aren't you? Anyway, as far as I know there's never actually been a Yeti captured or even photographed anywhere, so it could have green fur for all I know. As long as it scares the kids, that's what matters. And as long as everything gets finished to time and on budget, that's all I care about."

With the Yeti in place and uncoupled from the crane, it was clear for them to get back in the buggy and continue to the lab.

"What is it that you want to see, exactly?" Mary said as she steered the buggy down the access ramp towards the southern end of the park. "I thought you'd covered everything last time."

Zander had been vague when he'd turned up at the site un-announced and asked to see Mary. After all, Fisher had offered whatever help they could give.

But looking at the men's disappearance from a different angle meant he wanted to see what they'd been working on again, see if there was anything out of the ordinary which could be a threat to anyone.

"Just the files again. I only really spent a couple of minutes looking at them last time, and there's the question of how we ensure the work carries on."

Mary nodded, seemingly satisfied.

There were a few more people at workstations in the control centre when they walked in, people acknowledging Mary and saying hello as they both walked across the room to the corner where the scientists had been working. Zander logged on, then started scrolling through the files.

"Is there a way to see the activity on their swipe cards?" he said.

"How do you mean?"

"Well, we know Mike saved work here at just after half two in the morning, or rather the file was autosaved when he shut the computer down. And according to the delightful Mr. Banjo, the records show that both Jules and Mike used their swipe cards to get down to the dock about 11. I was wondering whether the swipe card records might tell us anything else."

"We could always ask Mr. McKenzie – Banjo. But he's not always the most accommodating, if you know what I mean."

"I kind of got that impression," Zander said. "Slightly odd choice for head of security, if you don't mind me saying."

"Don't mind at all. And he's not head of security. That's Jamie Dryden, ex Police Scotland. Banjo's something else, some kind of personal security adviser to Mr. Fisher, reports directly to him. He doesn't actually work for NessieWorld, but he's got Mr. Fisher's authority to have the run of the place. Not always the easiest man to work with."

"In that case, is there a way to look at the swipe card records without involving him?"

"Absolutely." Mary grabbed the phone on the desk, punched in a few numbers, and spoke to someone called Ben who joined them in a matter of minutes. He was young and assured, the way Zander remembered he used to be himself.

"Swipe cards records, yeah?" Ben said, then started tapping away at the computer, getting into Mike's account using administrator permissions. "What day you after?"

"Monday night."

"Oh yeah. Obviously," Ben said, then started tapping again. A list of numbers scrolled onto the left-hand side of the screen. Zander ran his finger down them, stopped at one.

"22:34:13. C4. The time's obvious, but what's C4?"

"It's that door over there in the corner," Mary said. "The way we came in."

"There's quite a few here between then and..." he looked down the list, "23:43:27. DK1?"

"That's the dock area," Mary said. "Think that was mentioned before."

"I thought it was nearer eleven, not nearly midnight. But that's the last one. There's no record of him coming back up here to shut down his computer. Do they shut down automatically?"

"Go to sleep, not shut down," Ben said.

"But this one was shut down, I think. Can you check?"

Ben opened some other tabs, did some checking.

"Yeah, it was physically shut down at 02:33:56 on Tuesday morning."

"Maybe Dr. Conway did it?" Mary said. Zander got Ben to check the records, but there was nothing on Jules coming back to the lab after he'd left it at 22:38:47, not long after Mike. There was a swipe at the dock door just after Mike's too, at 23:43:50.

"What do these other numbers stand for?" Zander said, pointing down a column at various times between just after ten thirty and eleven thirty. B2, B4 and B7 were listed several times each.

"B2 is the door at the bottom of the stairs on the way to the dock. B4 is, I think, the holding tanks, that's a restricted area. And B7 is...help me out here, Ben."

Ben pulled up a plan on screen.

"That's just an auxiliary area, spare tanks, overflow storage, water drain, that sort of thing."

"And both men were in there?" Zander said. Ben flicked back and forth between tabs.

"Yup. Through B2, then in B4 and B7 for an hour, back and forwards by the look of it, then out through B2 then DK1, the dock."

"So, they were in there for over an hour after leaving here, and before they took the boat out," Zander said. "What were they doing all that time? Funny no-one mentioned it before."

"Maybe that's where they kept their beer?" Mary said. "Fairly chilly down there."

"Only one way to find out," Zander said. "Fancy a walk, anyone?"

"I'm afraid we can't, not down there," Mary said. "As explained to you last time, it's a restricted area. It's kept under very specific conditions of temperature, cleanliness, to make sure it's safe for the sea life stock once it gets here."

"Yes, but I only want a quick look, though," Zander said, putting on his best smile. "Just a few minutes."

Mary took a long look at him, then shook her head, smiling.

"You are going to get me in trouble," she said, pointing at his chest. "Come on. Quickly."

They left Ben at the desk and headed through the doors and

down the stairs, down to the double doors with the 'Strictly No Admittance' sign above them. Mary swiped the door, then tapped in a PIN. The doors clicked and she pushed through, keeping them open for Zander to come through.

Lights came on automatically and Zander realised they were in a huge, man-made cave. It was about the same size as the one with the amphitheatre but was totally enclosed. In the centre was a vast glass-sided tank filled with water. One end of the tank was up against one of the walls, and Zander guessed it linked up with the amphitheatre's own tank with an underwater door of some kind. At the other end of the tank, two large pipes stuck out, one bending down into the concrete and the other heading straight out through the rear wall. The whole place was clean and chilled, and motors and pumps hummed in the background. A mini forklift lay still beside a crane connected to several pulleys, and unopened boxes around the walls promised more equipment ready for set-up.

"Not much to see at the moment," said Mary. "We're due to finish this within the month in time for the aquarium to get populated. The species that'll be on show, the dolphins, seals, orcas, maybe even sharks – I don't know if that's sorted yet – they'll be kept in the aquarium and transferred here for the shows themselves through these bloody huge pipes. That's the theory anyway. Not my department. There's some sea life experts who've been hired at great expense, I'm told."

Zander walked around the edge of the tank. It must have been the size of four or five tennis courts at least. Quite a feat of engineering. And the glass – that must have been six inches thick to be strong enough to hold back all that water. Give Frank Fisher his due – he was thinking big. This was all extremely impressive.

"And through there?" he said, pointing to another set of double doors on the back wall, just along from where the pipe from the tank joined it.

"B7. The auxiliary area. Just a much smaller version of this."

"Can I see it."

"Can't see why not. Now that we're here."

Mary moved towards the doors but was stopped by a shout.

"The fuck's going on here?!"

Mary and Zander both turned. Banjo and Easter were striding fast towards them, faces like fury.

"Who gave you permission to be here?" Banjo said, still in shouting mode, red-faced and breathless. "Restricted area. Out of bounds. You need to be out of here right fucking now."

Mary looked embarrassed and seemed about to say something, but Zander cut across her, putting his hands up.

"All down to me. Just wanted a look at the operation. Pretty impressive, it's got to be said. This is going to be massive."

"You've got no reason to be down here."

"Just wanted to see where Jules and Mike were."

"Showed you that. The dock, the boat."

"Yes, but they were in here too, that night."

"Says who?"

"Says the computer records. Thought you said the police had seen all that. They didn't mention it. Which is a bit odd."

Banjo seemed stumped for a second.

"Can't see what that's got to do with anything. Police have got everything they need. Right, now out of here. You are not authorised to be down here."

"But Mr. Fisher said if there was anything I needed."

"That you should ask. You didn't ask."

"I asked Mary."

"You didn't ask me."

"Okay. Can I have a look in that room over there?"

"No. Now, out. I haven't got time for any more of this shite."

Banjo and Easter started moving towards Zander and Mary, being menacing but stopping short of being blatantly aggressive.

Zander took the hint.

"In that case, I thank you for your very kind hospitality and your generous offer of help. If you'd now take me to see Mr. Fisher, please."

"Boss is busy. But I'll give you a lift to your hotel. See you safely home."

Zander decided he had to grin and bear it while he thought about what to do next. He followed the two men, Mary walking behind him. No more small talk. As he got in Banjo's pick-up truck, he saw him shoot Mary a look that was far from friendly.

Annoyed as he was, Zander felt he'd learned something valuable. If only he could figure out what it was.

CHAPTER FOURTEEN

Clubbing

It was all Sean Connery's fault, really.

Back when he was a kid, Frank Fisher saw a re-run of 'Gold-finger' in a James Bond double-bill at his local cinema. Obviously, he was impressed by the Aston Martin DB5 and its tyre-shredding, Rolls-tracking, baddie-ejecting brilliance. And he was transfixed by the tense laser beam scene – although it wasn't until he was older that he realised the real terror came from the prospect of having your tackle fried off rather than the subsequent sweet release of death by bisection.

But even all the gold, which he came to love in later life, wasn't what grabbed him the most at the time.

It was the golf.

That might sound strange for a child, given the many other attractions in the film. But young Francis Fisher was never a normal child. According to his parents, anyway. And the other kids. His teachers too.

The golf. It was the golf in 'Goldfinger' that got him hooked. There was something glamourous about it, the way Connery played it cool and made the game seem stylish and – although he didn't really understand this at the time – sexy. To be good at golf was to be like James Bond. Even though that aspiration left him a long time ago, as he began to favour the wealth, power and downright badness of the Goldfingers, Blofelds and Strom-bergs instead, golf was stuck inside him.

He started playing as a pre-teen with borrowed, battered clubs on public courses. By his late teens he could challenge the best players in local competitions. As he grew into an adult and all the politics, porn, clubs and gangsterism took an increasingly important role in his life, golf remained his big love.

And he hated to lose. Which was exactly what he was doing now.

Three holes to go, and he was four shots down against Chief Superintendent Neil Wilson, the Inverness area commander for Police Scotland, the most powerful cop in the Highlands.

Not that he couldn't have beaten him into the ground any day. The Chief Super's drives were a little weak and he had a tendency to slice his other fairway shots. His putting was sound, though, and this was where Fisher was able to disguise his own game and let the policeman get ahead. He'd deliberately missed some long but sinkable putts on previous holes, as he did every time he played against the man.

And although he hated losing, he liked having influence more. And you didn't get influence by belittling people in power – unless you had compromising material on them, of course.

Talking of which, Councillor Gordon Mackay was trailing behind them both, waddling along in too-tight tartan trews with a high score Fisher refused to lose to. He had him where he needed him. Still, it was important to keep him close until the licence was finally sorted.

The three men stood at the 16th tee at Tain Golf Club, a links course at the edge of a small old town twenty-odd miles north of Inverness. Not that they were trying to hide from anyone. Nothing wrong in local worthies getting together for a game of golf, after all - it was practically obligatory in the Highlands. But even though there were nearer courses such as Castle Stuart or Nairn, sometimes it was best to put some distance between themselves and Inverness, especially if there was business to discuss. Transactions to be made.

The wide-open space of the Tain course, with the beach and the Dornoch Firth stretching out towards Norway on one side, gave a reassuring sense of privacy. Difficult to overhear any conversations, let alone record any.

Not that all the talk was about business. As was the way of things, a lot of time was taken up with golfing chat and gossip. Fisher was in full flow about his plans for the launch party.

"It'll be like nothing the Highlands have ever seen. A lot bigger than those pissy festivals they used to have on the site. This will be mega. Absolutely mega. The event of the century for Scotland. Obviously, I can't confirm just yet, but strictly between you and me we have got some of the biggest stars in the world coming."

"Such as?" the Chief Superintendent said, examining his clubs, wondering which driver to choose for this relatively short hole. "Anyone I've heard of?"

"Well, you didn't hear it from me, and I'll deny it if anyone asks me about it, but don't be surprised if you're standing at the launch party and you suddenly look up and see.....Miss Beyonce Knowles. And her husband. His name escapes me for the moment, but I'm told he sings too. What do you think of that? Maria Carey? Michael Bublé? And I'm told there is a definite chance that Madonna might be available. Because of her links with the Highlands, the wedding in Dornoch. From the failed marriage, obviously, but I'm sure she can be professional and put that to one side for the evening."

"Anybody Scottish, though?" Councillor Mackay said, edging between the two other men on the flat tee. "Important to support Scottish music."

"Well, yes, obviously," Fisher said. "The likes of your Travis, your K T Tunstall, The Proclaimers, that boy that sounds Italian. All the top names."

"Rod Stewart?" said Mackay.

Fisher screwed up his face.

"I'm not really sure he's Scottish, though, is he?" he said. "I know he says he is, or he'd like to be, but not really. Anyway, I met him once. Celtic Park, the VIP lounge. Told me to piss off. Twice. In a very Cockney accent. No, he doesn't feel right for the whole image we're trying to project for the park. It's a family attraction. We don't want some skinny pensioner going on about how they're sexy and have hot legs. Varicose veins, probably."

The Chief Super placed his ball carefully on the tee and lined himself up, twitching the driver a few times before taking a swing and hooking his shot, sending the ball to the edge of the fairway about seventy yards away.

"Bugger. And so all these big stars are confirmed are they?" the Chief Superintendent asked him, knowing full well they weren't.

"Not all signed and sealed, no, but discussions are ongoing, you know what these stars are like," Fisher said, placing his own ball and whacking it straight down the middle of the fairway.

"Be a bit of a disappointment if you don't get them confirmed, though, eh? If you don't have a major headline artist," Councillor Mackay said. "Take the shine off the launch if it's just a few nobodies."

"Oh, don't you worry about that," Fisher said, raising his voice, irritated at Mackay's taunting tone. "The launch party will be stacked with celebrities, major fucking stars. Loads of household names to impress all the bigwigs. Great word, that – 'bigwigs'. You like a big wig, don't you Gordon?"

Councillor Gordon Mackay flushed pink immediately, put in his place, reminded of the hierarchy. He waddled to the tee, placed his ball, then shanked it into a thick clump of gorse bushes.

While Mackay went off to find his ball, Fisher moved close to the Chief Super and rested his hand on the policeman's elbow as they walked along the broad fairway.

"Something I wanted to mention actually, Neil. To do with the launch and such. Not quite about the launch, really. More the lead up. I mean obviously we've got this terrible situation with the two lads who've gone missing, the boffins - and thank you again for all the work your team is doing on that. The sooner we find the bodies and can give the families some peace the better. It's all been handled very sensitively so far. After all, we wouldn't want it to cast a cloud over the whole project, would we. It's worth so much for all of us, the local area, it would be a shame to see anything which damaged that."

"I wouldn't worry, Frank. It'll blow over soon enough."

"Yes, but what if it doesn't? That's my point. Now, take this guy they sent up from the university, this Zander Burns. Nice enough lad, but he's started to get a bit funny about it all, going around getting people riled up, questioning whether it was an accident. It's all paranoid conspiracy theory nonsense, but you don't need me to tell you where that can lead. One minute it's a tragedy, the next minute it's a cause. And then the media get involved, and who knows what damage the publicity could do. The hit to earnings, the economy. And all because of this one guy who's forgetting why he's here in the first place. I mean, the whole thing's pretty insulting to the police, if you ask me. Pretty much saying that you're not doing your jobs properly."

"Okay, okay, Frank, I take the hint. What do you expect me to do about it?"

"Just close him down. This kind of talk doesn't do anyone any good – not us, not the families, not the community."

"Fine. I'll get someone to have a quiet word with him. Nothing's come across my desk about it yet, but I agree – it's not in our best interests. I'll speak to Bobby Turnbull, it's his team looking after the whole thing."

"Appreciate it, Neil. Best to nip these things in the bud. That's a decent lie you've got there," he said, pointing to the Chief Super's golf ball, sitting up on a clump of grass. "With a fair wind you could hit the green in two. Not easy, mind."

The game continued. Fisher managed to stay behind the policeman, narrowing the score a little after sinking a difficult but doable putt on the 17th because he could. It might have been showing off, but he judged that it would make the Chief Superintendent value his narrow win that little bit more.

All three men had arrived in separate vehicles. Fisher walked with Wilson to his car, a two-year old dark green Jaguar saloon with private plates.

"Let me help you with those," Fisher said, shouldering the policeman's golf bag and placing it in the boot. At the same time, he slipped a fat, brown envelope into the bag. A quarterly brick of untraceable cash. For the Police Scotland Christmas party fund.

Once Wilson had left, Fisher turned to Councillor Mackay, his eyebrows raised.

"Yes," Mackay said. "Getting sorted."

"Good. Knew you could do it. Does he want anything?"

"Oh, the Convenor always wants something. Expensive tastes that man has. Too rich for me to handle. Might need to broker a meeting between the two of you."

"How much are we talking about?"

"He didn't say. But I think he sees this as a major payday. He's always had his fingers in loads of pockets, but it's a few grand here, a few hundred there. All adds up, right enough, but you know as well as anyone that your theme park is the biggest thing to hit this area ever. He'll get a cut from loads of businesses who make money off you and the park, but in a way he'd be stupid not to use whatever power he's got to leverage as much as he can."

"I kind of respect that - in a fucked-up kind of way," Fisher said. "Risky, though. Trying to fuck the golden goose. What if the golden goose doesn't want to be fucked? What if it flies the fuck off to somewhere else where it doesn't get fucked quite so hard?"

"He's not going to let that happen, is he. He needs this to work almost as much as you do. There's no way he's actually going to block it, but he needs to put the pressure on so you'll fork out. It's just a negotiating tactic. Fine, I didn't think he'd do this, I hold my hands up, but now that he has, and now that I know he's open to negotiation, I think it's sensible for you to have a chat with him."

Fisher thought about it as he shoved his clubs in the back of his orange Range Rover.

"Fine. Set it up," he said. "Quickly."

"Will do." Councillor Mackay turned away, then stopped. "Frank," he said. "That video...you're not going to...."

"At the moment, I'm thinking about getting big fucking posters and putting them up all over Inverness offering copies for 99p. Might even get t-shirts made, hand them out at Caley games. Big picture of you spuffing your load as the evil Baroness flays your arse to ribbons. They'll probably make up songs about you. Twenty years' time, if you go to the smallest fucking remote island in Papua New Guinea, you'll get a crowd around you shouting 'there's the spanky wanky Maggie hoor monster dildo cumface man'. So get your boss's fucking head in the right place, make sure he doesn't get greedy, and send him to see me. Then – and only then - can me and you talk about the distribution rights of You've Been Framed Like a Right Fucking Cunt. Understood?"

Fisher spun his Range Rover out of the gravel car park, leaving Mackay to brush the dust off his tartan golf trousers, trying not to weep. He failed.

CHAPTER FIFTEEN

A drive in the country

"You look like shit."

Zander rested his arms on the reception desk and turned his heavy eyes to Catriona. He felt weary, only now realising how tense he'd been on the awkward journey back from the theme park in Banjo's pick-up. Banjo staring at him half the time instead of looking where he was going. 'Watch the road,' he'd said to Banjo. 'Not me who needs to watch out,' Banjo had said back. And now the morale-boosting welcome at the hotel.

"Seriously, have they given you any training at all in the art of customer relations?" Zander said. "You're supposed to make the guest feel good. Make them feel at home."

"That's how we talk in my home. If you look like shit, we tell you that you look like shit. You should think of it as a compliment."

"A compliment? Saying I look terrible is somehow a compliment?"

"No, the fact that I feel comfortable enough to say it is the compliment."

"Oh, that makes it all fine, then. Not only do I feel like shit, I am now also well aware that I look as shit as I feel, and that your estimation of me is so low that you feel entirely comfortable with telling me all that. I've had better days, to be honest. And better compliments, believe it or not."

"You're welcome. Anyway, I'm just about to finish my shift."

"Not going to a class on kindness, by any chance?"

"No, I was thinking of heading up the Glen. You should

come with me."

"Up the where?"

"Glen Affric. It's up the back of the village. I sometimes go there when I need to clear my head. It looks like you could do with some headspace too. It's a beautiful place. Very quiet, very peaceful. There's a river, a loch, brilliant views. Come on – lunch is on me."

Zander thought about it. He had things to do. The university needed an update. He needed to speak to Hector about the memory card. He needed to see if there was any sign of Nigel, he needed to work through what he'd discovered at the theme park - and figure out why Banjo and Easter were so aggressive. He needed a break.

He thought of Catriona with the black hair and the piercings. With the pale blue eyes which didn't seem so cold now. A break.

"Ok. On one condition. No more compliments."

Ten minutes later they were in Catriona's battered green vintage Mini, winding up a single-track road through low hills draped in purple heather. They crossed a river then followed a wide valley, the hills on either side of the valley growing larger as they moved deeper into the countryside. The dark green squares of farmed pine trees parading across some of the lower hills gave way to more natural woods of birch.

They talked about the oddness of the situation as Catriona steered the car along the single-track road, Zander filling her in on the strange pattern of timings in the computer log and Banjo's very unhelpful way of helping.

"Old Donald said I should look for a motive if I think there might be more to it than Jules and Mike just dying in a stupid accident," Zander said as Catriona dropped a gear to take them around a tight bend in the road. "But I can't for the life of me work out if there's anything else going on here, or whether I'm just seeing things which aren't there."

"I mean, that is quite normal, isn't it?" Catriona said, glancing over at Zander as they hit a straight section. "People want answers. They don't like to think that death is just so ordinary and everyday and could happen to any of us at any time. But people die all the time. Car crashes, overdoses, illness, accidents. It's just that if it happens to someone you know, you want there to be a bigger meaning."

Zander kept quiet. He could see that Catriona was thinking, that she wasn't finished.

"Take me, for example," she said eventually, keeping her eyes on the road. "My mum died when I was a wee girl. I was eight. I realise now she'd been sick for a couple of years before she died, but to be honest I didn't realise at the time. And then she died. She was gone. And it was just....it was just impossible to take in. I was tiny, I didn't understand. All I knew was that my mum was suddenly gone, and I didn't know why. I wanted my dad to take me to church so I could speak to her, because if she was in heaven then that was obviously the place to go. But he'd stopped going to church by then. So I'd sometimes wander into the church on my way back from school or on the weekends, when it was empty. And I'd kind of whisper to her, and try and listen out for her, but I couldn't hear anything back. I don't know why I'm telling you all this." She gave a slightly nervous laugh. "But sometimes I'd think maybe she wasn't dead. Maybe she'd gone off on some important adventure that she wasn't allowed to tell me about, and one day she'd just come through the door and everything would be normal again. I mean, I didn't really believe that, but at the same time I kind of did. Does that make sense? I wanted to think there was some big important reason why my mum wasn't around anymore, why she left us. Sorry, that's all got a bit heavy. You probably just wanted to know if I had an answer."

She sniffed, and some tears escaped her eyes.

"Why don't we stop for a bit?" Zander said.

"Yes," Catriona said, half laughing, half crying. "I think that'd be a good idea."

She pulled into a small clearing off the road. A sign explained that the area was called 'Dog Falls'.

She turned off the engine and put her head in her hands. Zander rested his hand on her arm, not sure how much comfort it was ok to offer.

"Sorry," Catriona said again, sitting back up and wiping at her face with her hands, smiling in an embarrassed way. "I don't know what came over me then. I don't normally get emotional about it, not in public anyway, not these days. To be honest with you, I've never explained any of that to anyone before. It kind of caught me by surprise."

"You don't need to apologise for anything," Zander said.

"I know. I wasn't apologising," Catriona said, giving him a cool look. Then she smiled. "I'm joking, you fool. I don't know what it is about you, but I just felt like talking about it."

"It's my ruthless interrogation technique. And my generally shit-looking demeanour. Lulls people into a false sense of security. You'll be telling me your bank account PIN number next. Before you know it, I'll have cleaned you out and opened a bar on the Costa del Sol."

"You can finance a bar with a three hundred quid overdraft? Wish I'd known that before. Come on, let's take a walk. See if a bit of extreme nature helps us."

The unfolded themselves from the Mini's cramped seats and wandered down to the river. A path led down to the Dog Falls, which were more like gentle rapids as far as Zander could see. A wooden bridge over the river above the falls, tree-lined banks, views up to the hills. And silence, other than the flow of water over smooth rocks.

They stopped in the middle of the bridge and leant on the handrail, looking down into the water.

"The point I was trying to make," Catriona said, "before I was rudely interrupted by an uncharacteristic public display of emotion, was that I completely understand if you want or need to think that something happened to your friends, that it wasn't just an accident. It's difficult to process death, especially if it's sudden. In a way, it's natural."

"But is that what I'm doing?" Zander said. "I genuinely don't know. I wasn't big mates with Jules and Mike. I knew them a bit, but it's not like I'm suffering from major grief. I've never been a conspiracy theorist who sees big meaning in ordinary events. But all of this doesn't seem right to me. And although I'm not a conspiracy theorist, I'm not a huge believer in coincidence either. Too many weird things have happened in a short space of time in one small area. Even Donald thinks it's odd."

"So a retired policeman is on side. But not the actual police people who do actual investigations?"

"I haven't really put it to them in the terms I've explained to you. I haven't got any evidence as such. Or a clear theory or allegations or anything, really. Just a growing feeling that something's wrong, and that it's all linked somehow. But it's all a bit foggy."

Catriona watched the water for a while. The day was bright but not overly warm. Perfect for walking to the top of a hill in inappropriate shoes.

"Let's see whether we can clear some of that fog out of your head, then," she said. They got back in the car and drove another few miles alongside a narrow loch, reaching a bigger carpark at the end. Catriona grabbed a small backpack from the boot, then chivvied Zander into following her up a gravel path through hunched, ancient-looking trees.

The climb wasn't as grim as he'd expected. Even once the path ended at a stone cairn it was an easy walk through heather and long grass to get higher up the hillside, Catriona forging ahead in front of him. After twenty minutes or so she stopped by a clump of twisted pine trees. A grassy bank beside the trees faced down the hill and right up Loch Affric, a mountain still capped with snow rising up above it to the right. One of the most incredible views Zander had ever seen. He couldn't quite believe he was still on the same island where he'd spent all his life. He'd never really thought about the Scottish Highlands. It was so wild and peaceful. Not a person or a building in sight, and he could see for miles and miles through clear, clean air.

"Table for two?" Catriona said, squatting down on the grass and digging inside her backpack. She brought out some foil wrapped squares and handed one to Zander.

"Hope you're not vegetarian," she said. "Although it's fine if you are, of course. Just that you'll go a bit hungry. And I'll feel duty-bound to tell the Vegetarian Society about your meat feast breakfasts."

"No, not vegetarian," Zander said, taking the package from her. "And how do you know what I have for breakfast?"

"I've got spies everywhere. Well, Kirsty who does the breakfast shift told me."

"And why were you asking?"

"Who said I was asking? Maybe she was just keen to let people know about your needs. As a valued guest."

Zander snorted a laugh.

"Oh, that's what it was, was it? Obviously."

He opened the foil and took out the sandwich.

"Iberico ham and sliced avocado on olive focaccia, in case you were wondering," Catriona said. "What?" she said with a half-smile as Zander raised his eyebrows at her. "You think we all just sit around eating haggis and deep-fried Mars bars?"

Zander laughed again.

"Yeah," he said. "All washed down with lashings of Irn Bru."

Catriona shot him one of her cool looks again, then reached into her bag.

"Here," she said, throwing him an orange and blue Irn Bru can. "Shut up and eat your sandwich."

After lunch she rolled a thin roll-up and they sat back and enjoyed the view. A watery sun chased any remaining chill away. Catriona blew small clouds of smoke into a windless sky.

"So how did you end up as some slick PR man?" Catriona said. "Childhood ambition?"

"Not really," Zander said, smiling in a slightly sheepish way. "I more or less fell into it. I used to be a journalist. That's what I'd always wanted to be, since university anyway. I had this ambition to be one of those crusading-type journalists. Uncovering injustice, exposing corruption, fighting for the underdog, getting to the truth, that sort of thing. Then as you get older things get a bit more complicated. And not everyone can be a crusader."

"So you just gave up?"

"Well, not quite like that. But it's just....what is truth? There are lots of truths. You have one version on events, I have another – which one's the truth? There are millions of truths out there. And that old cliché about there being two sides to every story? Rubbish. There's usually far more than two sides. Life's a lot more nuanced than the absolutes you believe in when you're younger. But in journalism, you do have to pick a side to report on. There's only so much you can put in your story. It becomes a matter of judgement about what your readers or viewers want.

"For instance, one story I did, it was about an old bloke who found some Roman jewellery in a field when he was out walking. All very warm and nice, bit of human interest, makes a nice piece for the paper. But he was a right arse. He was rude, aggressive, wanted money for the interview – which obviously we wouldn't do for a little story in a local paper - then he insulted my photographer, who happened to be female. He was not a nice man.

"But do we do a story about 'sexist old bastard finds treasure, but we hope the Queen keeps it because he's a sexist old bastard'? Or is it a happy, positive 'local man finds Roman treasure' story with some smiling photos and a feelgood quote about him hopefully being able to keep some of the proceeds and doing something nice with it? Including giving some to charity. Although he didn't actually say that last bit – I added that in to get him back for being such a sexist old bastard. He complained, of course. But I'd written it down in my notebook at the time, so it must've been true.

"But my point being, what's the truth in there? There are some facts, which I mostly stuck to, but do the facts alone tell the truth? No, I don't think they do. There's a lot of truth you've got to miss out. And you realise eventually that journalism isn't about truth, it's part of the entertainment industry. What we do, in a nutshell, is provide content for newspapers and magazines and TV stations in a way that gets readers and viewers interested, which then allows our owners to sell more lucrative advertising space and make more money. It's not a noble crusade. And the opportunity came along to move into PR instead, which is more upfront about the choices it makes, and so I took it. Haven't looked back. Now I tell my employer's version of the truth. And I tell it in a way that attracts more funding and more students. And it doesn't do anybody any harm."

"Do you ever worry that you sold out your principles?"

"I've thought about it a lot. And I don't think so. I still believe that you've got to act ethically, you've got to tell a reasonable version of the truth, you shouldn't deliberately lie or mislead. I help people by giving them information, help them understand things which they may not currently understand."

"And is that what made you leave journalism, the fact that you hadn't become this fearless crusader for truth and justice?"

"That and the fact that I was getting tired with it. With the compromises, the intrusion, the stuff I'd find out. Some of the crimes you have to report on, there's a lot of information which never makes it into the news story, and you end up questioning human nature and the depravity which is out there. There are a lot of bad people around, doing a lot of bad things."

"But surely if you feel that strongly about those things, you'd want to expose them?"

"Does my exposing them make any difference? Just makes people realise there's more badness around, makes their world seem worse."

"Do you think you'll ever go back to it? Become a journalist again?"

"There's not usually a way back, not once you've moved to the 'dark side'. I don't think I'd want to anyway. My last job, I was reporting for regional TV and something happened which affected me. Kind of put me off the whole thing."

"What was it?"

"I don't really want to go into it, if that's ok. But it's just something that really affected my confidence for a while. That was a big part of me deciding to give it up and move somewhere else, get into PR. Just wanted to put it all behind me."

Zander looked off into the far distance, at the hazy violet hilltops, seemingly lost in thought.

"You punched a dog, though," Catriona said eventually. Zander's head jerked around to her, confusion all over his face.

"I....what?"

"We do have Google here, you know. And YouTube. Fair to

say a quick search of your name throws up some choice TV."

"I didn't know it was a dog!" Zander said, holding his hands up. "What was I supposed to do? I was standing there in the dark doing a live broadcast about a very serious issue and something jumps up at me. I was just defending myself."

"By punching a dog? In the face?"

"I didn't know it was a dog! Anyway, how did I know it wasn't trying to rip my throat out?"

"I don't think Labradors go in for throat ripping, if that's any help."

"It was a Golden Retriever. Actually. But anyway, yes, you're right. Knocking out a pet live on TV with a surprisingly effective right hook wasn't exactly a career high."

"There's some really good stuff on YouTube, though. Someone's slowed it down, set it to music. Who Let the Dogs Out. Eye of the Tiger. They've got quite creative with it."

"Yes, I'm aware that a lot of people have had a lot of fun out of my disgrace," Zander said.

"You're having a bit of a sense of humour failure about this, aren't you."

"Well, I know it seems kind of funny. But put yourself in my shoes. It's dark, I was in the middle of reporting something to the camera, there's a flash of quick movement in the corner of my eye, I've suddenly got something or someone jumping into me. Genuinely thought I was being attacked. You're quite pumped up anyway for a live broadcast, so I just did something natural. I didn't have time to think – I just did it, lashed out. And then I've got this Golden Retriever lying flat out at my feet, the owner's off to the side screaming and shouting, everything's kicking off, and I'm standing there thinking, Christ, I've killed a dog on live TV. My whole career flashed before my eyes and disappeared off into the distance. Totally humiliating. After that, I just wanted to get away. In most jobs, you make a mistake, you apologise and move on. It's forgotten. On TV, it's a very public mistake. And nowadays it's always there for people to see, so there's no chance that it can be forgotten. Ever. So even six or seven years later, a nosy person in the middle of nowhere can find it online and rip the piss out of me."

"That's a little unfair," Catriona said.

"In what way?"

"We're in the outskirts of nowhere, not the middle of nowhere."

"My apologies."

"Mine too," Catriona said after a moment. "Sorry. Didn't realise it was such a traumatic thing for you."

"Well, it was more traumatic for the dog, to be fair. Which was fine afterwards, by the way. Bouncer. The owner, not so much. Anyway, I can see how people might find it kind of funny. But it's not up there with the best moments of my life."

Catriona reached out her hand and touched Zander's, giving it a comforting squeeze, which surprised and pleased him. She left her hand there for a few seconds, then took it back. Then she slowly raised her finger to her lips, and with her other hand pointed up to their right.

Zander turned. A big red deer stood near the brow of the hill about thirty yards away, a mature stag with a fine spread of points on its antlers. It was magnificent. It lowered its head to nibble at the heather, then stood up proudly, silhouetted against the sky.

Then it seemed to sense something, jerked its head and leapt off through the heather and over the hill. It happened just as the tree next to Zander made an odd thud and splintering noise, and he was showered with small shards of pine wood. Then came the crack. The second shot was a lot clearer.

CHAPTER SIXTEEN

On the hunt

"Down!"

Catriona grabbed Zander's arm and dragged him to the sloping ground in front of the pine trees. The shooter was somewhere on the other side. For now.

"What the actual fuck?" Zander said, staring at Catriona, his heart hammering.

"Two shots," Catriona said, breathing hard. "The first hit the tree above your head. The second one, don't know."

She started scrabbling back up the bank. Zander tried to stop her.

"What are you doing?" he said, getting hold of her jacket. She shook him off.

"Trying to see what fuckwit's shooting." She crawled up the slope and into the trees, keeping very low. Zander considered staying where he was in the open, then followed.

They lay next to each other, very close, trying to see through gaps in the branches. Zander's nerves were fizzing. He wouldn't be surprised if she could feel him vibrating with nervous energy.

"There!" she said, pointing. About a hundred yards away a figure in green slung a rifle over their shoulder and climbed onto a quadbike.

"Quick," she said at Zander, and started sprinting through the heather.

"Hold on! Wait! What the hell are you doing?"

"The car!" Catriona said over her shoulder. "Come on!"

They ran, Zander glancing over towards where the shooter

had been, the quad bike now disappearing down a dirt track through a bank of pine trees.

Catriona had the car started as Zander reached it.

"Get in!" she said, pulling the gear stick into first.

"Wait! What exactly are we trying to do here?"

"I'm not fucking happy about being shot at, and I want to know who it was. There's not too many ways they can get off the hill. We can catch up with them. If we go now."

Zander stood holding the open passenger door.

"Yes, but. They still have a gun. We don't."

"They're not going to shoot at us again, though, are they? Obviously, they were going for the stag. I just want to know who it was. Can't let people get away with that kind of thing. Poacher probably. You don't shoot when there's people around. So. Get in!"

"Hold on. What if," Zander said. "What if they were actually shooting at us? What then?"

"Then they're crap at shooting. Look - I'm going. You coming?"

Zander held her furious stare for a moment, then climbed in. Catriona gunned the engine before his door was closed, reversed quickly and spun the Mini around on the gravel.

She skidded out of the car park and aimed the car down the single-track road. Zander gripped the arm rest with one hand and braced his other arm against the dashboard as the car picked up speed, veering around corners and taking off over humps in the road.

Faster and faster. Heading towards danger. Up ahead, a Ford pulling a caravan, heading right for them on the tight road. Catriona dropped a gear, sped up, and swerved into a passing place at the last second, forcing the Ford and caravan to brake, then rode two wheels up on the grassy verge to bring the Mini back onto the road with a bump. Zander's knees banged off the dashboard.

Catriona slalomed the car fast through a series of bends, nearly losing the back wheels at one point but spinning the wheel in time to correct it. As they crossed a low bridge she slowed hard, skidded the car in a sharp left off the road and up a dirt track.

"Where the hell you learn to drive like this?" Zander shouted above the scream of the engine, bracing himself so he wouldn't slide over into her lap.

"Misspent youth and some poor boyfriend choices."

They climbed higher and higher up the hill, the Mini straining more and more. Another path crossed theirs, and Catriona stopped, wound down her window. She looked down at the tracks in the mud and decided.

"This way." The tyres spun in the soft earth, then caught a grip, fishtailing the car up the track towards dense blocks of pines. The world darkened as they moved into the trees. Zander tried to think of a plan, what they'd do when they caught up with whoever they were trying to catch.

"You still think this is a good idea?" he said as they bounced through a deep puddle of peaty water.

"It's a brilliant idea. Some stupid bastard takes a pot-shot at me, they're going to get their arse kicked."

"So what do we do when we catch them?"

"Find their arse. Kick it repeatedly. We should be getting nearer....oh shit!"

As they turned a tight corner at speed the quad bike was set right across the track, the figure in green standing up on it, with some kind of protective mask, pointing a big rifle straight at them.

Catriona stamped on the brake, putting the car into a violent spin. The Mini missed the quad bike by inches but clipped a pile of pine logs by the side of the track. It threw the car spinning the other way, off the track and down the side of the hill.

Zander grabbed Catriona's arm, pulled her towards him as he elbowed his door open, shielding her with his body, using every bit of strength he had to drag them both out the door and onto the hillside before they rolled to a stop in the heather. The car kept sliding faster as the hill fell away, before hitting a rock, flipping onto its roof and dropping out of sight into a gulley.

Catriona looked up as the quad bike's engine roared. Whoever it was, they weren't hanging around. The figure in green set off down the track in a cloud of blue exhaust smoke. She tried to get up but yelled as pain shot through her hip. She collapsed down next to Zander. She looked over. He wasn't moving. Maybe something to do with the blood pouring from his head.

She scrabbled around in her jacket pockets, finding a pack of tissues which she used to wipe away the blood. There was a cut – a long scrape by his temple – and the beginning of a big blue bump next to it. He was totally out of it.

She looked around again, panicked. The single-track road back to Drumnadrochit was far below her down the hill. Too far to go for help. She wasn't sure what to do. She remembered something about keeping airways clear, slipped her fingers into Zander's mouth and opened it. Nothing odd, as far as she could see. She pulled him up so she was kind of cradling him, wiped at the would again, started rocking him.

"Shit, shit, shit, shit, shit."

This was all very fucked up. This shouldn't be happening. What was she going to do?

Zander stirred. His eyes opened, sleepy at first, then he half shouted, half moaned, and jerked up in a panic, clambering up out of Catriona's lap before the pain hit him and his hands went to his head.

"Easy! Easy!" Catriona said, catching hold of his arms, trying to soothe him. "You've taken a right bang."

Zander turned to her, squeezing his eyes as if the world was too bright. She reached her arms around him and pulled him in tight, and he put his arms around her too and they sat there holding onto one another, shaking with nerves and fear, calming each other.

Slowly, their breathing got back to something like normal. Catriona was the first to unfurl herself from the hug.

"That was...intense," Zander said. "Is this par for the course for all your lunch dates?"

"Not a date," Catriona said. "Definitely not a date." Then she dropped her eyes. "Sorry," she said.

"What for?" Zander reached up to the side of his head, checking the lump and the cut. Still bleeding.

"For nearly getting you killed there."

"Hardly your fault. I blame the man with the gun for the whole 'trying to kill me' bit. Did you recognise him?"

"No. It was all too fast. And he had some kind of mask on, like those ones you get in paintball. But I think we can forget about it being a poacher or some amateur. From what I could see, it looked like a hunting rifle, but I can't imagine anyone round here deliberately pointing it at someone. Anyway, I shouldn't have been driving the car like that. It was stupid. I was angry and stupid."

She sighed, stood up wincing, and started walking over to the edge of the hill. Zander got up and followed, feeling unsteady, his head throbbing and his eyes stinging.

They looked down into the gulley. The Mini lay on its side in a river about twenty metres below them, door torn off, roof bashed in, windscreen missing.

Catriona sighed again and shook her head.

"How do you even start?" she said. "How do you even start to get this pulled out of there? Way up here? I don't even know if it's possible."

She seemed on the verge of crying. Zander put what he hoped was a comforting hand on her shoulder.

"Hate to say it, but it's probably beyond saving," he said. "And it was pretty old. Bit of a wreck, to be honest."

Another sigh. Then she spoke quietly.

"No. No it wasn't a wreck. It was my mum's."

Zander turned his face up to the sky, praying for a lightning bolt to deservedly strike him down.

CHAPTER SEVENTEEN

Roaming

It took the best part of a couple of hours to get back to the hotel and find a doctor. First, they'd had to get Catriona's bag and keys from the car, which wasn't easy. Then climb down the hill to the road. Her phone had been broken in the crash, and Zander couldn't get service on his, so no calls for help.

A couple of tourists cars had passed them but wouldn't stop. They eventually got a ride with a farmer near Cannich, taking them the last five miles into the village.

The local doctor had dressed Zander's cut properly and carried out some basic tests to see if he might be concussed. He wasn't, the doctor decided. Catriona spent a while explaining the situation to her dad, who wasn't happy but was relieved that she was ok.

It was Catriona's dad – his name was Bruce Mackie, Zander discovered – who called the police. A squad car arrived within an hour, and Zander and Catriona spoke to two police officers in the empty lounge bar. It was the young policeman Zander had spoken to earlier, but accompanied by an older, senior officer, a Detective Inspector Turnbull. He sat back while the younger officer noted the basic information about the shooting. When Zander and Catriona had been through it all, the Detective Inspector spoke up.

"And you had permission to be on this land where the alleged incident happened?" he said, looking at Zander. Zander looked to Catriona.

"It's a public path," she said. "Well, to the cairn. Forestry Commission, I think. After that it's probably either Forestry

Commission or on the estate."

"The Balkinnoch Estate?" he asked, raising his eyebrows.

"Yes. Possibly."

"So you are informing us that this might have happened on private land?"

"I'm not sure what that's got to do with it," Catriona said, bristling. "It wasn't *us* that was doing anything wrong. There's the Right to Roam, after all. We're allowed to go walking where we want."

"Constable Brown," Detective Inspector Turnbull said, keeping his eyes on Catriona. "Explain to Miss Mackie in simple terms the main provisions of the Land Reform Act 2003."

The constable gave a nervous glance at his superior, flicked back in his notebook, read something, then addressed both Catriona and Zander.

"The Act provides a general public right of access to most land and inland water in Scotland provided the right is exercised responsibly, sir."

"Responsibly," the Detective Inspector said. "Responsibly - the key word. Thank you, constable. Miss Mackie, had you sought to establish whether any shooting or stalking was taking place on Balkinnoch Estate land before you took it upon yourself to exercise your 'right to roam'?"

"Well, no."

"Although that would have been the *responsible* thing to do, would it not?"

"I think a responsible thing to do is not to shoot at people when they're out for a walk in the countryside."

"But you'd agree that if shooting is taking place on private land, it is your responsibility to avoid encountering it, would you not?"

"Sorry to interrupt," Zander said. The Detective Inspector

took a slow moment to move his heavy-browed gaze from Catriona to Zander. "I'm not completely up to speed on Scottish land law, but I'm still pretty sure that shooting at someone is pretty illegal right throughout the UK."

"Ah, yes – both you and Miss Mackie claim that you were shot at. And you saw this person shooting at you, did you?"

"No," Zander said. "But we saw them riding away."

"And this was just after the shots – two shots, I believe you said - and just after the stag ran off, am I correct?"

"That's right. The first shot hit the tree above me, and I'm not sure where the second shot went."

"This shot – and it sounds to me like we're only clear about the one shot, here – the shot hit a tree near you? Presumably this was also near the stag?"

"The tree was right next to me. The stag was about twenty, thirty metres away."

"And this alleged shooter, you say he was some distance away. How far would you estimate? Up to one hundred metres, perhaps?"

"Difficult to tell, but yes, I suppose that's possible. And there's nothing 'alleged' about him."

"But it's not out of the question that they could have been aiming at the stag, missed, and hit trees nearby."

"Well, if it was all above board, why did he run for it?" Zander said, his voice rising. DI Turnbull wasn't happy at Zander's tone and waited a few seconds before replying.

"Perhaps he realised his shot was off. Perhaps he panicked. Or perhaps he left because the stag had gone, and he was going off to find it. There are, as I'm sure you're beginning to understand, a number of possible explanations here."

"And what about when he stood there pointing the gun straight at us?" Zander said, getting annoyed. "Not too many ways you can interpret that."

"This would have been once you had decided to chase this mystery man, am I right?" He looked at both Catriona and Zander, who nodded. "And once again, this was on Balkinnoch Estate land?"

"Yes, I assume so," Catriona said.

"Constable Brown, remind me of the provisions in the Land Reform Act 2003 as it pertains to motorised activity."

"Public access rights do not apply to motorised activities such as off-road driving, sir, and would need to have the landowner's permission."

"And should I take it that permission had not been sought in this case?"

"No, obviously," Catriona said, her face flushing with annoyance. "We were trying to identify the person that had just shot at us with a high-powered rifle. Getting permission wasn't exactly top of our agenda."

"So, someone who may have been quite legitimately on that land was put in a situation where they were being chased by someone they didn't know, and who quite definitely did not have permission to be there, and who appeared to be driving their car with reckless abandon. Who knows what went through the mind of that other person, and what sort of danger they may have believed themselves to be in?"

"Why am I feeling like we're being put under suspicion here instead of the psycho who was shooting at us?" Zander said. "Shouldn't you be out looking for him instead of sitting here accusing us of not following some obscure procedure?"

"But we haven't established that anyone was actually shooting at you, have we? The more likely scenario is that you wandered somewhere you shouldn't have, interrupted some perfectly legal hunting activity, and then threatened person unknown by means of an illegal off-road pursuit. And then there is the issue of Miss Mackie's vehicle, which is currently lying in what sounds to be a relatively inaccessible position on private land which she had no right to be on, in a river. Potentially polluting that river, which breaks a number of very important laws."

Detective Inspector Turnbull stood up, followed quickly by his constable and both Zander and Catriona.

"So, you're not going to do anything?" Zander said, getting angrier.

"Oh, I'm going to do something alright," said Turnbull. "I'm going to speak to the Estate to find out what action they wish to take on this matter. I'll also find out whether they had any stalking taking place on the hills today. But all these, ah, allegations." He shook his head. "May I have a word in private, Mr Burns?"

And with that, the Detective Inspector marched out of the lounge bar and out the hotel's front door, leaving Zander little option but to follow.

When he got outside, the policeman was standing by the squad car.

"Mr Burns, you seem to have quite the imagination," he said, staring off towards the loch, hands clasped behind his back. "These allegations today, and some other things I've been hearing. Stories that you've been spreading. About the accident on the loch, conspiracy theories. It's most concerning." Zander seemed about to speak but Turnbull held up his hand to stop him. "It would be entirely understandable if your distress at losing these two valued colleagues has put you under a great deal of strain. Completely normal in circumstances like these. But it can't carry on. You are not doing yourself or your university any favours by behaving like this. And it's not going down well locally either. Quite a lot of resentment building up at the things you've been saying. It's not good for the area, not good for business."

"I haven't been saying anything," Zander said. "But there are some strange things going on here. Men going missing, my room broken into, now this stuff today. Things I'd have thought the police would be interested in."

"And there you go again, Mr Burns. Look, this is a small place. People talk. You might say something to one person, they tell a few more, and pretty soon it's all over the place. How do you think I know about it? Your name is becoming mud here. You are losing friends very quickly, so if I was you, I'd wrap things up here sharpish and get on your plane back south. Best for everyone."

"And if I don't?"

Turnbull laughed, but there was no pleasure in it.

"You wouldn't be the first person to come here and lose their mind over tall tales. And probably not the last. But it'd be a shame, nonetheless. Do us all a favour – including yourself – and go home."

And with that, the Detective Inspector got in the car, hurriedly joined by the constable who'd been holding back in the hotel doorway. Zander watched the car pull out onto the road to Inverness, waiting until it was out of sight. Thinking.

Catriona had joined him – he wasn't sure when. She looked up at him with a question mark on her face.

"I'm no expert at this sort of thing," Zander said, "but I think I've just been told to get the fuck out of Dodge."

"And are you?"

He thought about it some more.

"Hell no."

CHAPTER EIGHTEEN

Get the big picture

"The very man."

Donald leant on his gnarled wooden walking stick and tipped his flat tweed cap at Zander.

"Donald, hi, how are you?" Zander said. He was trying to walk off the irritation he felt after the police questioning, do a bit of thinking. He'd wandered without any particular destination in mind and found himself by a wide expanse of grass, the home of Glen Urquhart Shinty Club, according to a sign by the road. He wasn't entirely sure what shinty was, but it was clearly something which needed a big field and a small pavilion for spectators. Donald was standing over near the pavilion when Zander spotted him, doing his best to throw a chewed tennis ball for Shep to chase and bring back.

"Fair for a Friday," he said, smiling.

"It's not Friday, though."

"In that case, who knows. Anyway, I'm glad I've bumped into you. We've got some news. Hector has something he wants to show you. Nothing to do with his genitalia, if that's what's worrying you."

"Well, I *wasn't* worried about it. Kind of am, now."

"It's these photographs from Nigel's camera. I think he's found something. He was very excited about it when I spoke to him. Well, as excited as Hector gets. We could wander over to his house if you've got time."

"Sure, why not?"

Shep came trotting up towards him, stopping a good ten feet away as if aware of Zander's nervousness. The dog dropped the tennis ball from its mouth and looked up at Zander, panting. For a second, Zander could have sworn it was smiling.

"Go on, give it a throw," Donald said. Zander felt he couldn't be rude and refuse. He kept uneasy eye contact with Shep as he bent down to pick up the tennis ball, flinching at its moistness. As soon as he picked it up, Shep started trotting around, ready to dash off. Zander hurled the ball as far as he could, and Shep sprinted off after it, catching it in his mouth before the third bounce. The ball was dropped right at Zander's feet this time.

"Got yourself a friend for life there," Donald said. "Usually bites people who touch his ball."

"You could've warned me."

"Call it a test. Good judge of character, that dog."

"Thanks for the vote of confidence." He threw the ball again, Shep chasing it.

The two men started walking down the length of the field.

"So, the sign says this is a shinty club? What is shinty, exactly?"

"Difficult to describe in a nutshell," Donald said. "Think of hockey mixed with football mixed with violence. Not for the faint of heart. Very popular round here. Bit too much blood for my liking. Had enough of that in my day job. But good that the youngsters want to keep it going, a traditional sport like that, when they've got so many other competing distractions. Sex, drugs, baking."

They talked a bit about sport as they walked. Cricket and football, mainly, but there wasn't much cross-over of interest. Then Donald came right out with it.

"As you know, I was quite the detective in my day. And from a few subtle tell-tale signs, I'd say you've had quite a serious bang to the head."

"Is it the big plaster which gives it away?"

"Mainly. That and....actually, yes, just the plaster."

"It's been quite a day."

Zander filled him in on the shooting and the crash.

"And you'd expect the police to take it really seriously," Zander said. "You'd think they'd get right out there trying to track down the shooter. But instead, I get this idiot Detective Inspector accusing us of being in the wrong. Playing the whole thing down. Then pretty much telling me I should get out of town."

"Who was it?"

"Turnbull, he said his name was."

Donald nodded.

"Idiot. Total idiot. Very confident young man – although he's probably not so young now. Was always very full of himself, took himself very seriously. But an idiot. And you're sure he's a DI?"

"That's what he said."

"God, they must be desperate. Although he's in the same Masonic lodge as a fair few important people around here, so that probably hasn't done his career any harm."

"And here's the odd thing," Zander said. "Well, odder than not being too bothered about a shooting. He said I'd been spreading rumours around, conspiracy theories, trying to make more out of the whole situation than was there. But I've been thinking about it, and I haven't really said all that much to anyone. Just you, Hector, Catriona, Mary – she works at the park, logistics or something. And, I suppose, Fisher's security man, Banjo."

"Ah yes, Banjo McKenzie. Quite an interesting character. I'm using 'interesting' as what you might call a euphemism. I really mean 'psychopathic'. When he first appeared on the scene, I made a few inquiries with some of my former colleagues down in Glasgow, people who knew a bit about Fisher's past. It turns out Mr Banjo McKenzie has quite the reputation in the Glasgow underworld. Providing close security for various lower-level gangsters over the years. Pretty much a shoot first, dismember the body, dump it in building site, cover it with concrete, ask questions later kind of guy. And yet there he is, standing at the right hand of our esteemed saviour, Saint Francis of NessieWorld, here to rid the Highlands of poverty and peace and quiet. Makes you wonder, doesn't it. I mean, we all know Fisher's dodgy as hell, of course. Made his money profiting from other men's weaknesses. But a lot of people up here need him to be successful, they are literally banking on it, and a lot of blind eyes are being turned towards his past. Yet he still has unsavoury people like Banjo McKenzie hanging around. Yes, it makes you wonder. And you said you mentioned some of your doubts in front of him?"

"Yes. Not everything, but probably more than I should've in hindsight."

"Anything you said to him would go straight back to Fisher. Which means Fisher has a line to the police in Inverness, which wouldn't be a major surprise. So how are you going to respond to this warning you've been given?"

"Probably in a fairly reckless and irresponsible way."

"That sounds eminently reasonable. Right, down that street over there and we'll be at Hector's house in two shakes of a lamb's tail."

They crossed the main road, but as they turned to walk down the street Shep sprinted off down the pavement barking manically at a car which had just passed them.

"Shep! Shep! Come back, boy! Ridiculous," Donald said. "Got this thing about black cars. Always chasing them. No other colour, just black. Maybe I've got a racist dog."

A couple of minutes later Shep trotted back to them having

failed to bite the car.

"Good boy," Donald said, fixing on a lead.

Hector's house was a neat modern bungalow with a plain lawn at the front. Hector led them into his lounge, which Zander noted was clean, tidy and organised, although with no particular personality. No personal touches – photos, souvenirs, nothing. It could have been a show-home for an out-of-date furniture store catalogue.

But he did have a big, modern TV on the wall, which surprised Zander a little. And then he realised that it was linked to a couple of boxes, possibly hard drives of some kind.

"Had a look at the photos," Hector said, getting straight down to business. He picked up a tablet, and in a couple of swipes he'd caused an image to come up on the big TV.

"The grey photos. The blank ones. It was mist. Messed around with filters, took out noise, played with structure, sharpened it."

Hector kept making adjustments on the tablet. Zander and Donald kept their eyes on the big screen.

"Zoom in bottom right. What do you see?" Hector said.

Zander could make out some lines, a darker shape than the grey surrounding it. In fact, there were lots of different grades of grey.

"Not really sure what I'm looking at to be honest, Hector," Zander said. Hector went over to the TV, started tracing his finger down the screen, drawing a shape. An outline.

"That's a boat," he said. He drew the outline again. When it was pointed out to him like that, Zander could begin to imagine that it looked like a boat, the front pointing to his left. But not definitely.

"I suppose it's possible," he said. "Very faint, though. And there are all those other patches of grey. Isn't that part of the same thing, whatever it is?"

"No," Hector said, quite definitely. He started drawing a different outline. "That's the other boat."

"The other boat?"

"The other boat."

Donald laughed and clapped his hands at the same time.

"Yes! I see it!" he said. "Wouldn't have spotted it myself, but now you point it out. Two boats, one behind the other. And knowing you, Hector, that's not the end of it."

Hector gave a little smile, so slight it would be easy to miss. He fiddled with the tablet again, and the TV screen split in half. On one side the grainy photo, on the other a shot of the boat the scientists had use of, The Kelpie. It was at a slightly different angle to the faint outline in the grey picture, but once Hector traced the outline again there was a potential match.

"It's the Kelpie. Pretty certain," he said. "Can't get it clearer, but there it is."

"And the other boat?" Zander said.

"Too faint. Not the point, though. Point is, two boats."

"Doesn't really prove anything, though, does it?" Zander said.

"Time," said Hector. He swiped at the tablet again and a list of data appeared on the screen. "From the memory card. Photo taken at twenty-three minutes past midnight the night the men went missing."

"Went missing supposedly on that boat," said Donald quietly. "Except there was another boat too, which no one has mentioned. Two boats. Only one found. Why would there be two boats?"

"You think someone else was involved?" Zander said.

"I don't know what to think," said Donald. "But if this shows the Kelpie and another boat out in the loch on the night your friends went missing, it means someone's not telling the truth.

Or someone knows more than they're telling. Same difference in the end."

"Nigel," Hector said. "Maybe he knew. Took the photos, anyway. Must've had a reason."

"That strange interview he gave before he disappeared," said Zander. "Was he hinting at this? That he knew something? Did he say something about another boat? I can't remember."

"And maybe it wasn't actually the camera your thief was after," Donald said. "Maybe it was that memory card. Those photos. Maybe someone doesn't want them out there."

"In that case, maybe we can flush out that 'someone'," Zander said. "I think I'm about to do something reckless and irresponsible. Can I borrow a phone?"

CHAPTER NINETEEN

The unhappy bunny

When three of the biggest newspapers in the country got a tip from a trusted source about a growing suspicion of foul play in the disappearance of the two Loch Ness scientists, they had to go with it.

It was a squeeze to get it into the first editions, but they managed – and other news outlets then scrambled to catch up. The key fact - evidence had emerged of an unidentified second boat near The Kelpie on the night the men disappeared. Rumours of photographic proof being sent to police.

The late breaking story caught out the Police Scotland press office, who were bounced into an ill-judged "no comment" rather than being able to kill the story with a firm denial. But that was part of Zander's calculation about the exact timing to set the story running.

The Edinburgh branch office of NessieWorld's big London PR company were also late to the party, only being approached late in the evening for comment. Their eventual panicked calls to Frank Fisher's home were not the easiest or quietest the PR people had ever made.

And now, here he was, Frank Fisher, standing at his desk staring at a spread of newspapers Banjo had picked up from the local newsagents that morning. Banjo and Easter stood to one side of him, picking up on his tension. Sensing his mood, Anne-Marie had sensibly gone off to find something important to do elsewhere.

The 'papers. All fairly similar in content and tone. Big new developments. Foul play suspected. Second boat mystery. Missing local Nessie expert – is it linked? Were the men silenced? If so, why?

The Inverness HQ of Police Scotland was now scrabbling together denials and clarifications, with orders from the top not to mess it up. That was after botched early attempt at clarification revealed that they had actually received new information – a late night email about the two boats, along with a grainy picture. Now the police's public position was that it was too early to tell whether any of the new information had a bearing on the case, which was still being treated as a tragic accident.

None of this, it's fair to say, had much of a calming effect on Frank Fisher. His mobile had been buzzing all morning, from well before breakfast. He'd ignored it.

His face was a shade of red Banjo had never seen before. The veins in his temple, which could become prominent at times of anger, were standing out so clearly that it would have been reasonable to give them their own names.

Frank Fisher was not a happy bunny.

New developments. Foul play. Spotlight on the troubled NessieWorld project again.

Fisher looked from one headline to another, at each caption under each photo, especially one using an old snap of him looking shifty with the strapline 'controversial developer'.

Banjo stood back. Mount Fisher seemed on the verge of erupting. He seemed to find it difficult to talk, his lips quivering but not opening. But it burst out eventually.

"Fucking Zander fucking Burns!"

He turned towards his two henchmen, fixing Banjo with a bulging-eyed stare.

"That fucking fucker's fucking FUCKED!"

Banjo nodded quickly, grabbed Easter's arm and dragged

him from the room. Best to leave before the mayhem began.

Zander Burns was pretty pleased with how his little bombshell had landed. Unmissable coverage in the media. He'd given a couple of radio interviews over the phone already, talked to a few more 'papers. He kept his quotes broad, keeping his finger-prints off the story's origins. One of the 24-hour news TV channels was interested too.

Now he was sitting on a wooden bench at the top of a small hill overlooking Drumnadrochit. He had a clear view of the loch and, in the near distance, the theme park. It was a good place to be, suggested by Catriona. Away from any questions by visitors to the hotel, but with decent mobile phone reception.

There had been a slightly sticky conversation earlier with Richard Gladwell, the Vice-Chancellor at the university. He'd had to skirt around the truth a bit, denying that he'd known the story was coming but admitting he'd briefed some journalists on background once they contacted him.

Gladwell wasn't happy that the story had hit him by sur-prise, that he hadn't been given a heads-up about it before he saw it in the papers. But he did admit that, in the circumstances, it was useful for Zander to be there on the ground if – as it seemed - the situation was changing.

There were some messages on his mobile demanding that he call Detective Inspector Turnbull. He would – it was only polite, after all – but not yet.

His next move was to brief the media about the shooting in-cident, to keep the story going. Also, encourage them to follow up on Nigel's disappearance.

Yes, this was all going nicely to plan. In as much as it could actually be called a plan. Clearly the endgame here was to get to the truth about Jules and Mike's disappearance. But other than forcing the police to put more effort into the investigation, if only to keep the media off their backs, Zander didn't have a particularly strong next move. As long as the police upped their game, there was little for him to do.

So why did he get the feeling that this wasn't over yet?

His phone buzzed. A text from local TV, wanting to do an interview. Might as well. No rest for the wicked.

It had been a decent day of tourist-bothering. Okay, perhaps not to the extent that anybody had actually turned back from Urquhart Castle, but some of them at least stopped for a chat and selfies. A few quid to spend later.

Hector Menzies put his new placard into a special carrying case and headed home. There was something bothering him, something that young Zander had said about his trip to Nessie-World, where Banjo McKenzie had almost forcefully ejected him.

The previous night, once Donald and Zander had left his bungalow, he'd tried getting into the CCTV feed inside the theme park. He'd managed to get into some of the more public areas where the feed was live – by the reception at Castle Fisher, in a few of the fast-food concession areas, a soft-play barn, the public walkways. But he hadn't managed to get into the feed at the nerve-centre, where Zander had been.

He'd expect good cyber-security these days, especially as it affected public safety, but even he was surprised by the blocks he found. There were a couple of programmes he couldn't crack, even with his experience.

But that wasn't the only thing he had experience in. And sometimes it was best to see things with your own eyes rather than through a lens. It was a challenge.

So, after a late tea of fish fingers and mashed potatoes, Hector gathered together some equipment in a small rucksack, loaded up information onto credit card sized pieces of plastic, swapped his polished brown brogues for black, rubber-soled walking boots, and drove over to the small village of Dores on the south side of the loch. He parked at the Dores Inn, a rustic old pub right on the water, and waited for darkness to fall.

The pub stood just outside the land owned by Frank Fisher and his NessieWorld development.

Hector knew, from previous visits, there was a security weakness in the fence between the Dores Inn car park and the theme park land. He'd popped in at night a couple of times, just to have a nosey around when there was nobody there except predictably lazy night-shift security guards at the main entrance – he'd even followed one around for a while, just for a laugh. But he'd never bothered with the buildings themselves.

This time, though. A proper challenge.

When it was dark enough, Hector checked on a tablet to see where the security guards were at that exact moment. He'd already checked the pattern and timing of their rounds but wanted to be sure.

Once he was satisfied that they were safely in the guard room at the front entrance, he squeezed through the loose metal rungs in the fence, protected from sight by shipping containers and hoardings at the end of the car park, and slipped into NessieWorld.

He crept through the bizarre shadows of rides and monsters, heading for the entrance to the arena. The front doors themselves would be physically locked, so he planned to go in one of the service doors around the side. The plastic cards he'd loaded up before leaving home should be good enough to trick ninety five percent of swipe machines to let him in. He just hoped the staff doors at NessieWorld weren't in the other five percent. Even if they were, he had a couple of technological tricks in his bag which should get him in safely, although it'd take a lot more time.

He waited in the shadows near a side door for a full five minutes, checking on the video feeds showing on his tablet. From the cameras he could get access to in the building, there wasn't any suggestion of anyone working late. Other cameras showed the guards drinking coffee or tea in their guardroom, although he knew one of them would do a circuit of the site in about half an hour's time.

He walked up to the door and swiped the card through the slot. A small red light flashed three times. The door stayed shut. Hector rubbed the card on his jumper, slotted it into the reader again and swiped it slower this time.

A green light. A click. He was in.

Now for a little wander.

CHAPTER TWENTY

Boffin boss man

Light mist lay over the loch. Zander was down by the shore, up early to work out a plan of action. It was one of those days when the loch was absolutely still, not a breath of wind and the water smooth as glass.

It was extraordinary, Zander thought. An outrageously beautiful place. And standing there, peering out at the flat water, he could imagine the sudden thrill of the surface breaking, some dark shape cutting through it for a second or two.

He could imagine what it must be like to believe.

Not that he himself could be tempted to believe, though. From everything he'd seen and read, it was clear the legend was a mixture of wishful thinking, hoaxes and misunderstandings. But the idea of it. Maybe Fisher was onto something after all.

Fisher. Where did he fit into all of this? Was there anything he knew about the accident but wasn't telling? Was there anything which might have affected his business? That's all he seemed interested in, after all.

A busy day yesterday. Zander hadn't seen the morning papers yet – the local shop wasn't open – but he'd skimmed through the online versions the night before. A decent spread of follow-on stories, although not all of them high profile.

He picked up a flat stone and tried skimming it across the water like he remembered doing as a kid. The stone hit the water once, flipped up, then dropped and sank.

If anyone knew any more about the scientists' disappearance – or about Nigel, for that matter – hopefully the media

coverage would flush them out. His tetchy phone call with Detective Inspector Turnbull wasn't overly positive. Leave it to us,
was the message, but it wasn't said with the urgency Zander
hoped for. It was still very much in the 'keep your nose out of
it' camp. And no movement on the shooting either.

He settled on his next move – sending the enhanced photo
of the boats to a couple of trusted contacts, one at a tabloid, one
at a broadsheet, with some off-the-record speculation that Nigel's vanishing act could be linked to the picture, which was
linked to the scientists. Which tended to point the finger back
towards NessieWorld. Frank Fisher would not be best pleased.
Zander smiled at the thought.

Keeping up the pressure. That was what it was all about.

Zander walked back up the public footpath through the
field, heading towards the main road. Time for breakfast. Maybe
there'd be haggis. Probably need a bit of stodge to keep him going.

As he reached Urquhart Castle car park his mobile rang. He
didn't recognise the number but took the call anyway in case it
was a journalist – or a tip-off.

"Zander, hi, it's Jim Leonard here."

Sir James Leonard. Chancellor of Addington University. The
boss, the main man, the big cheese, whatever you want to call
him. Not a call Zander would expect to get. Although he'd expect Leonard to keep across what was happening at the loch,
he'd do it through Richard Gladwell. Zander was too far down
the food chain for someone as grand as Sir James to speak to.

"Yes, Sir James, how are you?" Zander tried to sound bright
and positive.

"Look, cut to the chase, we've got to pull you out of there.
Not going the way we'd hoped."

"I...did Richard Gladwell mention the new developments? I

think it's quite important that I stay on."

"Developments this side too. I believe Richard mentioned when he originally briefed you that I wanted this all low-key. Best for the university, our reputation – you know all that. But here I am looking at an email with all the press stories from the last couple of days, and it's as far from low key as you can get. Concern here is that it's getting out of control. Best that you come back and look after it from base. We don't want the university's name dragged through this."

"But wouldn't you agree that if the whole situation keeps getting in the news, it's best that I'm here on the ground to help manage it from the university's perspective? There's a limit to what I can do from Addington."

"Yes, well I think that's rather the point, isn't it? Take you out of the equation, let the story die down."

"I hope you're not suggesting I'm behind those stories, Sir James."

"And I hope you don't think I was born yesterday," Leonard said, his tone becoming harsh. "I know people, Burns. I know people who *know* it was you. I'd rather do this in a civil way, get you out of there, smooth things over with the local business community, and we can get things back to normal. What none of us wants - or needs, quite frankly - is for you to be going rogue on us. You don't need me to tell you where that leads."

"That's sounding a bit like a threat, Sir James."

"It's an accurate reflection of your contract is what it is. Bringing the university into disrepute. Summary dismissal. Pretty standard. I'm sure you'll see sense on this one."

"But there's more to it than anyone's admitting to," Zander said, trying to keep calm even though his pulse was pounding. "There are questions about how Jules and Mike went missing, when they went missing, whether anyone else was involved. There are people who don't want those questions asked, but it's our duty to Jules and Mike. If we don't ask those questions, who will?"

"The police will, for God's sake. That's their job. As the Chief Superintendent kindly reminded me. Another phone call I could have done without. Look, there's a lot riding on this for the university. Our relationship with this theme park brings in a substantial amount of funding, and we can't afford to do anything to jeopardise it. No, you're on a flight back to Luton this evening. End of story."

"What do you mean jeopardising the funding? Is this Fisher? Is he behind this? Trying to get me out of here?"

"It's nearly £400,000 a year. It's funding we can't afford to lose. If he thinks continuing a link-up with us damages his business then we can wave goodbye to it, simple as that. That means jobs going, research going without funding. The money we get covers far more than this Loch Ness project. You know that. Richard will expect you back at the university tomorrow morning."

"But I feel I'm close to uncovering something here, something that matters. To us, to the families."

"There is little point in continuing this conversation. The situation is very clear. Tomorrow morning, report to Richard at the university. First thing. Any other action would have career-limiting implications. And that's the end of the matter."

And then Zander's phone was dead. No goodbyes, no take cares, no kisses.

It'd been a long time since he'd had a bollocking at work. It was not a nice feeling. As well as his thumping heart he felt sick, and his mouth was dry. He was surprised to find his legs were shaking too. He felt ashamed, like he was a schoolboy being told off for something. He wondered whether he should've stuck up for himself more, defended what he was trying to do. But he felt

like he'd been run over by a bulldozer. Leonard was right –
there wasn't really much of a choice here. If he wanted to keep
his job, he was going home. He'd been caught out, and was lucky
they were prepared to keep him on.

He stomped up the hill, trying to get the nerves out of his
legs. And with each step, anger kept building. At the situation,
at his timidity, and the helplessness of it all. At the injustice.

As he reached the castle car park, Hector spotted him and
came bustling over, shouldering his sign.

"Need a word. A quick word," he said as he reached Zander.

But Zander kept going, the blood roaring in his veins.

"Not now. Not the best time," he said, not even looking at
Hector.

Hector watched him go. What a pity he was in such a rush.
Something important to tell him. Well, maybe important,
maybe not. Interesting, at least. Oh well, he could always tell
him later.

Zander trudged on. Every step, more and more anger. All
the way back to the hotel.

As he reached the hotel, Bruce Mackie came out from behind the reception desk to meet him, his worried face even
more strained than normal.

"Ah, Mr Burns, glad I've caught you," he said, moving as if
to block Zander's path. "Your bill's all settled, everything's been
sorted. Just need your key for check-out. Would you like me to
book you a taxi for the airport?"

Zander stared at him.

"What? Who said I was checking out?"

"We had a call," Mackie said, gesturing towards the phone
on the reception desk in case Zander was in any confusion
about what 'a call' meant. "From the University, saying you
were leaving us this evening. And then Mr. Fisher's office
called, settled the bill – even the extras, the food and what have

you, so there's no need for you to worry about any of that."

"Fisher? Frank Fisher's paid for my bill?"

"Yes, sir. In gratitude for all you've done while you've been up here. His office asked for me to pass on his regards and thanks."

"Well, that's all very nice. But what if I don't want to check out?"

Mackie's worry lines deepened.

"I'm not sure I'm with you, Mr. Burns. Everything's been settled."

"Not with me, it hasn't. I might decide to stay on."

"That won't be possible, I'm afraid. Not in this hotel. All the rooms are..." Mackie seemed to search for the right term. "They're spoken for." He smiled, but it was less than reassuring.

"Right," Zander said, sighing. "In that case, I'll pay my own bill. I wouldn't like to be in Frank Fisher's debt."

As Zander reached for his credit card, Bruce Mackie shook his head.

"There isn't actually a bill to be paid, as such," Mackie said. "There's no charge. Mr. Fisher's waved all charges. It's his hotel, after all."

"Of course it is," Zander said, his jaw tight, his bubbling blood almost at boiling point. "I must thank him for it."

Then he spun around and headed straight back out the door.

CHAPTER TWENTY ONE

See you, Jimmy

Fisher could hear the simultaneous door-thumping and bell-ringing above the noise of his TV. Which was annoying, because Sandra and Tony from Bolton were sitting in a café in Tenerife trying to decide whether to splash a hundred grand on a wreck in the hills or a boxy townhouse. It was tense.

"The land, you fuckwits," Fisher said to himself, irritated. "Got to be the land. It's not like they're making any more of it, are they?"

The thumping continued. And the doorbell.

"Anne-Marie!? Anne-Marie!? See who the fuck that is and tell them to fuck the fuck off. Can't hear myself think in here."

Fisher tried to concentrate on the screen again. Sandra had doubts about both properties. Tony was happy to go along with whatever she thought.

Morons.

Anne-Marie stuck her head around the lounge door, her eyes wide.

"Who the fuck was that?" Fisher said. "Cheeky fucker. No-one bangs on Frank Fisher's door like that."

"Frank...." Anne-Marie said, but whatever she'd been planning to say was blocked out by the two large figures who brushed past her into the lounge.

"Jimmy!" Fisher said to the first one, standing up quickly. "Jimmy!" he said, turning to the second one.

The Jimmies.

"Good to see you guys," Fisher said, putting a big smile on his face although his muscles were trying their hardest not to.

He grabbed the remote off the chair, turning the TV off. "Come in, come in, take a seat. Can I get you anything? A drink, anything?"

Jimmy Donohue and Jimmy Nuts moved slowly to the centre of the room like bull elephants checking out a threat to the herd. They wore matching funereal black suits. Jimmy Donohue, the slightly smaller of the two large men, reached his right hand out.

"Francis. Long time no see," he said in a high, whispery voice at odds with his bulk. There was no smile. Fisher took the hand and shook it. It was soft and warm, and he could feel that his own palm was slippy with sweat. Anne-Marie ducked back out the room, closing the door behind her.

"Jimmy. Keeping well, I hope?" Fisher said, then turned to the other man, Jimmy Nuts. He'd been called Jimmy Nuts for so long everyone had forgotten his real last name. Fisher put out his hand to him.

"And you, Jimmy," he said, keeping his smile fixed. "Looking fit as ever."

Jimmy Nuts looked down at Fisher's hand without moving his vast, round head. He waited a couple of beats, then took it. Fisher could feel the restrained power in the thick, rough fingers immediately. He flinched, ready to pull his hand back quickly but there was no need. It was just a normal, if mismatched, handshake.

"Take a seat, gents," Fisher said, nodding at the big sofa. "Some drinks."

"We're not staying long, Francis," Jimmy Donohue said. "We'll stand."

Francis. Only his mother called him Francis. And his old priest, the dirty bastard. And Anne-Marie when she was mad at him. Francis, for fuck's sake. Jimmy Donohue always called him that, probably trying to make him uncomfortable, make him feel small.

Fucking worked as well.

What was it he'd said to Anne-Marie? If the Jimmies appear, you know you've fucked up big style. Long time enforcers for Tommy Gallagher, the big man of Glasgow gangsterism. In some ways Fisher's mentor, his patron. But not his friend. Business was business. And if he'd sent the Jimmies, it meant Tommy Gallagher was seriously unhappy with how business was going. You hear stories.

The Jimmies, both of them standing there making his huge lounge seem poky and claustrophobic. Fisher shifted his weight from one leg to the other, feeling self-conscious in his baggy loungewear.

"So, to what do I owe this honour?" Fisher said. He was struggling to keep the smile on his face, and he could already feel himself beginning to flush. This couldn't be good.

"Not a social call, Francis," Jimmy Donohue said. "Fact is, Mr Gallagher is less than pleased with what we might say are 'developments', and how they pertain to his business interests."

Pertain. Typical fucking Jimmy Donohue word. Trying to sound better than the fat fucking thug that he was.

"Developments? We had a minor hiccup, sure, but that's all sorted. Yesterday's news."

"A minor hiccup," Donohue said, letting each word have a bit of room. "A minor hiccup. Would this be in reference to the disappearance and suspected death of two of your employees?"

"Well, not my employees, but working with us, yes."

"Not your employees, but working with you? And this distinction is important, is it?"

"Well, no, not in that sense, no. But yes, terrible accident, but that's life. Over and done with. We move on."

"And the other man who's gone missing? The suspicion of

what the media predictably call 'foul play'? The new uncertainty about the licence? These are also included in your minor hiccup, are they?"

"They're just problems, Jimmy. Just problems. Problems get solved. That's what Frank Fisher does. If there's a problem, Frank Fisher solves it. Mr Gallagher knows that, he knows I've always delivered for him. And there's nothing here that can't be solved. It's inevitable that you get these hiccups. It's a big project, a gargantuan project. There will be problems. But you know what? You don't get rich by taking the easy road. It's what marks out men like Tommy Gallagher and me. You take the risk, you get the reward. And yes, that means there'll be bumps on the way. So what? No pain, no gain." Fisher shut up quickly, instantly regretting putting the word 'pain' out there.

"Bumps. Hiccups." Donohue took a long look at Fisher from under thick eyelids. "Another way of describing the situation might be that you are not handling it with any particular acuity." Fucking acuity. "Mr Gallagher might have reason to suspect that this is all just too much for you. The accidents, the headlines, not dealing with the powers that be in an efficient and satisfactory manner. It's exactly the sort of poor handling which leads to a lack of confidence."

"Now hang on, Jimmy. I have always delivered. Always delivered. I've always made money for Tommy. He knows that."

"Mr Gallagher is cognisant of your previous financial contributions, Francis." Cognisant? Fucking cognisant? "But this is on a much bigger scale, of course. The investment is much bigger. And people are beginning to suspect that it's a much bigger risk than previously thought. Mr Gallagher is beginning to wonder whether he and his associates should proceed with the final investment this week."

Fisher spread his arms wide, disbelief spreading all over his face at the same time.

"Now, Jimmy, come on. No, no, no. This is not the time for getting cold feet. That investment needs to happen. There are payments to make, everything's on a very strict and disciplined schedule. The banks, other investors, they're expecting this to happen. I cannot stress to you enough how damaging and dangerous it would be to pull out now. This is tens of millions of pounds we're talking about. It could kill everything we've been working towards for the last few years. The reason I came to Tommy with this opportunity is because it's a licence to print money. Once the park's up and running he can just spend his days trying to work out how much richer he's becoming every minute. And I know Tommy, there's no way he'd want to lose the seven million he's already put in. That's all at risk if we don't get the final investment."

"I think you're spot on there, Francis. I don't think there's any circumstance under which Mr Gallagher would be happy to see his seven million seed money disappear. I'm sure he'd want that back."

"I don't think you quite understand it, Jimmy," Fisher said, shaking his head and feeling the sweat drops fly off it. "That money has gone, all spent, it's in the bricks and mortar and land and staff. But if everything collapses because we can't get the final investment together, it's all gone. The final payments need to happen, Jimmy. The paperwork's all drawn up, the routes for the investment channels, the shell companies, everything's ready to go. Tommy presses the button in a couple of days' time, and we're all on our way to being richer than God."

Jimmy Donohue seemed thoughtful, chewing on a soft knuckle.

"You make some compelling and persuasive points, Francis," he said. "There is one thing, though."

Jimmy Nuts stepped forward and gripped Fisher's balls, his

massive hand like a grabber in a scrapyard. He crushed. Fisher screamed. A sick, poisonous pain flooded his body. Instinct made him throw both hands down to catch hold of Jimmy Nuts' wrist, but he was swatted away. He felt his legs going. Jimmy Nuts released the pressure but kept his hand curled around his gonads. Fisher wanted to collapse on the floor but couldn't, held up by Jimmy Nuts.

Jimmy Donohue put his mouth close to Fisher's ear so that Fisher could hear him above his hyperventilation.

"The thing is, Francis, Mr Gallagher doesn't like being put in a situation like this. He thought you were clear on that point."

Jimmy Nuts squashed. Fisher screamed again, followed by a long moan. Black patches formed in his eyesight. Nothing was clear. The whole world was pain. He gripped onto Jimmy Nuts' suit lapels. Jimmy Nuts got hold on one of his hands and bent two fingers back. Fisher let go. He was going to faint, he knew it. He couldn't tell if he was breathing or sobbing or both.

He tried to speak. Nothing came out. Drool dripped from his mouth.

"You were given a message," Donohue said. "You were disrespectful. You brought us here."

Jimmy Nuts clamped his fingers together tighter this time, letting Fisher fall to his knees with an animal wail, going down on one knee beside him so that he could keep a good grip.

Donohoe bent over with a little difficulty.

"Consider this a final warning, Francis. If this doesn't go right, you and everything you hold dear will cease to exist, but only after a long and painful exit from this world. You understand?"

Fisher managed to nod, snot and tears flowing from his face. Jimmy Nuts gave one more crush, accompanied by a twist as a final flourish, causing Fisher to spew his breakfast all over the shagpile carpet.

He lay there whimpering, unable and unwilling to look at the men.

Jimmy Donohue helped up the other Jimmy, who straightened out his suit, brushing at the lapels.

"And now that we're all clear about everything, we'll take your leave," Donohue said. "I really hope this theme park of yours works out. Jimmy's keen to see the dolphins, aren't you, Jimmy? Such gentle animals, don't you think?"

Then both men turned and walked slowly out of the room, Jimmy Donohue first, Jimmy Nuts following.

Fisher managed to push himself up onto all fours, then reached for a chair arm to help get himself up. His breaths came fast, and rockets of pain shot out from his groin to every extremity in his body.

He managed to get to his knees, then placed one foot in front on him but had another lurch of sickness before he could get up.

Anne-Marie came running into the room, tears gushing down her terrified face.

"Frank! Frank! Oh, Frank! Oh, ma darling!" she said, rushing over to him, stepping through the sick. "What have them bastards done to you?"

"Ice," Fisher said, his voice a strained croak. "Get me fucking ice."

Anne-Marie didn't know what to do at first, then ran for the kitchen, coming back with a bag of ice-cubes from the freezer.

Fisher, on his feet now, still shaking, grabbed the bag, slammed it down on the edge of his desk, pulled down his baggy leisure trousers and rested his red ball sack on top of the bag. A mixture of wails and sobs as the freezing cold met the tender skin and bruised balls. His arms were taut, resting on the desk on either side of the bag, his head hung low.

Anne-Marie was crying, shaking too.

"I told you," she said. "I told you, Frank. You shouldn't have been so rude to that other one. I told you."

Anger managed to break through Fisher's pain.

"This is not the fucking time...." he said, spinning round. The ice bag, fused to his scrotum, spun round with him, hanging on for a second before giving in to gravity and falling to the floor, taking three or four layers of ball-sack skin with it.

"Holy fucking mother of fuck!" Fisher screamed, falling to his knees again, then letting his head hit the floor. As he rocked back and forth, muttering over and over about his balls, Anne-Marie quietly backed out of the room.

Maybe best to give him some time alone. With his ruined spuds.

CHAPTER TWENTY TWO

Word gets around

Rush hour on the backroads. That's the way it felt to Zander, anyway. Two vehicles within half an hour. Traffic hell.

As he walked up the long, snaking road towards Fisher's house he had to dodge onto the grassy verge to avoid getting run over by a big, white Mercedes 4x4 driven by a hard-eyed man with a buzzcut. It had come from the direction of Fisher's house, and Zander could make out two bulky figures in the back seats through the smoked glass.

Then a little while later, Banjo and Easter zoomed up in their black pick-up truck, horn blaring to get him off the road as they dashed up towards Fisher's place. They didn't stop to offer him a lift, oddly enough.

It was a long walk, all of it uphill. It was all Zander could do to keep his anger going the whole way. The views were good, though, as he noticed each time he stopped to catch his breath.

Zander wasn't entirely sure what he was going to do once he reached Fisher's house, which he could see a few hundred yards away on a prominent plot on the side of the hill overlooking the village. A Costa-style villa, a bit out of place amongst the old stone or white-harled houses dotting the countryside around Drumnadrochit.

He was supposed to get a plane back home in a few hours' time, and shouting at Fisher wasn't going to change that. It might make him feel a bit better, though. Show that he couldn't just be fucked with, that he was prepared to stand up for himself.

As plans went, it wasn't brilliant.

While he made his steady way up the hill towards the house, a kind of war conference was going on inside it.

Frank Fisher was propped up in bed, still white-faced and nauseous, his genitals creamed and being cooled by ice safely wrapped in a tea towel this time. A sheet was pulled up to his pale pot belly to spare blushes all round. Banjo and Easter stood at the foot of the bed. Anne-Marie was in a padded velvet armchair at the side, her face a mix of worry and fury.

"I mean, what is the point?" Fisher said, his voice more strained than normal. "What is the point of having actual fucking henchmen if they don't actually fucking hench?"

"Boss?"

"Hench! Fucking hench! Do your job! What are fucking henchmen supposed to do? You're supposed to look out for me, protect me. Where the fuck were you two when fucking Jimmy Nuts was doing the hokey-cokey on my Christmas crackers? Fucking nowhere, that's where. Probably away somewhere pulling the wings off flies or whatever it is you do for pleasure in your spare time. Fucking nowhere. Christ."

"You should have been here, you two" said Anne-Marie, lighting up a cigarette, drawing deeply on it. Her hand was shaking slightly. "Not happy."

"But boss," Banjo said, ignoring Anne-Marie, facing Fisher, "you're not saying we could have done anything about the Jimmies, are you? Taking them on, that's a death warrant. They're coming straight from Mr Gallagher. You don't mess with that."

"Well maybe you should have known they were on their way, then. What do you talk about when you talk to your psycho friends in Glasgow? The weather? Price of fish? The fucking Archers? New torture techniques? You should be finding out stuff that's useful to me. You should have known about them heading North by the time they'd hit Loch Lomond."

"Sounds like it was kept quite tight, boss."

"Tight? You have no fucking idea how tight it was." Fisher tried pushing himself up on the bed but was hit by a wave of aching sickness. "Sweet Jesus," he said, slumping again. He waited until his breathing was under control and the sick feeling had faded a little.

"The important point, this all needs to be got under control pretty damned quick. Frat boy's fucking off back down to England tonight, so that's almost sorted. You just need to get hold of those photos, that memory card. Where is it? Who's got it?"

"I'm on it, boss," Banjo said. "Should know soon."

"Once that's done, we're on the home straight. As long as you can avoid the temptation to play at being a fucking sniper again. I mean, Jesus Christ! Day of the Jackal? Day of the Cockwomble, more like. Anyway, loose ends to tie up. No more fuckups, you two."

A banging on the front door interrupted him, the bell going too. Fisher flinched, hands going to his crotch automatically.

"Fuck, no!" he said. "Don't let them in! Tell them I died! Fuck!"

Banjo slid up to the window, peering out but careful to keep in shadow.

"It's that university boy. What do you want us to do?"

"Get fucking henching."

Banjo headed for the front door, Easter lurching behind him.

He opened the door but didn't say anything, just stood staring at Zander like a rat about to pounce on prey. He leant his body forward at an angle, forcing Zander to step back.

"Where's Fisher?" Zander said.

"*Mister* Fisher is busy."

"I need to see him."

"Why?"

"We've got things to discuss."

"Such as?"

"That's for me and him, not you. Is he here?"

"Did you make an appointment?"

"No, I....look, is he here. I need to see him urgently."

"Mr Fisher's whereabouts are none of your business. Now, time for you to leave."

Banjo moved forward, pushing his hand against Zander's chest.

"Get your hands off," Zander said, swiping Banjo's hand away from him. Banjo put it back immediately.

"I'm warning you, get your hands off."

Zander swiped at Banjo's hand, but this time Banjo caught it and twisted, pulling his arm behind his back. He followed up with a sharp kick to the back of Zander's leg, putting him down on his knees on the gravel drive.

Banjo let go of Zander's arm, and Zander struggled back to his feet.

"You were saying?" Banjo said, a sickly leer on his broken-toothed face.

This wasn't going how Zander had planned it. Even though he hadn't really had a plan anyway. He ran through his options quickly. Try and get past the men and get into the house, although he didn't know if Fisher was there. Or make a quick and only slightly humiliating retreat. One involved potentially getting the shit kicked out of him. The other, less so. But before he could do anything, Banjo moved forward towards him. Zander took a step back.

"Look, a man raises his hand to me, he's going to get a slap," Banjo said. "I could have done much worse to you there. The fact that I didn't, that's out of respect. You, the university, you've done business with Mr Fisher, so I'm taking it easy. You've got to face facts, though. Time's up. You're not wanted here. Tell you what, to show you there's no hard feelings, I'll give you a lift to the airport. Easter, help him into the truck."

Easter lumbered over to Zander in two giant strides, putting his oak branch of an arm around Zander's shoulders and pulling him towards the pick-up truck. Zander was too surprised to stop it happening. Before he knew it, he was in the back seat of the pick-up, the two thugs were in the front, and Easter was driving them down the hill.

"Hell of a lot of people seem to know I'm flying home to-night," Zander said.

"Small place," Banjo said back. "Word gets around fast."

Easter skidded to a halt in front of the Drumnadrochit Arms, and Banjo got out quickly, opening Zander's door.

"We'll just wait here for you," Banjo said. "Don't be long."

Zander walked into the hotel, striding past Bruce Mackie at the reception desk, and headed straight up the stairs.

It didn't take long to pack his carry-on bag. He zipped it up, had a quick check beneath the bed and in the bathroom to make sure he hadn't left anything behind, then closed the door, locked it, and went back down the stairs. He nodded to Mr Mackie, laid the key on the reception desk, and then ducked through the door next to the reception, down the short corridor, into the Drum bar, and out the pub door. He walked along the back street, nervous and jittery, wondering how long it would take Banjo and Easter to realise he wasn't coming out.

He suspected he didn't have long. And he didn't have a plan either. This was as far as he'd got – find some way to shake them and then go somewhere else. It was the 'somewhere else' bit that he was a bit stuck on.

As he turned the corner at the end of the street, he was surprised to find himself pleased at seeing a dog. It was Shep, who came trotting up to him and sat down, tongue panting in its smiley way.

"Hey, Shep," Zander said, rubbing the dog's head and under its chin. No anxiety, no nervousness. This felt normal. This felt good. "Where's your master?"

Donald came around the corner, head to toe in green tweed, swinging his heavy, gnarled walking stick.

"Young Zander," he said. "Heard you were away."

"Not yet. And why does everybody seem to know that I'm supposed to be leaving?"

"The old tartan telegraph. You've got to remember, there's very little of any consequence which happens here. So, we gossip like there's no tomorrow. If we didn't there'd be very little point in talking to one another, except to discuss the exact type of rain that's falling. What do you mean by 'supposed to'?"

"Frank Fisher seems to be keen to get me out of here. He's been on to my boss, who's threatening me with the sack if I don't go home. I've pretty much been chucked out of the hotel, and Fisher's two goons are sitting out front insisting they take me to the airport."

"That sounds like, in the words of the great Frederick Mercury, that you 'want to break free'. Am I correct?"

"Never had you down as a Queen fan, Donald."

"Oh, you'd be surprised. That song was quite the favourite at the police Christmas karaoke. So, what's your plan of action?"

"I don't really have one, to be quite honest with you. I don't have anywhere to stay, I probably don't have a job anymore, and there's a pair of psychopaths who'll probably rip my limbs off when they find me."

"But apart from that, everything's hunky dory."

Zander smiled.

"Maybe not quite," he said. "But I can't just leave with everything up in the air. Something's not right here, we all know that. And I feel I need to find out what it is. There must be answers. And because I also feel that people are trying to stop us getting those answers, it's made me all the more determined to find out what they are and why all of this is happening."

"Sounds like you're giving up a lot to pursue it."

"Am I, though? A quiet life in a dull job in a featureless town? Is that what I was born to do?"

Donald thought for a moment.

"Look," he said, "it seems like you have a few problems on your hands, but at least we can sort the first one straight away. If you like, you could come and stay at my house. I've got what you might call a 'granny flat', although it's not a terribly helpful name considering that my granny died back in 1974. She's not still in there, by the way."

"Seriously?"

"Absolutely. We had to bury her once the smell started bothering the neighbours."

"No, I mean about letting me stay."

"Of course. And there'll be no charge. Other than walking Shep occasionally if you think you could manage that."

"Yes," Zander said, grinning. "I think I could manage that."

"Although if I find out you've punched him, I won't be best chuffed."

Zander's face dropped.

"What?"

"The old tartan telegraph," said Donald, adjusting his tweed cap. "Better than the Twitter."

CHAPTER TWENTY THREE

A message

Zander felt the chill in the atmosphere as soon as he walked into the Drum. The low burble of conversation died down. Some of the locals glanced up at him, stony faced, then looked away. As he reached the bar, the hairy man he'd spoken to on his first visit, Shuggie, turned his back.

"A problem?" he said to Catriona, who was in the middle of pulling a pint. She made a 'one minute' sign with her finger, delivered the fresh pint to a punter, took their cash, then motioned Zander down to the end of the bar, away from most of the people.

She leaned over and kept her voice low.

"Some of the regulars are a bit put out. Thinking you're trying to sabotage the theme park."

"Well, if that's what it takes to get to the truth," Zander said, causing Catriona to raise her eyebrows.

"The truth? As I said before, most folks here are more interested in the money. And as some have made very clear, very loudly," she said, nodding towards Shuggie, "the longer you're around, the smaller they think their pay-packets are going to be."

"So basically, everyone in this town wants me to get out."

"Well. Maybe not everyone," she said. Zander immediately perked up. Was that a flirt? Was there a hint of warmth in the eyes? "But strictly speaking, I'm not really allowed to serve you."

"Why not?"

"My dad said. Or I think he said it. My hearing's gone dodgy.

Probably a reaction to getting shot at by some bastard. So, a pint of Black Isle Blonde?"

"Yes, thank you," Zander said, smiling. "Anyway, I won't be long. Just here to meet Hector. Donald said he had something to tell us."

He took his pint and kept to himself, sitting at the end of the bar. When Donald came in, he got him a drink and joined him at a table near the back. Twenty minutes later, Hector pushed open the door and spotted them. At the same time, Bruce Mackie came in from the link door with the hotel and took in the scene, stopping to stare at Zander. He turned to his daughter.

"A word, please, Catriona."

Catriona put her glass-drying cloth down on the bar and followed her father back through the door. Zander filled in his drinking buddies about the ban.

After a few minutes Catriona came back through into the bar and came straight over to Zander, putting her hand on his shoulder as she bent to his ear, talking quietly.

"I managed to convince him to let it go for this evening, but after that he says that's it. And if any of Fisher's staff come in here in here tonight, he'd appreciate it if you made yourself scarce. He just wants to avoid any trouble."

"Don't we all," Zander said. Then a sigh hit him, and he made a decision. "Actually, I'd rather not stay where I'm not wanted."

He stood up, downed the dregs of his beer, and placed the empty glass on the bar. Catriona followed him there, her face saying sorry but the words not coming out.

"Look, you don't have to go," she said eventually as he put his hand on the door. He half turned. He had things to say, important things. But maybe not right now.

He pushed through the door, out into the fading light.

Catriona looked down at Donald and Hector.

"I'm genuinely trying to help," she said, her voice tense, cracking with frustration.

"I understand," Donald said. "You're in a difficult situation, my dear. Caught between a rock and what-have-you. Can't be easy. Let me go after him, see if I can win him round. You stay here, Hector. Guard those drinks. Some shifty looking ne'er-do-wells hanging about here tonight." He tipped his head towards a couple of old boys in similar tweeds to him and Hector. Old Norrie and Young Norrie.

Donald eased himself up, putting weight on his knobbly stick to help.

Zander was still in sight when Donald got outside. Donald called out a couple of times, but Zander kept walking, so he stuck two bony fingers in his mouth and shrieked out a long, loud whistle.

It stopped Zander in his tracks. He turned and walked back the way, meeting Donald halfway.

"Thank God for that," Donald said. "Thought I was going to have to sprint after you. Not that I'm saying I couldn't have done it, mind. 1971 Highland Police 100-yard dash champion at your service. No, it's just that I haven't stretched my hams with sufficient diligence today. I'm sure you understand. Wouldn't like to do myself a mischief."

Zander was smiling.

"Thank you, Donald. I certainly wouldn't want to be the cause of you losing your place in the local athletics team. And I suppose you're going to try to talk me into going back to the Drum? Pretend it's all fine."

"Yes. In a nutshell. I could spend more time putting an argument together, but 'yes' helps us cut to the chase, as it were."

"Look, it's been a long, strange day, Donald. I'm tired and I'm fed up. And I'm clearly not welcome here. And you know what? I get it. I can see why having some uppity English bastard poking his nose into things would upset some people here."

"Ah, to be fair, I've never heard them say 'English' in those terms. 'Bastard', yes. Fairly frequently, now you mention it."

"Thanks for that clarification. Anyway, it's just the last straw, Catriona being like that. I thought she was on my side. I thought she wanted to get to the bottom of this."

"She is. She does. Sounded to me like she was buying you time. But don't forget, she's in a difficult spot here. Conflicting loyalties and all that. She's very protective of her father. I told you he'd been through some rough years since Catriona's mum died. To her credit, she's always stood by him."

"Rough years?"

"Hit the drink for a while, although he sorted himself out. Needed to, to look after the wee one. But what I don't think many people know is that he developed quite a gambling habit. Got in a bit over his head eventually. From what I understand it, he started taking money out of the business, which is partly why the hotel ended up in the mess it was and why Fisher was able to snap it up for buttons. But there's more to it than that. I'm told by some of my former colleagues that Bruce's gambling debts, which were pretty hefty by then, spread across three or four bookies, got paid off at the same time. It wasn't exactly clear whether the money he got for the hotel would've been enough to clear it all. It was quietly looked into at the time, to see if there was any evidence of it being a side deal to dodge tax, but it all came to nothing."

"Are you thinking Fisher paid off the debt? Took on the debt himself?"

"I mean it's possible, but no one could prove anything at the time, and it's not something I've given a great deal of thought to. I'm not sure what benefit would fall to Fisher from taking on the debt. He still employs Bruce to run the hotel, the bar. I haven't seen anything which suggests their relationship stretches beyond that."

"Maybe Fisher just likes owning people. Makes him feel big."

"Yes, I can imagine that. Anyway, Bruce has not had it easy over the years, let's put it that way. And his daughter is a strong support to him. And yet she persuaded her father to go against what I can only imagine is a direct order from the high and mighty Mr Fisher so that you could drink there in peace for one more evening and find out what it is that Hector is so keen to tell us about. She's gone out on a limb, so I would gently suggest that it is in all our best interests to go back to the Drum, sit down, accept Catriona's hospitality, and set our minds to creating a devious plan."

Donald had worn him down. Zander nodded. In hindsight, he felt a bit churlish, flouncing out the bar like that. But his barring had felt like yet another slap in the face after a day of very hard slaps.

"Okay, let's do it," he said, and they walked back along the road to the bar.

As they got to the door it was flung open, and Hector bolted out in a blur of tweed. He stopped dead when he saw them.

"My house!" he said. He held up his smartphone so that Donald and Zander could see the screen, which showed a green figure moving around a dark room. "Some bastard's in my house!"

Before they could stop him, Hector jumped into his old Morris Minor and took off.

"For God's sake," Donald shouted after the car. He turned to Zander, worry creasing his face. "Ridiculous. He's in no fit state to take on a burglar. He's an old man. Look, I'll try to get to him, you phone the police. Tell them it's Hector Menzies' house, 10 Woodlands Crescent. You got that? 10 Woodlands

Crescent."

"Donald, wouldn't it be better if I went and you phoned?"

"And you'd find your way there from here?"

"Well, no. I take your point. But I don't think you should go anyway. Let's get the police there. I'm going to call them right now."

"I can't just let him do this by himself. The old fool," Donald said.

Zander had his mobile out but was defeated by a poor signal. He ran into the bar, asked Catriona for the phone, and dialled 999. When he got through, he told them the basic details. Then headed back outside.

But Donald was gone.

CHAPTER TWENTY FOUR

The chase

He'd been stupid. He knew he'd been stupid. Thought he could scare away whoever was there. Thought they'd maybe grab a laptop and go.

And now he was running through woods being chased by two men who would do him harm when they caught him.

And it was 'when'. He was an old man, an old stupid man who should've stayed at the pub. He could hear them behind him, crashing through the trees.

Hector swiped away low birch branches scratching at his face. The light was almost gone, although it was still bright enough if you knew the woods like Hector did. This was his only chance, the woodland behind his house with the faint trails which led to all sorts of different parts of the village. He knew his way around, and he was pretty sure the men in masks behind him didn't. As if on cue, he heard one of them call out in pain.

He kept going. He knew where he could go, where he could hide. As long as his heart could hold out. God, it was pounding fast. His lungs, so sore, like they were on fire. Not far now. Not long to go.

Just as he reached the bungalow, Donald heard the cry from the woods. Not Hector's voice, he was sure of that. Maybe someone Hector was chasing? Silly old fool was probably trying to catch the burglar. What was he thinking?

Donald considered going through Hector's back gate into the forest, but he knew it would be too dark for him to see properly in the gloom of the trees. His eyes weren't what they once were. He'd been in the woods many times with Shep in the daytime, but he didn't know them as well as Hector. Always knew where to find the pine martens, always knew where the best chanterelle mushrooms would grow. He'd be fine in there. Safe. The intruder was probably young – they'd get away.

Donald took some comfort from the thought, but it couldn't erase the large smear of worry all over his face.

Should he wait for the police? How long would they be? Was there a patrol car near, or would it have to come down from Inverness?

Where would Hector end up if he kept chasing someone, refusing to give up in that stubborn way of his? Where did the woods go?

When Donald thought about it, thought about where this arm of the woods stretched out to, it was obvious. The castle.

He'd better go and help, in case Hector actually caught up with whoever had broken into his bungalow. Donald set off along the road, deciding not to wait for the police. He'd flag them down if he saw them, divert them to the castle. But he couldn't just stand there and do nothing.

It was too much. He was getting faint, the exertion putting too much strain on his lungs and his heart.

Hector tucked himself down behind an old oak next to a broken stone wall, the shadows deep and inky.

He needed to rest. Just a few minutes, just until he could calm his body down.

Sweat was coming down his forehead. He removed his cap, wiped his head with his sleeve, stuck the cap back on and froze. Twigs snapping. They couldn't be far behind.

He pulled his knees into his chest as far as he could, making himself small, pushing back into the tight space between the tree and the wall.

His breathing. If only he could slow it down, make it quieter.

"Wait," a voice said, nearer than he'd expected, just a matter of yards. Fear gripped his heart again. "He's stopped. Can't hear anything."

Hector put everything into controlling his breath, fighting what his body was screaming at him to do.

"Try over there," the voice said, and Hector heard heavy, clumsy steps crunching through the dry undergrowth, getting closer and closer.

Right behind him. Right by the wall. Hector held both hands over his mouth, trying to keep the breath in.

"See anything?"

Hector could feel the presence behind him, something looming. Rocks in the wall scraped and moved as the person leant on them.

Then a violent commotion, rocks spilling everywhere, a shout from the man behind him.

Hector's old guts almost gave out. It was too much. He got ready to bolt as best he could, knowing it'd be pointless. This was the end.

"Fucking wall," a different voice said, deeper.

"What the fuck are you doing?" the first voice said.

"Not my fault. Fucking wall. Fucking collapsed. Useless fucking thing."

"Stop arsing about and get up."

"Trying."

"Right. Come on. He can't be far."

Hector heard the men move away through the woods. He waited, letting his breath come out slowly, trying to keep his heart from bursting.

Very few options now. Get through the new hole in the wall, make it down the castle that way. A bit longer, but potentially more sheltered.

Hector got up, shook the ache out of his knees, and climbed over the fallen stones. He kept close to the wall, stopping often to listen for sounds of searching. Not far now. Safety was just around the corner.

Donald flagged down the first car that came along the road, Sheena McKinnon who worked in the souvenir shop down at Fort Augustus and was heading for home in Cannich. She hadn't wanted to stop, but it wasn't often you saw a well-dressed pensioner standing in the middle of the road waving a big stick.

"My friend's in a spot of bother," Donald said when Sheena wound down her window. "If you could whizz me down to the castle, I'd be much obliged."

It was the way he doffed his cap to her that convinced her. Donald folded himself into her Fiesta, then she did a u-turn on the wide road and pointed the car back in the direction of Urquhart Castle.

"And if you wouldn't mind putting the pedal to the metal, as it were," Donald said. "In a bit of a hurry. It's ok, I'm a former senior policeman. No-one's going to chastise you for pushing the speed limit a bit."

He got out in the car park before Sheena had stopped the car, throwing a 'thanks' back over his shoulder at her as he raced for the path down to the ruins.

Spotlights picked out parts of the castle walls, the ramparts, the wooden bridge across the dry moat. Donald scanned the shadows far down below him. He started down the long path, then caught a blur of movement in the gloom over by the woods. A figure, keeping low. The thief?

He walked down the path as briskly as he could, using his stick for balance, trying to keep his eyes on the figure. For a moment it moved into a spray of light from a spotlight set in the ground, and Donald saw who it was.

"Hector! Up here! Hector!" Donald waved his stick, although it was a useless gesture in the darkness. He tried to pick up the pace down the path as he saw Hector crossing the wooden bridge, holding onto the handrail to keep himself steady, and disappearing into the castle.

And then two other figures burst from the trees, running across the grass with shouts and curses. Which is when Donald realised – chased, not chasing.

"Oh, damn and buggeration," he said. "Silly old fool." He wasn't sure if he was talking about Hector or himself, because he felt every year of his age at that moment. In his bones, his lungs, his heart, his knees.

But he had to try. He kept going through all the aches and pains, cutting off the path and taking a straighter, if steeper, route towards the castle across the dark lawns. A few steps in and his foot found a hole in the ground and he tumbled over, rolling a couple of times before coming to a halt. Everything ached as he dragged himself back up and started limping down the hill again.

Last throw of the dice. Hector knew Urquhart Castle as well as he knew his own house. The many hours spent on countless visits, day and night. His plan was simple. Lure the men into the castle, lose them in the confusing warren of ruined rooms and corridors, then slip out the dungeon door down beside the loch – which only proper locals knew about. Follow the shoreline round to the right, then through bushes onto the main road and the safety of lit houses and friendly faces.

He huffed up some stone steps into a turret. He could hear the men shouting as they crossed the lawns, splitting up, one going across the bridge, the other running towards the southern end of the castle.

Hector paused for a couple of seconds, desperate for breath. Then into a dark tower room, through a tight corridor, up some winding stairs, out into the open again along a walkway. He risked a look back. A dark figure was standing still in the court-yard below him, watching. Damn.

He ducked through another passageway to the side, down some internal steps and along the inside of a thick wall which he knew would take him out on the rampart above the loch. At the end was the staircase which branched off into the dungeon. It was closed to the public, but Hector knew how to get in.

He risked a look over the top of the rampart into the castle. The dark figure was moving around, trying to find a way up.

Good. Only yards to go and he'd be as good as safe.

As he moved towards the doorway on the turret in front of him, something about it struck him as odd. The shape of it, the tone of the darkness.

Which changed into the figure of a huge man, ducking out from under the doorway's low lintel and coming fast toward him.

Hector turned, started to run back along the rampart. Until he saw that his way was blocked. The other figure had found a way up.

Donald heard the cry quite clearly, and it was quite clearly Hector. A cry followed by a big splash.

He'd reached the castle walls, but now, instead of going for the bridge entrance he followed the walls around to the water's edge and the narrow rocky shore.

"Hector! Hector!"

No reply. No sign of anyone.

He looked up at the ramparts above him and saw a couple of

heads peering over, but there was no way he could make out who they were. The heads pulled back before he could say anything.

He started out the black loch. He couldn't see more than a few metres in front of him now.

"Hector!"

His voice carried across the loch, but still there was no answer.

Until something caught his eye. Something floating towards him, small and round. He bent down as it reached the shore, picked it up. Hector's tweed cap.

Donald held it to his heart and squeezed.

CHAPTER TWENTY FIVE

Business is business

Taking the fourth painkiller before the champagne might have been a mistake. They were strong codeine pills, left-overs from a prescription Anne-Marie got after one of her body-sculpting operations.

With the night he had ahead of him, Frank Fisher knew he'd need help with the pain. And what a pain it was. A special kind of pain. A personal, bespoke kind of pain. The sort of pain that, until the codeine kicked in, he felt would be with him for all time.

After two of the pills the pain was still there, the deeply sick ache spreading from the root of his manhood up into his stomach, his lungs, his heart, his brain. So another two pills got sloshed down with a glass of Armand de Brignac, his champagne of choice ever since discovering it was a celebrity favourite.

He wanted a taste of the good stuff anyway, because he knew they'd be served third-rate prosecco at the reception later.

Frank Fisher stood in front of a full-length mirror examining how he looked in his dinner suit. Anne-Marie had helped pad his crotch with cotton wool and bandages to protect his tender plumbs, but the result was a bloated front to his formal trousers.

"Fuck's sake. Anne-Marie! Looks like I'm trying to smuggle a Christmas pudding in there."

Anne-Marie stuck her head out from the dressing room. She was in a sleek, shimmery dress ending high above the knee and low on her chest.

"You look fine, darling."

"Fine?" Fisher fiddled with his waistband. "Fine? Does looking like I've had some elephant balls stitched onto me look fine, does it? Does me waddling about like a duck that's had a right royal keestering by a sex-pest swan look fine, does it? Well, that's fine, then."

"Do you not want to go?"

"We've got to go, haven't we? It's my coronation. My final acceptance by these inbred bastards after years of chipping away at them. I want to see their faces when they have to stand and clap and admit that Frank Fisher is better than any of them in any way they'd care to consider. That Frank Fisher has achieved what none of those tiny-minded backwoods pound-shop arsewipes could ever achieve."

"But are you sure you're up to it? With your sore balls and everything?"

Fisher gave Anne-Marie a look.

"I think 'sore' might be underplaying the seriousness of my overall genital catastrophe, don't you think? My boys have been majorly traumatised. But I'd be letting them down if I didn't pick up my prize tonight. It's what they would've wanted."

"You've got your speech with you?"

Fisher patted his jacket pocket in response, smiling. The codeine was doing its work.

"The car ready?" he said. Anne-Marie went to check. One of the drivers from the park was going to take them to the event and back.

It was the highlight of the business year in the Highlands. The North of Scotland Business Awards, sponsored by a couple of trade bodies and some big companies, presented by a local TV personality, and attended by anyone who was anyone in the Highlands and Islands, plus some national politicians.

The most prestigious award of the night, the North of Scotland Business Personality of the Year, was being presented by the First Minister herself. And Frank Fisher had it on excellent authority, namely the chair of the judging panel who was deep in his pocket, that he was this year's recipient.

In recognition of his vision and the prosperity and fame he was generating for the Highlands in the year his theme park would finally open.

Yes, the years of political disgrace and shady connections, the porn and the prostitution, they were far in the past now. This was the culmination of a long-held dream, the fulfilment of his ambition. To be a respected businessman, honoured by his peers, acknowledged widely as a success, to have the so-called legitimate business world at his feet looking up to him. While he made millions and millions and millions of pounds into the bargain.

Frank Fisher – a king amongst men. He'd be able to hold his head up, look anybody in the eye and say with utter, unshakable certainty – I'm better than you.

But first, some business of the other kind.

The driver took them both to a point on the north side of Inverness, a quiet road leading out to the locks where the Caledonian Canal entered the Beauly Firth. At Fisher's instructions, the driver parked the orange Range Rover beside a white lock-keeper's cottage. Fisher got out, leaving Anne-Marie and the driver in the car listening to a local radio station playing 70s hits.

At the end of the canal two huge wooden lock gates held back the water, meeting in the middle at an angle to create a shallow V across the canal's ten metre breadth. White-painted metal guard rails on each side of the gates created a walkway across it. Standing in the middle of the walkway, leaning on the rail, looking out into the wide Firth, was a tall, grey-haired man in a long black coat.

Alasdair Thompson. Long-serving Convenor of Highland Council, arguably the most powerful politician in a 200-mile radius. In bow tie and dinner suit too. He'd be on the top table at the awards, of course.

Fisher looked back over his shoulder. He could see the Convenor's Jaguar sitting in the small carpark beyond the lockkeeper's cottage. The engine was still running. Fisher stepped onto the walkway crossing the canal and stood next to the man. The pain had more or less gone. He felt lighter, a bit spongey, slightly euphoric.

"Councillor Thompson," he said, holding out his hand.

"Mr Fisher," Thompson said, continuing to gaze out to sea, not looking at Fisher, not acknowledging the hand. Fisher lowered it, feeling a buzz in his head, his blood fizzing around his body.

"Thank you for agreeing to meet up," Fisher said. "Better to iron out any problems face to face, I always find. Although irons and faces aren't always a great combination, now I think about it. Effective in the right circumstances, though."

"Is that supposed to be some kind of a threat, Mr Fisher?"

"No," Fisher said, grinning. "It's just me blethering. Think it's the painkillers talking."

Thompson nodded slowly, focused on a point on the horizon.

"Are you a student of history, Mr Fisher? Do you know where you're standing?"

Fisher shrugged, sniffed in the sea air and seaweed.

"Somewhere smelly?"

"You are standing on the edge of an economic miracle. That's what people were told at the time, anyway, more than two hundred years ago. The Caledonian Canal stretches from here right across Scotland, sixty miles to Loch Linnhe in the west, effectively joining the two coastlines. One of the biggest engineering projects of its day. Boats wouldn't need to go all around the top of Scotland anymore, through the rough and dangerous waters. Shorter, safer trading routes, cheaper produce, thousands of jobs. The flood of people leaving after the Clearances would stop. New life and new prosperity for the Highlands. That was the plan."

"And I'm thinking, what's your fucking point here?"

Thompson looked at Fisher for the first time, peering at him like he was something slimy you'd find on the shore at low tide.

"I didn't think you'd understand. You never do, your kind. The point was," he said, looking back down the line of the canal, most of it now lost in the gathering gloom, "it didn't work. Not at first, anyway. It took years to finish. By the time it was built, shipping had changed, the world had changed, it wasn't needed in the same way. But Highlanders are resourceful. We adapted. The canal actually became a tourist attraction in Victorian times, people coming here and using it to look at the scenery. And then the trains came in, linked up with the pleasure boats. And so the Highlands did flourish after all. Not as originally planned, but flourish just the same. Because of the beauty, the peace, the sheer majesty of the hills and glens.

"These gates that we're standing on, they hold back a big weight of history. I come here sometimes just to feel it. The Highlanders here before me, they created something that lasts. Something with long term worth, that became part of the living fibre of the Highlands."

"I hate to interrupt, but are we going to stand here wanking on about canals and boats and how brilliant Highlanders are, or are you going to tell me how much money you want?"

Thompson turned slowly towards Fisher again.

"You're a vulgar man, Mr Fisher. A vulgar little man who

will taint the Highlands with your vulgarity and your showiness and your seediness and your money-grabbing depravity. Your pleasure park, or whatever you call it, has no place in the Highlands. You will attract the wrong type of person, the wrong type of image."

"The wrong type of money?"

"And there you go again. The vulgarity never far from the surface. Money isn't everything, Mr Fisher. Those who value it above legacy and history are not the sort of people that I would regard as fit and proper custodians of Highland culture. Is your funpark destined to last? Or is it a get rich quick scheme, scarring our precious landscape with a hulking great white elephant when tastes change? And you and I will be long gone by then, and it'll be left for future generations to clear up the mess. You might not care about that, but I do. And that's the big difference between you and me. I feel the responsibility of guardianship. I've got the interests of the whole community and the history of that community – past and future – right at my heart. I'm not persuaded you have a heart at all."

"Ok, so I'm getting a bit confused now. Could be the painkillers, could be the sea air, could be that I'm getting bored senseless by some wittering old bastard wittering on about some shite that I completely lost the point of ten minutes ago. Correct me if I'm wrong, but we are here to do a deal."

"A deal," Thompson said, sniffing. "How grubby that sounds. We are here, Mr Fisher, to come to an understanding."

"And would that understanding involve me putting a large sum of money into a numbered bank account of your choosing in return for you not being a total obstructive bastard about my development, by any chance? Because if it's not, I've got somewhere else I need to be."

"Let me be very clear, Mr Fisher. I don't like you. I don't like your kind, what you stand for, how you operate. I don't like your development and what it'll do to Inverness and the Highlands. I don't like your attitude or your past, and I have more than a few doubts about your morals. But I am also a practical man. I know a lot of people want to see this theme park nonsense go ahead, and that there's a lot of money riding on it. But I have my principles. I also have my price."

Fisher wondered for a moment what would happen if he just nudged the Convenor over the guard rail and into the canal basin. Deep, dark water. High sides. No-one to hear him scream.

Except his driver, sitting over there in the Jag. Oh well.

"Glad you got that off your chest, are you? Made your little speech in front of your conscience? Good. Right, what's your price?"

Thompson paused, looked back out to the lights coming on across the Firth.

"One million."

The surprise caused Fisher to snort, cough and laugh at the same time.

"A million? A million fucking pounds? Are you actually serious?"

"That's my price. Take it or leave it."

"A fucking million? Are you on drugs?"

"Principles come at a high price, although I'm sure that's small change to you."

Fisher shook his head, laughing softly.

"So this is it, is it? You think you can step in right at the last minute, put me in a spot where I've got no option but to pay up? That I'll be a soft touch? That you hold the sword of, what the fuck's it called, fucking Hercules over my head? Do you know where I grew up? Glasgow, yes. East End. Different world to here. I bet you grew up around here, farms, countryside, clean air, all that shite. I didn't. We used to play in all these rundown houses, abandoned, some of them junkie dens. The smell of some of them, Christ, it'd melt your eyes. And there was always rats. Rats everywhere. Fearless little fuckers, too. Until we kicked shite out of them, used them for footballs. But you know one thing we were taught, right from when I was about as small as you can get? Never corner a rat. If you do, it will go for you. Any other time, you might get away with it. But see if you back it into the corner of a room? It'll go right for you, tear right through your face if necessary. And that's what you're doing to me. You think you've got me in a corner, that I can't get out. But I'm the biggest fucking rat you'll ever come across. And I will literally eat your fucking face off to get out of this. I will pull your eyeballs out, fuck your soggy brain through your eye-sockets, and then crawl right through your head to get through the other side. Nobody puts Frank Fisher in a corner. Not if they want to keep their face. And not have their brains fucked."

Thompson seemed to have difficulty swallowing. His mouth had gone a little dry, but he kept his gaze as steady as he could.

"The tough guy. You don't frighten me, Fisher. You're nothing but a cheap gangster, a Poundland Al Capone. Whereas I have what you don't have – influence and power. And that includes influence and power over you, whether you like it or not. Which is why you will pay me what I want. One million. Not a penny less."

"You're right, you're right - I'm a gangster. Hands up. You got me bang to rights. But that is exactly why you need to be a little smarter here. You do realise, don't you, that for as little as ten grand I could have you disappeared? Cut up into one-inch cubes and fed to pigs in Fife, never to be seen again. For ten grand. And yes, before you ask, that is a threat."

"And you do realise, don't you, that if I hold this up, you

stand to lose multiple millions of pounds – maybe even every-thing."

"Which is why ten grand would be ten grand well spent. I mean, I understand greed – believe me, I do. I even respect it in a man. But you've gone blasting off to some weird Planet Greed in the sky where everything is upside down and the trees are made of jelly, and....fuck it, I don't know where I'm going with this. The point is, you block this deal, you don't just cause pain to me, you cause it to my investors. Now, that'd put you in the bad books of some big, shiny financial giants in Edinburgh. So what, boo hoo, you might think. Massive reputational hit for the Highlands, take you years to recover, but that's your choice. But you'd also piss off some people who are far from being Pound-shop Al Capones like me. You're talking about the Harrods of bad guys, people you don't want knowing your name. People who include close personal colleagues of mine who will make you watch as they rip your ancient, shrivelled balls off, then stuff them in your gob and make you chow down on them. For starters. Which is why you'll take a hundred grand and thank me for it."

"Half a million."

"You don't get it, do you," Fisher said, laughing again. "You're not very good at this. I know you've been a low-level corrupt prick for most of your life, but you're playing with the big boys here. You lot, you're just a bunch of small-town ama-teurs. Bet you love it, don't you, swanning around here, thinking you're the big man. People running up to shake your hand at the golf club, developers schmoozing up to you, freebies getting chucked at you all over the place because you're the guy to know, you're the guy who says whether something happens. Yes, but in the middle of Buttfuck Nowheresville. Nobody out-side your little circle of happy sheepshaggers cares about you and your position and your shiny fucking car. So don't fuck with me. I know you're getting stars in your eyes hearing about all the millions flowing around with NessieWorld, but it's all just numbers moving around in the ether. I don't have half a million just sitting around waiting to jump into your bank account. Even if I did, I wouldn't give it to you. You said you have principles. Well guess what – so do I. And mine include not allowing myself to be bent over and fucked roughly up the bahookie by some jumped up tinpot tartan mini-Mussolini. Right. I've had enough of this. Last, final and deadly serious offer. Two hundred grand. In your account tonight. And we both walk away and live happily ever after. Instead of you becoming gristly pig shit."

"Two hundred and fifty."

"Fuck you with your two hundred and fifty. Do I look like some fucking Moroccan fucking carpet salesman in some fucking bazaar or something, selling you little boys on the side, you fucking paedo fuck? This is not a haggling situation. It's a deal. An 'understanding'. And you better understand if you don't say yes right now then I'm walking away, and I will not be held responsible for the consequences. Which will be pretty fucking devastatingly earth-shattering and final for you, by the way. I'm trying to be a nice guy here. This is not how I wanted or expected our conversation to go, but it started off all weird with that guided tour of canal history shit. So that's where we are. In two seconds, I'm going to walk to my car. I haven't got time for this shit."

Fisher stared at Thompson, keeping his eyes as still as he could, which was more difficult than he thought it would be. Those painkillers. Quite a hit.

A few seconds passed. Thompson broke first. He looked down.

"Fine." He took a slip of paper from his coat and handed it

to Fisher, who glanced at the handwritten numbers.

"What's this?"

"Bank details. Sort code."

"Sort code? For where?"

"My account. Bank of Scotland."

"Your what? Bank of...are you joking? I can't just land that amount of cash in there. There'd be red fucking flags going up everywhere. Get yourself an offshore one, Switzerland, wherever. Fuck's sake, do I need to run corruption seminars or something? Local government graft for beginners? Look, get an offshore account, give me the number, it'll be sorted. Might take you a bit of time, but trust me. You have my word. But – and this is the really important bit - if I don't hear by tomorrow lunchtime that you've withdrawn all concerns and questions and blocks on my baby, it's war. You like your history, don't you? Remind me - how did the war end for Mussolini? See you later."

Fisher walked slowly back to his car a bit bow-legged, careful not to let his groin padding chafe his thighs. Anne-Marie leant over in her seat and opened the door for him. He climbed up, nodding at the driver to go.

"These fucking simpletons," he said to Anne-Marie once they were back on the road. "Like doing business with Forrest Gump's stupider cousin. Could've stung me for a lot more if he knew what he was doing. Small town, in-bred, swivel-eyed fuds. Got any more of those pills, by the way? Pure buzzing, doll."

CHAPTER TWENTY SIX

A problem shared

A stiff word and a stiff drink.

The stiff word was for Donald. He'd wanted to help search for Hector himself, get involved in the burglary investigation. He was getting in the way, as the senior police officer told him in very clear terms.

The stiff drink was also for Donald, but he was joined by Zander and Catriona in his front room downing generous measures of 10-year-old Glenmorangie whisky, made at a local distillery.

At least the police seemed to be taking it seriously. They'd seen signs of forced entry on Hector's back door, signs of disruption inside – although without Hector's help they couldn't know if anything had been taken or whether the burglars had been scared off. They'd tried to access Hector's home security programme to look at camera footage, but his computer systems were well protected, encrypted to the hilt.

By the time the police got to the castle there was nothing to see. The figures Donald saw were long gone, and there was no sign of Hector. The police said they'd look further in the morning, and after a lot of persuasion they eventually agreed to question Banjo and Easter at some point - even though Donald admitted that he hadn't actually seen the men's faces.

Catriona persuaded Donald to go to bed, promising to wake him if there was any news. She and Zander retired to Zander's studio, the 'granny flat' Donald was letting him use, the upper part of a garage in his driveway. Zander was grateful for it but reckoned Donald must have had a very small granny.

You could swing a cat in it. But you'd probably kill it.

Catriona brought the Glenmorangie and glasses with them. She poured a healthy top-up for herself then offered the bottle to Zander. He shook his head. He'd had enough for now.

They sat together on the small, worn sofa, the lack of space in the studio forcing them to sit close together. Neither of them seemed to mind.

It was the first time they'd been alone with time to talk since the shooting.

"I'm sorry," Zander said.

"What for?"

"All this. This mess. Dragging you into it, getting you involved."

"I wasn't dragged into anything. I'm perfectly capable of making my own decisions, you know."

"Yes, I realise that, I didn't mean....well, what I meant was, if it wasn't for me digging away at everything and making myself public enemy number one around here you might be having an easier time of it. I can see the way people around here are looking at me, and I can't really blame them. But it wouldn't be good if you're tainted with that too. You've got to live here."

"So what? You've convinced me that something bad's going on. The way I was brought up, if there's something you can do to make it right, you do it."

"Even if it involves pissing off the whole village?"

"Especially if it involves pissing off the whole village. Don't get me wrong, some of them are nice, but some of the others..." She shook her head. "Anyway, you know the old saying? A problem shared..."

"...is a much bigger problem because now two people are stuck not knowing what to do."

"Yes, that's exactly the old saying I had in mind," she said, making Zander laugh.

They were quiet for a while, an ease settling between them.

"Did you mean what you said earlier?" she said eventually. "About doing what it takes to get to the truth?"

"Yes."

"And this from a man who didn't think there was any such thing as truth anymore?"

Zander smiled at himself.

"Maybe I just forgot. Maybe I was overthinking it. There's a truth - somewhere - about what happened to Jules and Mike. To Hector, to Nigel. About all the weirdness happening here. It's not necessarily all that complicated. But we'll never find out what the truth is if we let the liars get away with it. They're lying for a reason, and it can't be good."

Catriona moved around on the sofa, tucking one leg beneath her, so that she faced Zander. She scrutinised his face, seeing a different man from the one she'd noticed when he first arrived at the hotel. They looked at each other. And then there was a moment, with sitting so close together, the lateness of the hour, the aged whisky in their blood. Zander found himself wanting to reach out and stroke her cheek. Catriona wondered what his lips felt like. But they both thought about these things, wondering what the other was thinking and how they'd react, for a little bit too long. The moment passed.

"One thing that's been bothering me," Zander said, picking up his empty glass for the sake of something to do, "is how they know things."

"How do you mean?"

"If Fisher is trying to stop us finding out something, he's doing it on the basis of good information. It was something I talked to Donald about recently, about Fisher knowing about me spreading rumours, wondering how he managed to find out. We thought I must've said something in front of his two goons, rat-face and the giant, and I probably did. But it's been nagging away at me, because it's more than that. If we think this is all connected to Fisher – and I know it's still a big 'if' - how did he know about Nigel and the photos? About us going up the glen that day? About when Hector wouldn't be in his house, so they could have a root around? It's like I'm walking around with a bug on me. If Fisher is behind this, he seems to know what we're doing and thinking almost before we do. But apart from maybe a couple of things I said in front of those thugs, and maybe Mary at the theme park, I've only talked about this to you, Donald and Hector."

"Mary? Who's Mary?"

"Logistics at the theme park."

"And you know her how exactly?"

"She's shown me round a couple of times."

"Has she, indeed."

"The theme park."

"Of course. What else did you think I meant?"

"She was really quite helpful."

"Accommodating."

"And I got the impression she wasn't a massive fan of Fisher's."

"Because she said so?"

"Not in so many words."

"Oh, so this was in a non-verbal bit of interaction?"

"It was more a feeling. A non-physical kind of feeling."

"So, you got a feeling she's not a fan of Fisher's, and that justified you telling her everything?"

"Not everything. Just the weirdness about the timings in the lab. Sorry, why has this suddenly turned into a Mary-fest?"

"We don't know her from Adam. Or Eve. Why should we

trust her? How do you know she isn't running back to Frank Fisher as soon as you've both finished exchanging non-verbal sweet nothings?"

Zander gave her a disappointed look.

"I haven't mentioned anything about any of the other stuff to her," he said. "And when you think about it, Fisher's lot found out about us heading up the glen pretty quickly. I can't even remember if I mentioned it to Donald or Hector. And I hardly think they're in league with Fisher anyway."

"So what you're saying," Catriona said, sitting up a bit straighter, "is that Fisher's getting fed information from somewhere, and that it's either from me, you, Donald or Hector, and you've eliminated Donald and Hector, and presumably yourself. So you think it's me."

"What? No!"

"That's where your logic's taking you."

"No, no, not at all, that's not what I'm thinking. It isn't you, though, is it?"

Catriona looked like she wanted to throw her glass at him, her face blushing pink and her jaw going tight.

"Did you seriously ask me that?"

"I'd didn't intend to. It was you that brought it up, not me. And if you stand back, look at it objectively, how am I supposed to know? How do I know who to trust?"

"They shot at me! I totalled my car, my mum's car! I'm in this with you. I can't believe you're even asking me the question."

"Sorry, sorry," Zander said, trying to retreat as fast as he could. "I genuinely don't think you've got anything to do with it, it hadn't even occurred to me to ask. It's just that it came up. I'm sorry I went there. It was stupid, insensitive."

"Piggish."

"Piggish, yes."

"Dickish."

"Yes, okay, dickish too. Can I stop now?"

"Fine." She folded her arms, keeping a tight hold of her whisky in one hand. She dipped her head, lifted the glass, took a small sip.

"So where do we go now?" she said.

"I don't know. Genuinely don't. It would be better if we were one step ahead of Fisher instead of the other way around. I'll check with Donald in the morning, but I'd assume he hasn't been talking to anyone about all of this – unless it's to some of his old police buddies. But that doesn't feel likely."

"And just to be absolutely clear, to set your mind at rest, I haven't mentioned any of this to anyone either," Catriona said. "Apart from my dad, obviously."

Zander needed a second to compose himself.

"Your dad?"

"Yes. Why not?"

"Well, don't take this the wrong way, but doesn't he work for Fisher now?"

"So what? So do I, sometimes. What's that got to do with anything? He's my dad. Of *course* I tell him stuff."

"Yes, but maybe he'd mention things to Fisher or his goons. Innocently, of course. But things he thought they'd be interested in." Zander didn't know where he was going with this. It had just come to him, so he wasn't sure how far to push it. Not very, it turned out.

"Can't believe this," Catriona said, standing up sharply. "You seriously chucking my dad into this? Watch my lips. They. Shot. At. Me. If you think for even a tiny splinter of a second that my dad would ever have anything to do with that, after everything..."

And then she rushed for the door before Zander could stop

her. He couldn't be sure, but he thought she was crying. She door slammed behind her, and he forced his feet to move. He grabbed the handle, opened the door and started down the steps outside. Before he was even halfway down Catriona's hard voice came out of the darkness.

"Don't even think about it."

He stopped, catching sight of her as she passed under a dim streetlight, middle finger raised. And then she was gone.

Zander moved back inside, slumped down on the sofa and put his head in his hands. Well done, Zander Burns. How to win friends and influence people. You arse.

CHAPTER TWENTY SEVEN

Top prize

On balance, Frank Fisher wasn't sure whether to refer to himself as a visionary or a legend.

He had the notes all ready for his 'thank you' speech. He'd run through it with Anne-Marie earlier in the day. Luckily, he'd been thinking about it for a while, or else the speech might have ended up as a meditation on throbbing testicles.

The effect he was aiming for was humble superstardom. He'd come to the freezing North, seen how the simple folk lived in their mud hovels with their ancient superstitions, and he'd brought them into his big heart. And that he was leading them to a land of milkshakes and honeycomb ice-cream, shiny burger joints and heart-stopping rides.

Along those lines, anyway. Not in those exact words. In short, he'd seen an opportunity, one that had been lying out in the open waiting for someone to pick it up. And it was him. He'd had the vision, the determination, the ambition.

And although it wasn't for him to say, he wouldn't be surprised if in fifty years' time a visitor to Inverness would find a huge statue of a noble-looking man at the top of Academy Street with the inscription 'Frank Fisher – the visionary who saved the Highlands'.

And that's where he was having a wobble. Maybe 'Frank Fisher – Legend' had a better ring to it. Simpler. Clearer. Easier to carve on the bottom of a statue as well. Although people might think he was a posho with a double-barrelled name. 'Well, hello, Mr Fisher-Legend, would you like some caviar with your quail's egg?'.

Mind you, maybe he'd be a 'Sir' by then anyway. Not that he was bothered by titles. In strictly political terms, he was against them. But a 'Sir' would be nice. Or 'Lord'. Lord Fisher of Loch Ness. Now there was a title worth having. Get you tables in a few restaurants, that would.

Fisher checked his watch. Not long to go. Some of the smaller awards had already been handed out, the hotel of the year, small business of the year, start-up of the year, that kind of thing. They were on a break at the moment, and Anne-Marie had gone off to powder her nose. Or have a dump. One of the two. He wouldn't be surprised, dump-wise. The food had been a bit heavy. Chicken breast stuffed with haggis in a whisky sauce. He'd almost sent his back with a question for the chef – had he actually tasted this monstrosity before he'd served it up to five hundred of the biggest cheeses in the North of Scotland?

Not that he was hungry anyway. The painkillers had stolen his appetite. And made the world a little soft and foggy. He was happy, though. Some people would be nervous about going up on stage in front of all these people to get given the most highly regarded accolade in the Highland business world, presented by the First Minister herself. But not Frank Fisher. This was the sort of thing he was born for. This was his right.

Fisher looked over at her, the First Minister. There she was, glad-handing with the great and the good of Inverness. And the simpering and the puny. Look at them, prostrating themselves in front of her, as if she was royalty. Wouldn't catch Frank Fisher doing that, no fear. He'd made Prime Ministers cry. He would kow-tow to nobody. Be good to get a photo with her, though. Be good for the media coverage, the profile. But tonight it wasn't about her - it was all about him.

He looked around at the other people on his table, his guests, the people he'd invited to share his glory. Getting the table had cost him a couple of grand. Good position, right at the front near the stage, next to table number one with all the big nobs on it. Easier for him to get up to receive his award. He'd known he was getting it when he bought the table, of course. Tipped the wink by the chair of judges not long after he'd tipped a bucketload of cash in the boot of his Mondeo.

He hoped they'd get on with it. He wasn't feeling at his best, to be honest. Happy, but a bit out of it. He knew he hadn't been sparkling company. His guests hadn't made much of an effort themselves, though.

Glum bunch of bastards. Boss of the local BMW dealership, chair of the Inverness pub association, the president of the main golf club, the local MSP, the editor of the local rag. All with wives, husbands, whatevers. A good spread, but not a barrel of laughs. Looked like they didn't want to be there, half of them. Sour-faced gits. Maybe it was just the pills. Maybe they were making him a bit paranoid, because when he was doing his own glad-handing at the miserable prosecco reception earlier, he could swear some people were avoiding him. Anne-Marie said he was imagining it.

Anne-Marie came back to her seat just as an MC on the stage warned that the next part of the event was about to start.

"You ok?" she said.

"Fine, doll. Just fine. What do you think – should I say visionary or legend? I want to set the right tone."

"Say both. Why not? It's true, isn't it?"

"You are wise beyond your years, doll." Fisher leaned over to kiss her cheek, misjudged it and ended up with an earring in his mouth instead. He sat back in his seat. No-one had noticed, he was sure of it.

The lights dimmed. Once everyone was settled back at their tables, the MC took to the stage again and announced that it was now time for the highlight of the evening. The North of Scotland Business Personality of the Year. Then he said what an honour it was to have the First Minister present at this event, inviting her up on stage to make the announcement. Fisher checked his inside jacket pocket again, making sure the prompt cards were there. He adjusted the trousers at his crotch – he didn't want them puffing out too much when he got up.

The First Minister stood at the podium, smiling, waiting for the applause to carry on for a sufficient length of time before encouraging people to stop.

"Thank you for that welcome, and can I just say what an honour it is for me to be invited to this event tonight, and to present this most special of awards. Anyone who knows me knows that seeing Scottish businesses and Scottish businesspeople do well brings joy to my heart. We are a wee country, but we've always had big dreams, and we've often shown the world how to do business the right way."

Fisher relaxed into his seat again. Of course. It wasn't an introduction. It was a speech. It wasn't about business and the award winners, it was about the government and how much it had done and was doing for business. Oh well, that's the price of getting a VIP to your do – give them a platform.

He only half listened to the rest. Incentives, stable operating conditions, fair regulation. Partnership, growth, sustainable jobs. Stuff he'd heard a thousand times before. He'd said a lot of it himself, way back when, come to think about it.

"And that brings me on neatly to this evening's award," the First Minister said eventually, causing Fisher to sit up straight again. Anne-Marie reached out and squeezed his hand.

"The North of Scotland Business Personality of the Year is not just about a person. It's about what they stand for, what they have been able to create not just for themselves but for the wider community around them. It's about understanding the special responsibility they have to the people who rely on them, and who help them realise their ambition with their own sweat and toil. It is about leadership and vision." Fisher squeezed Anne-Marie's hand back.

"And the winner of the award tonight is nothing short of a visionary," the First Minister said. "For the opportunity they saw, the dedication they then applied to it, the refusal to be beaten down when all the odds were stacked against them. For staying true to a dream, which I'm sure is something we can all learn from and take heart from."

Fisher felt that little rush of adrenalin, a little judder at the back of his neck. Excitement rather than nerves. He started to move his chair back ever so slightly, ready to stand.

"I know this award is seen as the pinnacle of many a career in the North of Scotland, and quite rightly so. But I feel there is a lot of energy left in this person, and this is just a step towards even greater things. Ladies and gentlemen, I am very proud to be able to present the award of North of Scotland Business Personality of the Year to..."

Fisher flexed his legs.

"Jennifer Balfour, Chief Executive of Fearn Renewables!"

There was clapping. Clapping, some cheering, some swirly lights, some pumping music. None of it got through the roar in Fisher's ears, the inner scream he was doing everything to keep in. He grabbed a fork from the table and pressed it into his thigh. Harder and harder, to stop the explosion. He was vibrating with anger. Anne-Marie grabbed his arm.

"Oh, Frank," she said, but she could see it wouldn't help. Nothing would. His face was a deep purple, begging to burst. His teeth bared, the best approximation of a smile he could manage under the circumstances.

There were flashes from the stage, photos with wide grins

destined for the 'papers. A local TV news team was filming the event, getting ready to do interviews for the morning bulletins. It wasn't right. It was supposed to be him up there. There'd been a mistake. They'd got it wrong.

The event was over, the MC said goodnight, everyone applauded again, conversation burbled around the vast function room. Then he saw him, Scott Kennedy, chair of the judges, lurking in the wings of the stage.

"Little shit," Fisher said, shooting out of his chair and heading for the curtain beside the stage.

He pushed through the curtains, came up behind Kennedy, grabbed him by the neck and pushed his face into the wall.

"What. The fuck. Was that?" he said, punctuating it with more face bashes. He spun Kennedy around, forced him back up against the wall and shoved the fork up under his chin. "What the living fuck just happened there?"

"Frank, Frank, I can explain," Kennedy said, his voice high and panicky, on the verge of soiling himself. "It was her, the First Minister." He tried nodding in the general direction of the main room, but the fork made it an unwise move, the tines poking into him. "Her office said she wouldn't come unless it went to someone else. Said there were some issues."

"But it was my fucking award! Mine!"

"What can I say, Frank? It was taken out of our hands. I don't know if it was political or what, but we were told. Her or you."

"Then you should've chosen me. That's what you were paid handsomely to do. And I fucking deserved it too. Nobody's done more for business up here than I have."

"Totally agree, Frank, totally agree. Would you mind getting that sharp thing out of my neck, please? It's hurting."

"Hurting? You don't know the meaning of pain."

Just then Anne-Marie came through the curtain and inserted

herself between Fisher and Kennedy.

"Dignity, Frank," she said, moving the gripped fork away from under Kennedy's chin. "Leave with your head held high. We know who the real winner is here tonight. You've got nothing to prove. Come on, I've phoned the driver to meet us out the back."

She held his stare, saw something in it change. Fisher bowed his head.

"You're right. You're right." He gave a last hard look at Kennedy, then he started walking with Anne-Marie towards the area behind the stage. "Hang on, there is one thing, though," he said, as if he'd forgotten to take his mint from the table. He turned back, walked onto the stage, and took the MC's microphone off its stand.

"Excuse me? Excuse me, can I have your attention, please?" he said into the mike, but it was lost in the hubbub of chatter in the room as the tables mixed and finished the free booze.

Fisher took the microphone over to one of the large speakers at the side of the stage, put it up against the mesh front. Feedback screeched out, going on and on, making everyone turn, stopping conversations dead. Fisher smiled. An old trick from nightclub days.

All eyes were on him now as he walked back to the centre of the stage. They were all there. The bigwigs, the politicians, the award winners. All quiet, waiting. Wondering.

Fisher took a long, deep breath.

"I'd just like to say," he said, smiling wide, taking them all in with a slow sweep of his eyes, "you're all cunts."

Then he winked, held his arm out to the side and dropped the mike.

As he turned to leave, his foot caught the falling mike in an accidental drop kick, spinning it out into table twelve where it burst the nose of the third most successful insurance broker in

Nairn.

Anne-Marie stared at him open-mouthed, not for the first time. She latched on to his arm and dragged him out the back door to the car park where their driver sat with the engine running.

"Out of here, quick as you can," she said to the driver as soon as they'd both climbed in. She turned to face Fisher, her face like stone.

"Happy now?"

Fisher made a non-committal humming sound and sat back in the leather seat. There was always this little voice inside his head, a voice that said 'don't do that, that wouldn't be right, that's not sensible, that's just weird, normal people wouldn't do that'. And over the years he'd learnt to rely on that voice. He relied on it to remind him what was proper and decent and respectable, and how proper, decent and respectable people behaved. And then he'd ignore it, because those things were for the little people, the ordinary people, the ones who'd never taken a chance in their lives. No-one ever achieved greatness by being normal and sensible.

Fisher kicked the empty passenger seat in front of him. Then he kicked it again. Then punched it, then kept punching and kicking, faster and faster, harder and harder, letting the rage flow out. The driver kept silent

"Why! The fuck! Is everything! Going! Wrong!?" He let go three final punches to the headrest before slumping back in his seat.

The car was caught in Inverness's one-way system, and Fisher noticed they were about to drive past the hotel's front entrance, guests from the event spilling out into the night.

He hit the button to lower his window, raised himself up and stuck his head out.

"Muthafuckaaaaaaaaaahhhs!"

He eased his head back in and sat back down.

"Yup. Much happier now, thanks."

CHAPTER TWENTY EIGHT

Locally caught

What was the opposite of the 'walk of shame'? The 'walk of innocence'? The 'walk of righteousness'? The 'walk of teeth-grinding frustration'?

Catriona wasn't even sure it was an opposite. Yes, she could have stayed the night, had things gone differently. But her return to Zander's crash pad in the morning wasn't an attempt to rekindle whatever might have been about to happen. And she was still mad at him. It's just that there were more important things to think about. Such as Hector, and where he was.

She decided it wasn't a walk of anything. Just a walk.

As she neared Donald's house, Shep came running down the drive to greet her, a black and white blur jumping up at her to say hello. She rubbed Shep's head with her free hand, and then the dog got interested in the paper bag she held in her other hand.

"Not for you," Catriona said, easing Shep's nose away from it. "It's a peace offering for your lodger. Although it's all his fault. Shall we see if he's up yet?"

She rapped on the glass door at the side of the garage, while Shep sat down and waited, looking between Catriona and the door, panting as usual.

Zander came down the short flight of stairs, rubbing a towel on his damp hair. He was surprised and happy to see Catriona, but tried not to show it, wondering if she was still mad at him.

"Hi," he said, opening the door. Catriona held out the paper bag.

"Present for you," she said. "Wasn't sure whether you'd had

time to get provisions in."

Zander peered inside the bag. Two white rolls, filled with something brown and grey and grainy-looking.

"Haggis?"

"Haggis. Locally caught. Served in the traditional way, sliced, in a morning roll, guaranteed to soak up any residual whisky taken to excess the night before. I've had mine already."

"Do you want to come in? I've just put the kettle on."

Catriona nodded and brushed past him. Shep stood up too, but Zander stopped him.

"Sorry, Shep," he said, reaching down to scratch under the dog's chin. "Grown-up talk."

He shut the door and climbed the stairs. Catriona was already sitting at the tiny breakfast table beside the kitchenette.

"Look," he said, feeling very awkward. "Last night – I didn't mean anything. I was just thinking out loud. Sometimes my brain filter doesn't work."

"It's fine," Catriona said quickly, clearly keen to avoid the topic.

"Sorry anyway. I didn't mean to be a bigger idiot than normal."

"Eat your haggis. It'll get cold."

Zander smiled and sat down, opening the bag and taking out one of the filled rolls.

"Am I supposed to put anything on it? HP sauce, ketchup?"

"Not if you want to live," Catriona said. "Can you imagine if that got around the village? They'd come after you in a mob, burning torches, the works. Bad enough as it is. Don't want to make it any worse."

Zander took a bite, chewed.

"That's....that's not bad," he said. "Unusual. Not what I was expecting."

"What were you expecting?"

"More sausagey."

"It's got some of the same ingredients. Plus some other stuff."

"Quite peppery."

"It's for the best."

"So what else is in it?"

"Did you say the kettle had just boiled? I could do with a tea."

"Of course," Zander said, putting the roll down and getting up, grabbing a couple of mugs from a low cupboard and searching around for tea bags. He found some in a glass pot. He sniffed at them, wondering how old they were. Did tea bags go off? He shrugged, chucked them into the mugs and poured boiled water over them.

"Ah," he said, checking the mini fridge. "No milk. Or anything at all, really."

"It's fine," Catriona said. "I don't think Donald was geared up for a full-on bed and breakfast scenario. Have you seen him this morning?"

"Not to speak to. I saw him through the window earlier, out in the garden. I was going to go down as soon as I was ready."

"How do you want to play it today?"

"I'm going to spend a lot of the morning dodging calls from my less than happy ex-employer, who is less than happy that despite threating me with becoming an ex-employee if I didn't do what they said, I have now become their ex-employee by not doing what they said. If you catch my drift. Anyway, they want a 'clear the air discussion', apparently. Involving HR."

"Tempted?"

"Not very. Anyway, there's too much to do here. I tried to speak to the police first thing about Hector but couldn't get through to anyone sensible. Going to try again in a minute."

"Maybe Donald would have more luck? We should pop over to see him. Bet he hardly slept last night, worrying about Hector. Probably wouldn't admit it, though."

Zander finished his haggis roll ("I might keep the other one for later"), slurped down some hot, black tea, and pulled a shirt over the top of his t-shirt.

Shep was still waiting at the door as they left, trotting alongside them as they walked the thirty metres to Donald's back door.

He let them in, offered tea, sat them down in his sitting room. He was subdued, a little unsure of himself.

"Did you sleep, Donald?" Catriona asked him.

"Yes and no," he said. "Not that unusual, these days. Biscuits? No, a bit early for biscuits. Have you had breakfast?"

"All fine," said Zander. "Donald, we were thinking about this morning, what we're going to do about Hector. I've been trying to get the police interested, but I'm not getting through to the right people. I thought maybe you'd have better luck with your contacts."

"The sort of contacts who were supposed to phone me back first thing this morning and haven't?" Donald said. "Nearly quarter past eight and not a word so far. Pretty disgraceful if you ask me. After all, this isn't a missing person's case. This is the potential..." He paused for a moment, gathering himself. "This is the potential injury of someone being pursued by aggressive housebreakers. This should be top priority. I'm going to give one more call then go out there myself and look for him. It's not good enough. Simply not good enough."

"And we'll be right with you looking for him," Catriona said.

"Although," Zander said, shooting a quick look at Catriona, "are you sure that's for the best, you looking for Hector yourself? Might be better to check with the police, make sure they're on it."

Donald sighed.

"Yes," he said, grim-faced. "You're right. I'll give them a call."

He went out into his hallway, picked up the handset and dialled his contact in the Inverness police HQ. Zander and Catriona strained to listen to one side of the conversation, mainly Donald asking questions. After a few minutes he hung up and came back into the sitting room, taking a seat in a wing-back chair by the unlit fire.

"They've got a team on their way, apparently," he said, not sounding too convinced. "Going to do a sweep of the castle grounds, the shoreline, back into the woods. They're treating his house as more than just a burglary crime scene now, so they say."

"That all sounds positive," Zander said. "Sounds like they're taking it seriously, anyway."

"Yes, but what are we going to do," said Donald, a note of desperation creeping into his voice. "He's out there somewhere. I've got to hope that he's alive. I can't just sit here waiting for news, it'll drive me absolutely round the bend. I know exactly what you're going to say, the same as my contact said – leave it to them. But what sort of man would I be, what sort of friend would I be, if I just sat here and did nothing?"

Zander started to speak but stopped at manic barking from Shep as the dog sprinted from the back of the house round the side to the front, spraying gravel from the long driveway as he went. They could all hear the sound of an engine on the road at the bottom of the drive. No prizes for guessing what colour the car would be.

"I'll start again," he said, smiling. "Everybody understands why you want to do everything you can to help, it's just that...."

And then a thump, a piercing animal cry, loud yelps, an engine revving, a metal door slamming. Then a revving again, a car taking off.

"Oh God, oh God!" Donald said, leaping to his feet, his face ashen. He dashed for the door, closely followed by Catriona and Zander. All three rushed outside. Nothing to hear except a car engine, getting further away.

"Oh, God, they've taken Shep!" Donald said, running down the drive. "They've taken Shep!"

Zander and Catriona raced ahead of him, getting down to the road first. And then stopping dead.

"Oh Christ," Zander said, feeling the breath squeezed out of him, putting his hands on his knees. Donald was just a couple of seconds behind him, spared for that short time of seeing what Zander and Catriona had just seen.

On the pavement, ten metres away, lying on his side. Very still.

"No, no, no, no!" Donald rushed over to Shep. "No, boy, no! Not this! Not this!"

And then the tears came and the cries roared out as Donald kneeled down, bowed over Shep, hands on the dog's fur, trying to find a way to bring him back. "My boy, my boy! How could they do this? My boy!" He tried to raise Shep to cradle him. "Silly old fool! Chasing things, getting into trouble. Stupid, stupid, stupid! I'm sorry, Shep, I'm sorry, son. I'm sorry, I'm sorry."

And Donald buried his face in Shep's fur, stroked his old friend's head, and wept his heart out.

Catriona went over to him, rested a gentle hand on Donald's shoulder.

Zander stood, feeling a fury in his veins like he'd never felt before. And remembering what he saw. The car speeding off into the distance.

A black car.
To be precise, a black pick-up truck.

CHAPTER TWENTY NINE

Unconscious potatoes

It was the call he'd been waiting for.

His inside man in some big posh London finance house, the place outwardly respectable and solid and boringly conservative. But inside, some of the country's top experts at moving dodgy money around the world. Money which started its journey as filthy and tainted, often with blood, but which finished up as sparkling and crisp.

The call was short, just letting Fisher know that all the arrangements were in place for the transfer of money from Tommy Gallagher's shell companies later in the day – not that it was spelled out so blatantly on an open line - and assuming everything went smoothly there should be confirmation of the transfer by the evening with all the digital and actual paperwork finished.

Which meant he was on the home straight. Opponents out of the way, money in his hand, ready to charge towards opening day in a few months' time.

This was the sort of news to blow his hangover away. Although some more painkillers helped too, of course.

This was going to make him a king. Nothing and no one could be allowed to get in the way of it today.

He looked out of the picture window in the lounge, the sweep of the hill down to the village, out over Urquhart Castle, into the black loch.

Sure, there had been a few blips recently.

But Frank Fisher was back in control.

He let it sink in, that special winning feeling.

Nobody fucks with Frank Fisher.

He grabbed his mobile off the desk, speed dialled Banjo.

"Listen, big day for me today. Nothing and nobody is to be allowed to do anything to spoil that, understand? Nothing and nobody. Zero tolerance towards fuckwits and general fuckwittery."

Fisher listened for a few seconds, starting to feel a little edgy.

"Not on the plane? How could he not have got the plane? You were supposed to take him to the airport? Why not? When did this happen? And you were going to tell me when, exactly? I don't care, you should have called anyway. I need to know these things. What do you mean 'a warning'? Actually, I don't want to know. I just want you to make sure him and his freak show mates are kept as far out of the way as it's possible to be today. Understand? Don't want to see head nor hair of them. They can dance a fucking samba on my lawn tomorrow as far as I'm concerned, but not today. Clear? Right."

Fisher cut the call, not feeling as great as he had been five minutes previously.

Still. Problems would always occur. The mark of a great man was how you handled them.

Let the little people worry about problems. Frank Fisher was above all that. Frank Fisher was a total fucking legend.

Zander waited with Donald while Catriona went to find her father to see if he could help. They'd called a vet, who was getting there as fast as she could. Shep's pulse was weak, and they were pretty sure there were broken bones. But there was life – for now at least.

Poor Shep's bones weren't the only things broken. Donald could barely speak. He wouldn't leave Shep's side. The dog was lying unconscious on a blanket on the sofa while they waited. Donald kept his hand on Shep's coat, stroking him gently every so often.

"Vet's five minutes away," Zander said, looking at the text he'd just received from her. "It's going to be alright."

Donald shook his head.

"No. No, I don't think so," he said, keeping it quiet. "Shep's old. I'm not sure he can make it through something like this." He shook his head again, letting out a sigh. "It's too much. I can't do this. First Hector, now Shep. I shouldn't have got into all of this. I'm too old for this. I'm not up to it. Trying to pretend I've still got it, once a copper always a copper. Got myself in above my head with folk who play dirty. Well, they've won. Not ashamed to admit it. They've beaten me."

"Don't say that," Zander said, trying to sound supportive, but feeling like he wanted to hide Donald away somewhere safe. "We can't let people like Fisher and his thugs beat us. If they win, what's the point in everything? We just hand the world over to bullies and criminals and the corrupt. I know it feels rough at the moment, I can't imagine how badly you're hurting. But we need to carry on."

"No, no I can't," Donald said. "It's different for you, you're young. I'm an old man. A foolish old man who's got carried away. And look where it's got me? My dearest friend, my companion, everything I've got in my life. I've put it all at risk. It's stupid and foolish and I'm putting a stop to it right now. You do what you have to, but I just can't anymore. Everything I've got, it's been used up. I'm empty. There's nothing more to give."

Zander moved over to the window, keeping an eye out for the vet. No sign yet.

"I'm going to end this, Donald. You're right – it's come at too high a cost. It was my fight and should've been my fight alone. I'm sorry I dragged you all into this – I wouldn't have done it if I'd known it would get as brutal as this. It was selfish and short-sighted of me to accept your help, to put any of you in harm's way. As soon as I realised it was getting dangerous, I should've made sure you were all well out of it. And now..." he looked down at Shep, unable to finish, both men knowing the point.

A green van pulled up in the drive, Highland Vets written on the side. A middle-aged woman with short grey hair got out, slinging a heavy medical bag over her shoulder. Zander jogged to the front door to let her in, then showed her into the living room.

As she kneeled down and talked to Donald about Shep and his injuries she took items from the bag, laying them on the floor next to her. Then she started checking Shep's pulse, eyes, legs, ribs, feeling for breaks.

Zander mumbled that he'd leave them to it, and backed out of the room, easing the door closed behind him. He let out a deep breath.

Okay, time to end it. And if that meant going for Frank Fisher, so be it.

He started walking with purpose along the road, heading towards the centre of the village, determination building in his bones. He'd confront Fisher, and this time he'd be ready for his two goons.

He was getting near the Drumnadrochit Arms, and he thought he might check on Catriona, tell her that the vet had arrived. But he was still public enemy number one as far as the hotel was concerned. He stopped on the corner, checking his phone so he could call Catriona instead. No service.

"Standing on a street corner like a jezebel turning tricks. Disgusting," old Bessie said, sliding up to him.

"Not now, Bessie. Not in the mood."

"Oh, you're always in the mood, you young 'uns. Sex, sex, sex. All you think about. I expect you'll be trying to seduce me into one of your foursomes, you dirty pervert."

"Other things on my mind, Bessie. Now, if you'll excuse me..." Zander started walking off.

"That's it, away you go, off to see that other pervert, Bruce Mackie, no doubt. Him and his two chums, always trying to get me interested in a gang-bang. Not that I wouldn't turn down that big lad."

Zander stopped, turned.

"Beg your pardon? Who?"

"Perverts. Bruce Mackie and his two chums, always hanging about the car park there, plotting ways to entice respectable women into dogging sessions, I'd imagine."

"You said something about a big lad?"

"That's right," she said, straightening up. "I can't lie, I wouldn't say no to that. I've always favoured the larger cock."

Zander flinched.

"Bit too much information there, Bessie."

"The girth, you see."

"Way *way* too much" he said, holding his hands up and trying to shake the image out of his head. "So, you're saying you've seen Bruce Mackie with these two? And this is, what, quite often?"

"Quite regular, yes. That one with the teeth, always trying to undress me with his nasty little eyes when I go past. There should be a law against it."

"Yes, probably," Zander said, wondering. Bruce Mackie with Banjo and Easter, it had to be. More than just a passing acquaintance, if Bessie's fevered memory could be relied upon in any meaningful way.

Only one way to find out. Zander decided to take advantage of his current bullish mood, his justified anger. He nodded goodbye to Bessie and started striding along the road towards the hotel.

Straight in the front door and into the empty hallway. No-one at the reception desk. He walked up, pinged the old-fashioned bell on the reception top, waited for thirty seconds, then slid behind the reception and in through the 'Staff Only' door.

Which is when his world exploded into blackness, and he hit the floor like a sack of unconscious potatoes.

It was harder to drive with swollen achy balls than he'd expected. He still had the padding and bandages on, because even though the uber-strong painkillers were doing a decent job of masking some of the agony, he didn't want to risk his battered boys swinging free in his trousers when they were still in a delicate state.

But that meant an awkward driving position, so awkward that he'd have called out someone from the park to drive him if he'd realised.

He was propped up in the driving seat on a cushion he'd brought from the lounge. Anne-Marie was still in bed. She'd be no use to anyone until lunchtime at the earliest. The hangovers were hitting her harder these days.

Whereas Fisher, aided by pharmaceuticals, was feeling kind of fine, kind of happy, but still with a smidgeon of nervous excitement about the day ahead. And swollen achy balls, obviously.

He came to a straight bit on the loch-side road, saw a clear stretch ahead, and stamped down on the accelerator. The Range Rover lurched forward, swinging out from behind a caravan pulled by an old Peugeot which had been annoying him with its sloth for the past couple of miles. As he pulled alongside the car, he slid the front passenger window down and flicked the finger at the balding driver.

"Get a hotel room, you cheapskate bastards!"

He sped up again, pulling sharply to the left to avoid an oncoming lorry which had been coming faster than he'd thought. He was rewarded with a blare of horn from the Peugeot behind him. Fisher checked his rear mirror, saw the balding man mouthing silent obscenities at him.

"Not very fucking polite," Fisher said, then dug his heel into the brake pedal. The Peugeot filled his mirror, the man's mouth open in terror. The caravan swung into the other side of the road as the man slammed on his brakes, just missing a Volvo estate coming the other way.

Fisher laughed and sped off again, leaving the Peugeot standing.

"Cheap French car fuckers."

He hit the touchscreen for a bit of music, and one of his favourites came thumping out of the speakers. 'Simply the Best' by Tina Turner. Kind of an anthem of his.

It was still playing, Fisher still belting out the chorus through open windows, as he was waved through the front gate at NessieWorld without stopping. His phone rang as he pulled up in front of his office at the Victorian castle. He tapped the car's touchscreen to answer.

"Yo," he said, cheeriness personified.

"You on speakerphone, Francis?"

Fisher scrambled to get the phone off handsfree, dropping it in the process. He half slid down his seat, sweeping his hand around on the floor until he got hold of his phone and brought it up to his face.

"Not anymore, Jimmy. Good to talk to you."

The sudden rush of adrenalin made his gonads pulse. Which wasn't ideal. Not a pleasant sensation. It's as if they remembered. Recognised the voice.

"Just a courtesy call, Francis," said Jimmy Donohue, his voice whispering through the handset. "I know our people and your people are speaking, everything's reaching a conclusion. Just wanted a final assurance that everything's under control now at your end."

"Beyond control, Jimmy. We are talking total fucking lockdown. If I was any more in control of the situation, I'd have to declare myself Emperor of this place."

There was silence on the line, and Fisher wondered for a second whether Jimmy or his boss had heard about his little jape at last night's awards. Suddenly it didn't seem like such a smart business move to call a roomful of dignitaries, including the First Minister, cunts.

"Fine, Francis," Donohue said at last. "That's what we want to hear. Keep it tight."

"Will do, Jimmy," Fisher said, but Donohue had already hung up.

Tight. Quite.

CHAPTER THIRTY

Deeper and down

Tightness. Aching. Black, everything black. Something scratching his face. Mouth dry, hurting, can't swallow. Chest stretched, arms pinned. Can't move, can't move! Drowning! Drowning!

The panic kicked in as Zander came to. On a chair, hands tied behind him, ankles strapped to the chair legs.

Complete disorientation. He tried to cry out. Something across his mouth, he couldn't do it. Tried to stand. Fought against the force keeping him in place, the ropes and tape. The chair tipped, then fell on its side. Zander's right shoulder hit the concrete floor just before his head. A strangled yell, the agony of his forearm trapped beneath him, between the chair and the floor.

And everything still dark, something in front of his eyes, across his face, over his head.

Footsteps. Quick footsteps down stairs. Dim light through the cloth over his face. Zander felt hands drag him and his chair upright again. Heavy breathing. Zander tried to get his own breath under control. Fight the panic.

The smell. A stale, damp smell. Low humming, mechanical.

Zander tried to speak again, couldn't. Struggling for breath. Pain crushing his head, nausea, choking.

He was aware of someone walking behind him. Whatever was over his face, a rough sack he guessed, was yanked away. A hand gripped the top of his head, holding it still. The cloth gagging him was pushed down around his neck, a plastic bottle of water forced into his mouth.

He tried to drink but coughed it up, his throat raw and dry.

Nothing to see. Dim light from above and behind him. Shapes against walls, round, pipes, all in deep shadows.

The bottle touched his lips again, gentler this time. He drank, managed to keep some down.

He tried to ask for more, but the gag was being pulled up again. He shook his head as fiercely as he could within the strong grip of the person's hand.

"No, please, no. Can't breathe with it," he said, rasping the words out as quick as he could. "Can't breathe properly."

A pause, then the gag was pushed back down around his neck. The rough sack covered his head again, blocking out what little light there was.

The sound of steps on the stairs.

"Why?" Zander said, heaving the breaths in. "Why are you doing this, Bruce?"

The footsteps stopped.

"Quiet."

"But Bruce, this isn't right. You don't need to do this."

The steps came quickly again, the sack pulled off, the gag tugged up. Zander fought it as much as he could, getting a punch in the head for his trouble.

Then the gag was on again, the sack back down over his head, and Bruce was gone.

Zander was dizzy, sick and reeling. He struggled to control his breaths again, trying to calm himself and his racing pulse.

Time lost meaning in the dark. He realised he must be in a cellar, stored down with the beer barrels and pumps and boxes of whatever. Cold and musty, although the smell might have been from the sack.

It could have been twenty minutes, it could have been an hour or more. A door opening, footsteps down wooden stairs, someone standing behind him.

Was this it? Was this the end? Who was behind him? Was it Banjo, ready with a sharp knife, dying to slice it across his throat? Or maybe Easter, stretching his hands in preparation for snapping a neck?

Cold fear gripped his heart. His breaths were quick, shallow, jagged. Every second stretched out.

The sack was wrenched off his head. Zander nearly let go of his bladder. Then the gag was pushed down, and the sack shoved back on.

He sensed the figure moving to the side. There was a scraping noise across the floor, then some quick creaks, weight pressing down on a wooden chair.

Zander waited, listened. Nothing but the mechanical hum from a pump unit in the corner, and the heavy breaths from a few feet away from him.

The metallic rasp of a lighter, then the sweet smell of cigarette smoke. A deep inhale, a deep exhale.

Zander had to risk it.

"Bruce, I don't know what's going on here, but you know this is wrong."

Nothing. Just the steady breathing, the trace of a wheeze. Another drag, the crackle of red-hot tobacco.

"Bruce, you don't know what you're getting yourself into, this is..."

"Stop talking," Bruce said, cutting across him.

"Is it the money? Fisher paid off your gambling debts, didn't he. I take it there wasn't enough from the sale of the hotel to cover it. You owe him. But that doesn't mean..."

Zander reeled as a hand slammed into the side of his face. He hadn't felt Bruce move. It was all so quick. A ringing in his ears now. Blood in his mouth.

"I said," said Bruce, low, close to his ear, "shut it."

The noise of the man sitting down again, more deep drags

on the fag.

Zander waited, getting his bearings again. What was going on? Bruce had taken his gag off, but didn't want him to talk? Was he thinking straight? Was there something to play with here?

Fighting against other instincts, Zander decided to go with one in particular, an old one from when he was a journalist. If you're interviewing someone who wasn't used to it, who's uncomfortable about it all, give them time. Let them speak when they're ready - don't force it, however tempting it is.

So he waited. In the damp smell and humming machine noise and stale beer and sawdust and strained breathing. The sack scratched his face. The rope ties on his wrists and ankles cut into him too much. Numbness started taking hold on his hands, toes. But he waited.

He waited, and eventually it came.

Another scrape of the lighter, another cigarette fired up, another long inhalation.

"You people," Bruce said, almost to himself. "No idea."

Zander kept still, kept his mouth shut.

"No fucking idea. You come up here, you think it's all some tartan wonderland, don't you. Grouse and whisky and haggis and heather. Kilts and curling. All the tourist crap. All very beautiful, God isn't it beautiful, we should buy a second home up here, some bothy or croft. Hear it all the time. People like you."

Another pull on the cigarette, a big one. Silence for a while.

"You've no idea how hard it is, making ends meet. This hotel, doing okay once. But just the summer, a little bit over Christmas, New Year. But the rest of the year? Hand to mouth. Very fine margins. Too fine."

There was a chuckle, but not a happy one.

"Yes, too fine in the end. When I went off the rails a bit. And there are not too many ways out of the kind of debt I had. Not the sort of thing you can get a bank loan for. And people greedy for their money, not willing to wait.

"Did he take advantage of me, Fisher? Buy this place cheap in exchange for taking on my debts? When I was weak? *Because* I was weak? Or was I using him, getting him to take the heat off me, finding a way out of my problems? Who knows? Who the fuck cares in the end? We are where we are. I owe him, I work for him, I do extra when called upon. Above and beyond the call of duty. But not above the call of debt."

Zander decided to risk it.

"So it was you after all, feeding all that information to Fisher and his friends? About Nigel and his photos, what our thinking was, where we were going to be at any given time? All from things Catriona had said to you. She doesn't believe it, by the way. She won't hear a word said against you."

"Yes. Yes, it was me. Of course it was. Why wouldn't I pass it on? If it benefits Frank Fisher, it benefits me and my family."

"And you told them me and Catriona were going up the glen? You let your own daughter get shot at?"

"That was nothing to do with me! They were only supposed to follow you. Do you think I'd have let that happen to her? She's my...everything."

Zander heard some strange hiccupping noises and it confused him for a moment. Then he realised. Bruce was sobbing, trying to hold it back, sitting forward trying to suppress it but failing. Zander let it go on.

After a few minutes, Bruce seemed to have calmed himself. The sobs faded out. Zander judged it was the right time to try again.

"And what if she came in and saw what was going on here?" he said. "What would she feel about all this?"

"She's not."

"How do you know? She could come down here any second."

"No she couldn't."

"Why not?"

Bruce went quiet. Zander felt unease growing in his gut.

"Why not?" he said again, louder.

"Because they've got her, that's why."

Everything started rushing into Zander's head at the same time. Blood, panic, fear, a pounding beat going from his chest, up his spine and into his skull.

"Who's got her?"

"That evil bastard Banjo. Him and his mate. Holding her. As security."

"Security? What for?"

"To make sure I follow my orders properly, do what I'm supposed to do. I do that, they let her go, we're all friends again."

"And what are your orders?"

The spark of another cigarette being lit.

"Just one order. To kill you."

CHAPTER THIRTY ONE

Bread, butter and caviar

Shorter miniskirts? Maybe an inch higher? Fisher watched as two young women, both blonde, both tanned, crossed in front of his buggy. Having tartan uniforms had been his idea, but it was Anne-Marie who'd piled in with specific fashion advice on how they should look. How snug, how high the hems, the cut and fit of the blouses and little matador-type jackets. Keeping it just on the classy side of tarty.

Fisher thought it looked good on the girls, but he still wasn't convinced by the boys' get-up. Tight, stretchy tartan dungarees? So tight you could clearly see the meat and two veg on some of the lads. Must have a word with HR on dress codes. Mask the tadgers, please.

But maybe not. After all, it was all carefully worked out by those marketing bunnies from London, the uniforms and the people to go in them. Something for the mums and dads to enjoy while the kiddies were off gorging themselves on gunk and screaming themselves into a delirious boak-fest.

It was all a bit Eastern European budget airline cabin crew, though. Still, at least no-one was dressing up as a fucking rodent. Dressed as a cuddly Nessie, a cuddly Bigfoot, a cuddly Yeti, yes – after all, there was a lot of cash in cuddly merch – but no actual vermin.

Fisher was on his way to the Highland Fling. They were testing it with some of the technical staff, and he wanted to see it in action to make sure it was working okay – especially as he'd been told that they were still having issues with Nessie's Revenge.

He steered the buggy around the central plaza, then down a fake Highland high street. Halfway down his phone rang.

Security at the front gate.

"Sorry to bother you, Mr Fisher. Man here says he needs to see you urgently. Couldn't get hold of you at the office."

"Who is it?"

"Says he's from the council. Gordon Mackay."

Fisher huffed. Councillor Gordon fucking Mackay. The Maggie-hoor shagnasty bastard. What did he want now? Five minutes – that was all he was getting.

"Yes, let him in," he said. "Send him to the castle. He can wait there."

Fisher turned the buggy around and headed back for the castle and his big, panelled office. Councillor Mackay was sitting on a big Chesterfield leather sofa outside the office as Fisher got there, jumping to his feet as soon as he saw him.

"Frank. Excellent news," Councillor Mackay said, grinning, holding his arms wide as if he expected a hug.

"What is?" Fisher said, walking straight into his office, Mackay forced to dash after him. "They've discovered a cure for being an Inverness mutton-poker? Happy days."

"It's Thompson," Mackay said, holding out his phone towards Fisher.

"On the fucking phone?"

"On the...yes, I mean no, I mean...in the Courier."

Fisher grabbed the phone off him and examined the screen. The Inverness Courier's news app, with their top story. Convenor backs NessieWorld.

"Comes out in support, blah blah, final hurdle, blah blah, rumours that he wanted to block it, blah blah blah," Fisher said, scrolling through the story. "Says here he's finally decided that it'll be good for the Highlands. Nothing about me, though," he said, throwing the phone back to Mackay, who fumbled and had to pick it up from the thick tartan carpet. "Would've been nice if he'd, you know, actually given some fucking kudos to the person who's actually making all of this positive shit happen."

"Yes, I know, I know," Councillor Mackay said, shaking his head as if shocked. "I think it's just that he's putting a bit of distance between you. It's sensible – he doesn't want to give the impression that he's too close, does he? And there's the other thing, some people a bit unhappy at some things which might have been said last night. At the awards, and so on."

"Oh, that. Thin-skinned bastards. That's the trouble these days – can't have a laugh without people getting serious and going all 'pillar of the community' on you. Well, they can sit on my big greasy pillar, that's what they can do. Anyway, it's good that he's finally seen sense and realised which side his bread is buttered on. Fucking butter. More like the finest fucking caviar."

"Anyway, Frank, that's everything set now. Full steam ahead, as you wanted. Licences sorted, all obstacles removed."

"And it's very kind of you to come here to tell me that in person, Gordon, even though I have people on the staff paid handsomely to give me that very information. So, remind me, why the fuck are we standing here having this conversation?"

"Well, it's just that I've fulfilled my end of things. Got it all through, like we agreed right at the start."

"Oh, *you* got it all through, did you? Nothing to do with me having a word with your Convenor, sorting it all out?"

"A meeting I brokered, let's not forget," Mackay said, sweat shining the top of his pink forehead.

"A meeting you brokered because you couldn't deliver what we agreed. Let's not forget that."

"We can argue the whys and wherefores of it all, but whichever way you look at it, I have delivered in the end. And I think that deserves some recognition, at the very least."

"Right. Fine," said Fisher. "And this recognition, it wouldn't happen to have lots of pictures of the Queen on it, would it?"

"In the circumstances, I think a modest bonus would be fair, don't you think, Frank? Now that everything's sorted, like I say. My part in making a success of this whole process has not been insubstantial."

Fisher laughed.

"You fucking teuchters," he said, smiling. "Biggest bunch of money-grabbing bastards I've ever come across."

He walked over to his huge wooden desk, unlocked one of the drawers, took out a wad of cash and threw it to Mackay. He caught it in one hand. No fumbling this time.

"There you go. You're right, we're through the choppy seas and safely into calmer waters. And I'm feeling particularly generous today, so consider that a gift from me. A thank you for all the hard work and effort you put in."

"Very kind of you, Frank. Very kind," Mackay said, trying hard not to glance at the wad but failing. £50 notes. There had to be a few grand there.

"Think nothing of it, Gordon," Fisher said, ushering him towards the door. "Anyway, I'll make more than that in profit on the DVDs."

Mackay stopped dead and turned towards Fisher.

"Ah, now Frank, you're just having me on, aren't you? Always the joker, eh? Now you mention it, about the DVD - I really think, now that we're through all of this, I really think I should have that film you made. And the copies obviously."

"You think so, Gordon? You really think so? Because I can't think for the life of me why I'd want to let go of something like that. It's almost a piece of performance art. I've become very attached to it. I'm thinking of calling it 'Gordon's Ravaged

Dung-funnel'. Quite catchy, don't you think? Might even put it in for the Turner prize. They love that kind of stuff. Gaping sphincters and the like."

"But being serious now, Frank. This isn't where we should be now, this isn't what we agreed. I come through for you, you come through for me. Fair's fair."

"I completely understand your concern, Gordon. I mean, who would want something like that hanging over their heads? Something like that in the hands of someone like me. Ok, I give you my absolute assurance that this DVD will never see the light of day. As long as it's in my possession, no-one else will ever see it. Ok? The only way it'd ever come to light is in the extremely unlikely event of you majorly fucking me over on something. And that's just not going to happen, is it? You will always do the right thing by Frank Fisher, I am utterly confident of that. This never goes away. Unlike you. I've got things to do. Off you fuck."

Fisher patted him on the shoulder, turning it into a gentle shove and propelling him through the office door.

Things to do, people to bribe and threaten, thrill rides to watch. Work, work, work, work, work.

Damp concrete. That's all she could smell. She knew she was in a room, a strange room, but she didn't know much else.

She hadn't seen where they'd taken her – she'd been blind-folded, stuck in the boot of a car. And she hadn't fought back when they'd grabbed her, because she'd seen the look in her dad's eyes. She knew she had to go along with this for him. He just had to do something for those disgusting men, that's what she'd heard them say, although she didn't know what the thing was. But if he did it, she wouldn't come to any harm.

But if she was going to guess, she was somewhere in Nessie-World. A storeroom, somewhere out of the way.

She'd felt her way around in the pitch dark, finding the edges of the room. The door, which was metal and had an immovable solidity to it, set in the wall about a foot off the floor like on a ship. The room sloped up the way at one end, and at the other end there were metal panels in the concrete floor. Nothing actually stored in the room, if it was a storeroom. Maybe the place was too new to have anything to store.

As well as smelling of damp concrete, the floor was cold and clammy. There was nowhere comfortable to sit, so she hunkered down on her haunches and rested her back against the wall. That was cold and damp too, but it was better than standing.

It was just a matter of waiting. Let her dad do what he had to do, and then she'd be free.

And yes, of course she was scared. Scared for her dad, scared because something serious must be going down or they wouldn't have kidnapped her and held her prisoner. Because that was pretty bloody serious, crossing a whole bunch of red lines. And she was bloody angry too, furious at those men putting her and her dad in that situation.

Whatever her dad was involved in, it must be shady enough that the men were confident she wouldn't go to the police about it afterwards. Which wasn't a good sign.

Was he in trouble? Had he done something stupid? Why was he mixing with those two thugs anyway?

Was she missing something? Was her dad closer to those two than she'd realised? Why would he be?

There were too many questions, and too much time to ask them. But there was nothing else for her to do.

So she waited. Angry, scared, cold and alone, her head stuffed with questions.

But it'd be okay. Her dad would sort it. He'd do what he had to do. And then everything would be just fine.

CHAPTER THIRTY TWO

The axeman cometh

Zander Burns had never really wondered whether an axe to his neck would hurt. Or whether it would just chop right through his spinal cord before his nerve endings could shoot pain signals to his brain.

Did it matter that his neck was near his brain? Did the shorter route mean the pain signals would just manage to sneak in there, blaring out a massive burst of agony for a moment before the bliss of oblivion?

And then there was the issue of despatch itself. He was being presumptuous about an axe. Could be a knife across the throat, gun to the head, suffocation, strangulation, garrotting with a wire.

It's just that Bruce seemed an axe kind of guy.

If Zander had been allowed to choose the manner of his death, it's unlikely that he would have opted for one which involved spending the last hour of his life wondering how he'd be killed and how excruciating it would be.

And as urgent as those thoughts were, they were battling for attention with a thousand or more issues bouncing around his brain in the last, panicked minutes of his life.

Had he done enough with his life, had he been a good person, had he loved enough, had been true to himself? Would he be mourned, would disappearing be better or worse for his family and friends? Should he have cherished them more, should he have thought more about settling down, starting a family? Would he have been a good father? Did any of what he'd been doing actually matter?

Could he get out of this? Could he escape?

So many questions, so few answers. His mind chattering in overdrive, emotions dragged from terror to regret to misery and back again, again and again. Unbearable.

At least he knew why. It was about the money. It was always about the money. Whether it was Fisher's money or Bruce Mackie's lack of it. All the deaths, including his own, it was all down to cold hard cash. Not the most noble way to go.

And now the end was near. And now he had Frank Sinatra in his brain, crooning on about 'my way', drowning out more important thoughts, and this was not how he wanted to go. He didn't want to go at all, but if he was going to go, if he was going to have a soundtrack to his death, he wanted something better than a cliché killed by a million cheesy club singers. He wanted 'All My Life' by the Foo Fighters, 'Highway to Hell' by AC/DC, 'Auf Wiedersehen' by the legendary Cheap Trick. Something with a bit of guts and glory.

Then the door opened, the heavy, slow footsteps down the stairs. Not the tread of a happy man.

Bruce was back.

Was this it now? Was this the end?

Zander heard Bruce slump down in his chair again. Zander's muscles were all screaming at him, jittering with nerves and fatigue, the stress of the last couple of hours twisting up inside his limbs.

"Is this it?" Zander said through the sack covering his head. "Just tell me, one way or the other."

The repeated scratch of a lighter, maybe Bruce struggling to get a flame out of it. Then the smell of fresh smoke, the sighing, wheezing breath out again.

"Bruce? Bruce, talk to me."

"Quiet. I'm thinking."

"Bruce, whatever it is you think you need to do, there's got to be another way. There's always another way. We've just got to work out what it is and how we get there."

"There's nowhere to go."

"There's always a way, Bruce. I can help you. We can put all of this behind us. Neither of us want to be in this situation."

"It's too late." Bruce's voice was dull and tired, as if all the humanity had been sucked from it. "I'm in too deep with that lot, Fisher and them. Helping them out with orders for stuff that never arrives, paying bills for work that hasn't been done, hiring 'ghost' staff who don't exist. It's ridiculous. If you could see my books, you'd think I was running the Gleneagles Hotel, not the Drumnadrochit Inn. All crooked as hell. Apparently, I send all my sheets to a firm in Glasgow to get laundered. Not the only thing getting laundered around here. And then there's the other stuff."

"Like what?"

"Doesn't matter. Nothing too dreadful. Sometimes go up to Inverness to hand an envelope to someone. Sometimes go to pick something up. Bagman stuff. Not happy about breaking and entering, though. Doesn't sit right with me."

"What?" Zander said, suddenly getting it. "Hector's place?"

"Yes, Hector's place. He was here at the pub, I tipped them off. Didn't expect the old bastard to burst in through the door on them. Soon as he saw Banjo and Easter he hared off into the woods and they went after him."

"What happened to him?"

"Don't know. They never said. I just want to keep out of all of this, get through it, get my debt paid off."

Zander's brain was going ten to the dozen, trying to work out ways to change Bruce's mind. He didn't feel like he had too much going for him, but the one point in his favour was that Bruce wasn't some professional gangster. He was just a man in a difficult spot. Zander needed to connect with him as a person. Eye contact might help.

"Bruce, could you do me a favour?" he said, trying to sound a whole world calmer than he was feeling. "Could you take this bag off my head, please? It's playing hell with my eyes and my throat."

"I'd have thought that's the least of your worries."

"Please, though, Bruce. Just let me breathe the air a bit clearer, before I go. It's not much to ask."

Zander waited, not sure if Bruce would go for it. But he'd been good about the gag, so maybe it would be easier for him to take this next step. Sure enough, Zander heard Bruce get up, shuffle over a few steps, then pull the sack off his head, throwing it down to the side of the room before taking his seat again.

Zander blinked a bit, adjusting his eyes to the different gloom of the cellar compared to the almost pitch black he'd been in up to now.

He looked at Bruce, who was leaning forward staring down at the cigarette burning between his fingers. Zander tried to keep in his mind what Donald had said, that Bruce was a good man. What he saw in front of him was a man who, if not completely broken, was seriously fractured. Everything about him – his strained face, the way he slouched, the nervous drags on his cigarette – they all screamed that this was a man on the edge.

"Bruce, look at me," Zander said, then waited for Bruce to raise his eyes, which he did but only briefly. "Do I look like your enemy? I'm not the person you should be fighting. I haven't done you any harm. It's not me who's taken Catriona."

Bruce snorted out a cloud of smoke.

"And I just stood there while they took her. My own daughter. I did nothing. Nothing! What sort of a man is that? What sort of a father is that? I should've made a stand, done something. But I didn't – I was too scared, I chickened out. It's pathetic."

"It's not too late. You can make a stand now. You can refuse to let them win. We can go and get her together.

"Why should I listen to anything you've got to say? I don't know you. The fact is, I do what I'm supposed to, Catriona goes free."

The whole time, Bruce kept his eyes on his boots, the floor, his cigarette, his hands, anywhere but look at Zander again.

"Tell me something – do you feel you let her down?" Zander said.

That got a reaction, Bruce's head jerking up, his face twisted with anger, looking Zander right in the eyes.

"What do you mean?"

"It's just that people have told me you did a fantastic job bringing her up. She's a really good, decent, person. That's obviously your doing, how you raised her. Decent values, doing the right thing. That's why I was wondering whether you feel you've let her down, possibly getting caught up in murder. Is that the sort of father you tried to be?"

"I'm the sort of father who wants to protect his daughter. And if this is what I've got to do, this is what I've got to do."

"But what about Catriona? Is this the sort of father she expects you to be? Is that the sort of father she'd look at with pride, someone who'd do this? People around here told me about your wife, and I'm really sorry about it, it's a terrible thing to happen. But people tell me she was a really good person, a kind person. What would she think about all this?"

"You leave her out of this! You didn't know her! You've no right!" Bruce broke off, sobbing. He leapt to his feet, pointing at Zander, struggling to control his voice. "That's why....that's why everything is about Catriona, everything I've ever done, everything I do. It's all about her. You've no idea what it was like, the birthdays, the Christmases, the holidays, and that poor little girl without a mother. Trying to bring her up, trying to help her, guide her. And I've done the best I can, but I'm weak, I know I'm weak. But if I can just get through this, get her back, get out from under Fisher's thumb, I can make it right."

"Not with the guilt hanging over you. Is that something you want to live with? Is that what you call making it right? She'll see it in your face, the guilt. You've said you're in too deep already. Well, stop digging. For goodness' sake, Bruce, you don't want to kill me."

"Don't be so stupid, of course I don't want to kill you. If I wanted to, don't you think I'd have done it by now? I don't want to, but I have to."

"But you don't. Me and you, we can go and get Catriona together, rescue her."

"And how in the hell would we do that? We don't even know where she is?"

"*I* do. I think I know exactly where she is. I think I know where they *all* are – Catriona, Jules, Mike. And I've got a plan."

"Not interested. As long as you're breathing, you're a threat to my Catriona's life. And if it's a choice between your life and hers, it's no contest. Sorry, but that's just the way it is."

Zander lowered his head, letting out a deep sigh.

"Then I need to die."

CHAPTER THIRTY THREE

The face of a killer

Bruce Mackie didn't feel like a murderer. When he'd examined his face in in the mirror, while washing his hands once everything was over, he didn't think he looked like one either.

But that was the point, he supposed. You could never tell. You never knew what people were capable of doing in certain situations, under mountains of pressure.

He steered his old VW Golf around the last bend before the works entrance to NessieWorld. The theme park glowed in the late afternoon sun. Beams of golden light caught the tops of the rides and the fake mountains and castles. It almost looked beautiful.

He stopped at the security gate.

"Here to see Mr McKenzie," he said out the window. The security guys knew him, knew his registration, and he'd texted Banjo in advance, so there was no problem. The guard checked his iPad anyway.

"Yes, Mr Mackie. You're to head down to the control centre. He'll meet you there."

Bruce nodded, and drove slowly along the internal roads, heading down towards the lochside and the vast domed structure holding the control centre, the auditorium and the empty aquarium.

As he reached it, he turned the car off at the side of the building, pulling up outside a service entrance. Banjo was standing there, holding open an emergency exit door. He had a strange look on his weasel face, which Bruce reckoned might be a smile of some kind.

"All done?" Banjo said as Bruce got out of the car. "Didn't think you had it in you. Show us, then."

He stuck his hand out. Bruce flicked through his phone to find the right bit, then gave it to him.

Banjo looked at the photos, four of them. Three different angles of the lifeless body on the cellar floor, a dark stain spreading from underneath the head, the hair matted with blood and gore. Then a shot in a forest, a patch of disturbed earth.

"And this is it, is it?" Banjo said. "No video or anything?"

"I wasn't exactly in the mood to make a movie. Other things on my mind."

"Aye, it's always strange, the first one. You get used to it. So where's this?" he said, holding up the photo of the grave.

"In the woods up past Gartally. No-one's going to find it up there, not for a long time anyway."

Banjo started fiddling with the phone.

"What are you doing?" Bruce said, stepping over to Banjo, reaching for his handset but Banjo moving away, keeping it out of his reach.

"Just sending myself some mementoes," Banjo said.

"No way," Bruce said. "These are being deleted as soon as I get Catriona back. No evidence."

"Well, we'll see about that, won't we Brucey? Whole new conversation that is. But fair's fair. You've done what was asked of you. You'd better come in."

He nodded at Bruce, indicating that he should go through the door. Bruce waited until Banjo handed him his phone back, then went into the building. Banjo followed, letting the door slam behind them.

Curled up in the Golf's boot, aching but alive, Zander slipped his phone from his pocket. He watched the clock on the home screen, letting a couple of minutes go past. Then he started typing a text to Mary, letting her know he was ready to come out.

He'd arranged it with her earlier over the phone, filling her in on the sketchy plan. He'd skipped over the bits about faking a death scene with oil, ketchup, mince and steak from the hotel kitchen, then faking a grave in woods nearby. The main point she needed to know was that Bruce was going to drive to the theme park with Zander hidden in the boot. While Bruce picked up Catriona and took her to safety, Zander was to slip into the building to free his two colleagues.

He was pretty sure he knew where they were being kept prisoner, and Mary was the key to getting them out of there. She could help him get to the right part of the building, through the various security doors. Not a fool-proof plan by any means, but the best he could come up with in a short time with limited options. And it had been good enough to persuade Bruce not to become a killer. Which was nice.

He'd asked Mary to hold back, out of sight, until the text came in. He finished writing it – Open the boot now please – and hit send.

It wasn't long until he heard movement outside the car. Hands on the boot, the release button being pressed, and the hatchback boot door opened.

Zander unfurled himself and looked up. Straight into the huge grinning mug of Easter, who reached in, grabbed both of Zander's wrists in his vice-like hands, and dragged him out of the car.

Pain shot through Zander's arms as Easter twisted them behind his back and forced him up on tiptoes. But through the agony, he was able to notice one thing. Mary, standing over to the side of the building, phone in her hand, apologetic look on her face.

"Sorry," she said, waving the phone at him. "Got to pay the

bills somehow."

Zander was too stunned to speak. There was no Plan B. This was his best shot. Turned out he'd been shooting blanks.

He felt all energy and hope flood out of him as Easter forced him through the service door and down a long, dim corridor with pipes overhead. After a while, on the right, a set of metal stairs heading down. Easter kept Zander's right arm up his back, using his left hand to grab him around the back of his neck, directing him downwards.

He'd genuinely thought he'd stood a chance. Now it was all gone. His great plan had lasted a matter of seconds before betrayal and brute force destroyed it. All the people relying on him – Catriona, her dad, the scientists – he'd let them all down.

At the bottom of the stairs, another corridor, even dimmer than the other one. The number of pipes was even greater here, making it seem more like an access tunnel than a proper corridor. They came to a large metal door set deep in the wall, up a few concrete steps.

Easter pushed Zander right up against the door, face flat to the cold metal, then swiped his security card at a panel on the side. The door hissed and swung open. Easter shoved Zander through the dark doorway. He fell a couple of feet, landing on a cold, damp concrete floor. The door shut quickly, blocking out all light.

Zander threw himself at it, banging on the metal with his fist, then the palm of his hand when he found out how much it hurt. The door was firm, immovable.

"Shit! Shit! Shit! Shit!" he said, slapping the door with each shout. He leaned forward, putting his forehead against the cool metal, spent.

"I think he prefers the name 'Easter'," said a voice behind him. "Which is understandable."

"Catriona?!"

They both found each other in the dark, Zander gripping Catriona in a hug as tight as his sore bones and muscles would allow.

"Woah, there, cowboy," she said, hugging back anyway. "I'd like to keep at least some of my ribs unbroken." She pressed her head into his chest, heard his heart thumping, felt him shaking. "You okay?"

"It's just, you've no idea how glad I am to see you. Although I can't actually see you. Glad to feel you. That came out wrong."

"That's fine," she said, keeping a tight hold of him. "Glad to feel you too."

They stayed like that, holding each other in the darkness, until Zander felt calmer.

"Anyway, what are you doing here?" Catriona said as they broke off, still holding onto each other's hands.

"Rescuing you. Kind of," Zander said. "Doing a spectacular job of it too, even if I say so myself. Once I figure a way out of this room, we're sorted."

"Good luck. I've been over every inch of it, the walls, the floor. It's a bit weird – the floor goes up at one end and there's a kind of grill on that low bit of the ceiling, but you can't shift it. No way out, other than that door. It's got some sort of hydraulics on it, so unless you've got some specialised equipment handy, we're just going to have to wait."

"I'd rather not. We need to get out of here as soon as we can."

"It's fine. I'm not too happy being cooped up in here, but I'm sure we'll be out soon enough. My dad just had to do a job for Fisher, and they're keeping me as insurance to make sure he does it. Something dodgy, no doubt. All a bit melodramatic, but I'm sure he'll be along in a minute, once he's done it."

"Yeah, about that," Zander said, deciding not to tell her everything. "I don't think things went quite to plan."

"What do you mean? Where is he? Is he alright?"

"Yeah, I'm sure he's....look, I talked him into coming here and saving you and helping me free Jules and Mike. I thought I'd worked it all out, that Fisher was keeping you all in a big storage room behind the huge pool where they're going to do all these water shows with dolphins and all that. Obviously, you're here rather than there, so I was wrong about that. But I'm pretty sure that's where they are. Banjo was incredibly keen to keep me away from there, even though the computer records show people going in and out of that room on the night Jules and Mike disappeared. I still don't know why he's keeping them prisoner, but it'll be something to do with money. The important thing is that we get them out."

"The same way you rescued me?"

"Similar to that. Similar, not exactly the same. Might build in more escape options."

"So what's the plan?"

"Well, the plan was for your dad to take you away, I'd get down to the storage room, get them out of there, get out of the park, live happily ever after."

"That's not really a plan, though, is it? More a wish-list. Not much detail."

"Oh no, there was detail. I'd thought through how to get to the storage room, how to bypass security, how to sneak them out of the park. Just didn't want to bore you with all the minutiae."

"Bore away. I've got time on my hands."

"Well, at the core of the plan, an absolutely essential element, was to get Mary..."

"Mary again."

"...was to get Mary, the logistics person..."

"Very practical, I'm sure. Good with her hands."

"...anyway, she was going to use her security pass to get us through. It was a pretty fundamental part of the plan."

"And?"

"And it turned out she's a bit of a cow."

"As in, she criticised your dress sense in front of other people? Made you listen to opera?"

"More a kind of traitor cow kind of cow. Thought she was on our side, turns out she's not. Led me right to Easter, which is why I'm in here."

"So where's my dad?"

"He went off with Banjo, all very friendly. I'm sure he'll be fine."

CHAPTER THIRTY FIVE

Send in the clones

Frank Fisher was, not for the first time, worried about his balls. His ball-sack too, of course, but mainly his balls.

He'd just come off a round of calls with investors and financial wizards, lawyers, suppliers and contractors, the days getting busier as the opening of NessieWorld got nearer. And today, of course, busier than most because of The Deal.

He had staff to handle most of the issues, but he always liked to make some of the calls himself, show them that Frank Fisher was bossing it all.

Now he was propped up on the big leather Chesterfield in his wood-panelled office, taking a break, flinching as Anne-Marie spread new antiseptic cream on his ball-sack scab and changed the gauze and bandages around his groin.

"Do you think they're broken? My spuds?" he said.

Anne-Marie tutted, wiping her rubber gloves with a tissue to get the cream off.

"Don't talk daft. They can't break. They're balls."

"But maybe they've burst or something. Still sore as fuck. Swollen too. What if the apparatus is damaged?"

"Apparatus? What are you going on about, 'apparatus'?"

"The apparatus. The workings, the mechanics, the whole spuff-making business. I'm just conscious that we haven't done the dirty since my nick-nacks got paddy-wacked. Maybe we should do a trial run. Maybe you should try to prime my pump a bit, see what happens."

Anne-Marie huffed, looked around her, saw her hand-cream

bottle in her handbag on the floor and grabbed it, squeezing a dollop into the palm of her gloved hand. She got hold of Fisher's flaccid member and started trying to stroke it into life.

"For God's sake, woman, not with your rubber glov.....actually that's not bad. That's not bad at all. Good idea. That's it, that's it. Hang on, I think there's some stirring down below. The beast is emerging from the deep. Careful, now, not too brisk. That's it. That's a good boy, look at you. Now that's what I call a Loch Ness monster. Here, doll, I've got an idea - let's do the full test drive. My engine's revved up, let's see what I've got in my tanks. You just get yourself on all fours, that's probably the easiest. Get yourself ready, if you know what I mean."

Anne-Marie knew what he meant. She squeezed out some more hand-cream, the nearest available lubricant, hitched up her skirt and got herself ready.

"Come on, then," she said.

"Right," Fisher said, shuffling behind her on the long sofa, eyes bright with excitement. "The old purple-headed custard-chucker is ready for action!"

He jammed himself inside her, but three quick thrusts were enough to make him regret it.

"Oh, Jesus, no!" he said, withdrawing slowly, keeping one hand on Anne-Marie's back to steady himself, fighting a wave of nausea. "Christ, that's unpleasant. Sorry, doll, not your fault. Misjudged the whole knackers bashing off your bahookie problem. Didn't think that through. Christ!" He wiped a sheen of cold sweat off his forehead. He crawled back to one end of the sofa and curled up. Anne-Marie sat back on her heels, looking less than impressed.

"Is that it?" she said over her shoulder.

"That's it," Fisher said back, hands cupping his crotch. "The marines are retreating to barracks for a while, doll. God, that was horrible."

"Fuck off," Anne-Marie said, chucking a cushion at him, wishing it was something harder.

"I'm not saying it was any fault of yours, am I?" Fisher said. He took a few deep, slow breaths, checked his gauze and bandages, adjusting them so they were in the right place, then swung his legs onto the floor. He gave himself a moment. There was still a sick dizziness to contend with.

"This is no use," he said, a wave of mild depression breaking over him. Maybe they were broken after all, whatever Anne-Marie said. "I can't just sit here stressing about my danglers. Send me completely doolally. I'm off around the park. You carry on yourself if you want, don't mind me."

He shuffled across the office carpet, grabbing his loose grey jogging bottoms from a chair and tugging them on. Anne-Marie watched him go, unable to find the energy to complain.

Not even a burst of Tina Turner on the car stereo was enough to lift Fisher's mood as he drove around the internal roads in the park. Today should be the day, his day, a day of unparalleled triumph. He should be feeling like the king of the world. Instead, he was low and anxious. About his banjaxed bal-locks, certainly, but also about deal day. It had been a rocky week, and was he really completely confident that everything was going to go smoothly?

Easter slung the coil of thin rope over his head and across his broad left shoulder, wearing it like a bandolier of bullets. The storeroom had loads of useful-looking stuff, but he could only recall Banjo mentioning rope, chains and padlocks. There was a short chain, but no padlocks that he could see, and he decided not to take anything else. He was better with strict instructions than using his initiative, although the instructions could some-times be a bit difficult to remember.

He wandered back towards the office where they'd stuffed Bruce, thinking about how he was going to tie him up. Was it better to truss his hands and feet together hog-style? Behind him? In front of him? Run the rope around his arms to restrict his movement? He wished he'd asked Banjo before he'd left.

When he got to the corridor with the empty offices, he couldn't remember which one they'd stashed Bruce in. There were numbers on the doors, but he hadn't noted their one before going on his rope search.

Didn't help that all the windows onto the corridor had blinds pulled down, so he couldn't even take a sneaky peak to see what was inside.

There was nothing else for it. Easter used his security pass to open each one, starting at a random door on one side, then going down the corridor a bit, checking one on the other side, and so on. No pattern or system evident, but it maybe made sense inside his head.

All the offices were empty, in that they had basic office-type fittings – desks, chairs, filing cabinets – but no people. They'd come later, although Easter didn't know when. He wasn't really across that sort of detail.

No people, including Bruce.

This was getting frustrating.

One of the office doors seemed to be slightly open, which he was sure wasn't allowed. He shoved it right the way back and looked inside. Empty, just like the others. Was this the one they'd put Bruce in? It was difficult to tell. They all looked so similar. It was like being back in Basra.

But there had been some slight disturbance, he could see that. A couple of chairs in the wrong place, a desk askew. And, yes, there – the carpet a bit scuffed. This was where Banjo had given Bruce a kicking.

Easter smiled, pleased with himself that he'd found the right office. Then he was annoyed again. Because something wasn't right, something important. Bruce – that was it. Bruce was supposed to be in there. He was supposed to tie Bruce up. And now it looked like Banjo had changed his mind and taken Bruce somewhere else.

All that bother getting the rope, all for nothing. Although it was nice to have it. Maybe he'd keep it. Never knew when it'd come in handy.

"What do you mean 'hiding', Hector? Hiding where? Why?" Zander said, helping Catriona through the doorway and down the steps, into the corridor where Hector stood with a little smile on his face. His hair, unencumbered by a cap, was white and spiky.

"Hiding. From those bad folk. The ones who were after me. Hiding here."

"But what happened?" Catriona said, stroking Hector's tweed-clad arm. "Up at the castle and all that. We thought you were...."

"Sean Connery? I get that all the time. Think it's the moustache, mainly. Anyway, they chased me, those two bastards, Banjo McKenzie and his big dumb chum. Down to the castle, cornered me, thought I was done for, ended up over the wall, into the water, hid beneath an old jetty, kept quiet. Once they were gone, took a rowboat, headed over here to hide. Keep the photos safe, the evidence. Loads of places to hide here, cubby holes, service shafts, all sorts. Could hide here for a hundred years and no-one would ever know. Apart from maybe the smell. From your rotting corpse, and that."

"Yes, well, thank you for that, Hector," said Zander, trying to squeeze water out of his shirt. "Anyway, how did you know where we were? And how to open the door?"

"Heard you shouting and banging. Used my cloned card to open the door. Takes a while, though. Won't open until the water's gone – had to use the pad over there to open up the sluice gate. Pretty irresponsible of them to put you in there, actually. It's some kind of draining chamber for the big pool up top. You could've been drowned."

"I think that was the main idea," Zander said. "How do you know so much about this place."

"Been spending my time here having a wander through their computer systems. Seeing how things work, how it's all laid out. Pretty smart stuff. All linked up. Good security. Not impregnable, mind."

"Hang on, did you say you've got a cloned pass? Like, a security pass? That can open up all the doors?"

"Yes, pretty sure it can open everything."

"Then I'm doubly happy to see you, Hector. Because we need to get to a big storeroom off the main hall with the water tanks. I'm pretty sure that's where they're holding Jules and Mike. When I came here before, Banjo was incredibly strange about letting me near that room, made a big deal about me not being allowed in there. Wasn't sure why at the time, but I think it's pretty obvious now. Can you get us there?"

"Yes, I know the place," Hector said, an odd look on his face, a bit reticent. "Actually, there's something there you might be interested in seeing anyway."

"What?"

"Easier to show you."

"Fine. Well, let's get down there, see if we can find Jules and Mike, and your dad, obviously," Zander said, turning to Catriona. "And then let's get the hell out of here."

Traffic flowed out of the main gate as Fisher passed it. Home time for most of the workers on site. That would change when the place was actually open, with teams of staff there 24 four hours a day, readying the park for a 7.30 in the morning opening until a last chucking out at 11 at night, 363 days a year. Closed Christmas Day and New Year's Day, but other than that – kerching!

As he pulled up outside the main control centre office down in the Nessie's Lair building, he saw Banjo and Easter arguing by the front door. Well, more Banjo pointing a finger in Easter's face and shouting, which all stopped as they noticed Fisher's car.

"Everything all right here?" Fisher said to them as he climbed out of the Range Rover, not wanting to get involved in whatever problem they had, but also not being too pleased at his personal employees having a ding-dong where everyone could see. Not good for the image. Not that there were many people around now, but that wasn't the point. Discipline was the thing.

"Boss, no, everything's fine," said Banjo, his face still red from shouting.

"Best not to air your dirty linen in public," Fisher said. "You two got a problem, sort it out away from prying eyes."

"Definitely, boss. Understood."

"Right, I've got things to sort out. Going to find someone who can show me how they're getting on with fixing that Nessie's Revenge ride. Want to make sure they're definitely on it. Any sign of that Zander guy, by the way?"

"Haven't seen him, boss," Banjo said. "Not expecting to. He's out of the way."

"Okay, well make sure it stays that way. Remember, this is a big day for me, a big day for this whole place. Big day for Scotland, actually. So keep it tight. Make sure there are no fuck-ups, and that nobody interferes with what we're trying to do here.

Any questions?"

Banjo shook his head.

"No, boss. All clear."

Banjo caught a movement out of the corner of his eye, but it took him a moment to realise what it was. It was an arm. Easter's arm, with his big meaty hand on the end of it. And he was holding it up.

Even Fisher looked confused.

"Ah, yes, Easter. You've got a question?"

"Yes, boss," Easter said, keeping his hand up. "When we catch him, do you want us to hog-tie him? Because I got rope."

Easter tugged at the thick spool of rope draped over his shoulder, in case the boss hadn't noticed it.

"Catch? What do you mean catch? You can put your hand down now, son. Catch who?"

"I think what he means, boss," Banjo said, cutting in, "is if for whatever reason, which won't happen, that we see this Zander clown – which is not even on the cards, it's all sorted – do you want us to restrain him in some way."

Easter snorted and made a noise that might have been a laugh.

"No, not him," he said, like it was the most ridiculous thing he'd ever heard. "The other one. Bruce from the hotel."

"What? What's the fuck's he talking about Bruce for?" Fisher said, looking at Banjo, his face creased in utter confusion.

"Lost him," Easter said before Banjo could react. "Funny story, though. We both thought the other had him. Didn't, it turns out. He kinda escaped."

"I'm probably being really thick here," Fisher said. "But I'm still not clear why Bruce needs to be caught, why he has to escape from anything or anyone."

"Pretty straightforward, boss," Banjo said, trying to assert himself and take back control. "Bruce was supposed to sort something out for us, he didn't, so we're teaching him a lesson."

"Today? Today of all days? Here? What the fuck are you thinking? I thought I made myself very clear – no hassle today. Nothing can go wrong. So, what, you tried to keep him prisoner somewhere and he's managed to give you two geniuses the slip? And now he's roaming around here, talking to God knows who about being kidnapped, presumably? Brilliant. Well done. Any other major fuck ups you want to make me aware of on my special day?"

"No, boss, we're just sorting...."

"Zander Burns is here," Easter said, butting in.

"For fuck's...you and your big fucking mouth!" Banjo said, giving Easter daggers. "He doesn't need to know about that."

"He's here? You said he wasn't here," Fisher said, pointing at Banjo.

"Ah, to be fair, boss, I said I hadn't seen him. Which I haven't. It was Easter who saw him."

"In Bruce's boot," Easter said, nodding.

"In his boot? In his car boot? You mean Bruce topped him, stuffed him in his boot?"

"Naw, he was alive. Hiding," Easter said. "Bruce was in on it with him, drove him here."

"Why?"

"Dunno. Needed a lift?"

"And where's this Zander Burns now?"

"Put him in some tank. Probably dead."

"Probably?"

"Probably. Might've escaped, though. Doubt it, but you never know."

"He's very chatty today," Fisher said to Banjo, tilting his head at Easter. "Don't get me wrong, it's nice that his confidence is building so that he can come out with more than the odd grunt occasionally. But I'm thinking maybe today's not the day for it? Especially with the sort of things he's saying. You know - the fuckity-up bits. You get me?"

"Got it completely, boss," Banjo said. "Easter? Shut it, now. Need to focus on what to do." He looked over at Fisher, hoping for an instant plan.

"So let me get this absolutely crystal fucking clear. You've got a pissed off Bruce Mackie running about, and possibly that Zander Burns bastard too. If he's not dead. On a day when I absolutely cannot have something like that happening. Does that fully and accurately describe our immediate problem, do you think?"

"On the nail, boss."

"Right. Grab the guns from the truck. Lock and load, boys. Time to go hunting."

CHAPTER THIRTY SIX

Violent tendencies

Zander lost count of the twists and turns as Hector led them along corridors, through maintenance tunnels, up and down stairs and ladders. The man must've had an inbuilt sat nav.

At this time in the evening there was no-one to stop them or question what they were doing. They seemed to have the run of the place.

Even so, they were careful at corners. Typically, Hector would poke an eye around the edge, then motion them on.

"Not far now," he said, as they came to an opening, a sort of hallway with four corridors leading off it.

Too late they discovered that someone was in the corridor on the right, hidden from them until they emerged into the centre of the hallway.

Mary. And she didn't look happy. Unless she normally scowled when she was chuffed.

"Where do you think you're going?" she said, stepping in front of them, addressing Zander.

"Going to free my friends," he said. "Not sure you're familiar with the concept of 'friends'? People you like and trust and want to help."

"He sounds bitter," Catriona said to Hector.

"I can't let you," Mary said, holding her arms out as if to block them.

"I don't remember asking your permission. I remember asking for your help, but not your permission."

"Very bitter," Catriona said out of the side of her mouth, but not very quietly.

"Who's Little Miss Sarky-arse here?" Mary said to Zander.

"A friend. The sort of friend you can rely on. Now, if you'll just move..."

Mary put the flat of her hand against his chest and pushed him back against the wall.

"You're going nowhere."

Catriona stepped forward.

"Get your damn hands off him," she said, reaching for Mary's arm, but getting her hand slapped away.

"You have no idea what's going on," Mary said, right up in Zander's face. "I'm NCA."

She stepped back, dropping her hand.

"What you do in your personal life is none of my business."

"You do know what NCA stands for, don't you?"

"I'm *pretty* sure. But if you wouldn't mind saying it out loud, just to check we're talking about the same thing."

"National Crime Agency."

"Yup, I knew that. That's what I thought it was. Hang on, so that means you're..."

"Police, yes. DS Mary Duffy. And we've spent years to get to the stage we're at. We are minutes away – literally minutes – from nailing Frank Fisher and confiscating hundreds of millions of pounds of criminal assets, and I'm not going to let you stuff it all up."

"Is Mary your real name?"

"Yes. Although that wasn't the really important bit in what I was saying."

"But you're not really in charge of logistics here?"

"Yes, I am. But undercover. Look, it's taken an age to get people in the right places inside Fisher's organisation. And now we've got teams on standby waiting to seize his property, his assets, bank accounts, everything. He's going to jail for a very long time, and a lot of very bad people are going to lose a lot of money. Money they've made from drugs, people-smuggling, sex slaves, you name it. So – and this was the really important bit – I am not going to let you fuck it up. You are to stay here until we've got confirmation that we can move on Fisher and his team. Everything you've been doing over the last few days has jeopardised an operation that's been years in the planning. And if you don't just back off and sit tight, God help me I will restrain you with a level of such pain you will not believe."

"You'd be surprised at the pain I can put up with. It's been quite a day."

"She's quite the sweet talker, isn't she?" Catriona said. "I can see what you saw in her."

"Ok, so you've got some big police thing going on," Zander said to Mary, flicking an irritated glance at Catriona. "Didn't seem to help Jules and Mike, or Nigel. Or Hector when we thought he was dead. Or me and Catriona when we got shot at. Didn't see much police action going on there. So forgive me if I don't give a shit about your big plans, because I'm not just going to sit back while lives are at risk. Fisher's got Mike and Jules, and I'm pretty sure I know where. I don't want their lives to be in danger for one second longer than necessary."

"*Thousands* of lives are in danger," Mary said, snapping at him. "Thousands have lost their lives already. From poisoned heroin, or stuck in airless lorries, beaten to death by some pimp. These men, Fisher and the people he works with, the people he accommodates and enables – they don't just have a few drops of blood on their hands. They've got swimming pools of the stuff. These are bad bastards. They don't give a damn how much damage they do, which is why we've got to stop them. And we're about to do that, because Fisher has persuaded them to put huge chunks of their money into this monstrosity. They're just about to hand it over, and we're just about to grab it. So, no, you're not going off on some hero knight in shining armour crusade. You're staying right here."

Zander nodded.

"When you put it that way," he said, putting on a solemn, serious face. Then sprinted off down the left-side corridor as fast as he could.

Catriona and Hector cottoned on quickly, each dashing down different corridors.

"Shit," Mary said with a big sigh. "Fucking civilians." Then, deciding he was the one worth catching, chased after Zander.

If Frank Fisher had a pound for every time someone had said to him that 'violence doesn't solve anything', he'd have £27. Give or take.

He could never understand why people said it. It was spouted, almost inevitably, by someone who was having violence threatened upon their person. And always, the violence – either the threat of it, or the delivery of it – got Fisher all or most of what he wanted.

But the people who said it – did they genuinely think it was persuasive? Did they have any useful experience about the effectiveness of a well-placed threat or kick? Because if they didn't, and they were dealing with someone who clearly did, why did they think saying that would be enough to suddenly make their tormentor say, 'oh, yeah, you're right, let's sit down with an Earl Grey and talk this through instead'?

They were, Fisher was convinced, usually halfwits who needed to have some sense kicked into them.

Having said that, Frank Fisher was not a personally violent man. He had a temper – anyone who knew him knew that, and it could be fearsome and destructive. But he preferred other people to do the violent stuff. Even from his early days as a

trainee hood in the East End of Glasgow, he always found people who'd let him lead them, including leading them into
trouble which they'd need to use fists or weapons to get out of.
But Fisher's knuckles would remain unscathed. He would in-
spire people to do violence on his behalf. Frank Fisher was
above the rough stuff. Leave it to the street-fighters and born
thugs.

Which is why he made a habit of going unarmed. Not like
his henchmen. He preferred them to have some decent tools to
back up their naturally violent instincts. Fight dirty or die, as
one of his old mentors used to say.

Banjo had his high-powered hunting rifle, Easter had a
pump-action shotgun. They held them across their bodies, mil-
itary-style, as they marched either side of Fisher through the
vast manmade cavern holding the show pool and thousands of
banked seats. The cavern was so big it reminded Fisher of the
hollowed-out volcano in a James Bond film. Except without a
massive rocket. Or a mad wee baldy bastard strangling a cat.

Fisher was sure the intruders would head for the anteroom
with the huge glass storage tanks. That's the impression they'd
picked up from Mary earlier, according to Easter. And if that's
where they thought the action was, that's where they would
head them off. And deal with them.

As Fisher and his goons passed through the large doors into
the storage tank room, a flurry of movement had Banjo and
Easter raising their weapons to their shoulders. From one side
of the large room, Hector and Catriona came bursting through
a door, and then from the other side, Zander came running out
of a corridor closely followed by Mary.

All four of them skidded to a halt in the middle of the room,
suddenly away of each other, Fisher and the guns pointed at
them. Zander, Catriona, Hector and Mary stood shoulder to
shoulder, staring at Fisher.

Fisher grinned.

"Where the fuck's Scooby-do?"

Another door opened, and Bruce Mackie came stumbling through.

"Ah, there he is. The faithful hound. Must remember to have him put down."

"It's over, Fisher," Zander shouted. "I know what you've been up to."

"And I'd have gotten away with it if it wasn't for you meddling cunts. That what I'm supposed to say? Something like that? Just checking – you've clocked the huge fucking guns, haven't you? The ones pointed right at your actual fucking noggins? You're on my property, probably caused loads of criminal damage – and if not, we can make it look like you did – so I'm no expert on the law, but I'm probably entirely within my rights to shoot the fuck out of you right here right now."

"Listen, violence doesn't solve anything."

£28.

"Fucking does, though, doesn't it? Always worked for me."

"All I want is to get my colleagues out of here. Let them go, and we will walk out and not say another word. That's all I'm after. Hand them over, and that's the end."

"Sorry, who are you talking about?"

"My two colleagues, Jules and Mike. The scientists."

"Oh, them. And you've got it into your head that I've got them hidden away somewhere."

"You've got them. I don't know why, and I don't really care. I just want them safe and sound, out of here today."

"So where am I supposed to be keeping them?"

"I'm pretty sure it's in there," Zander said, gesturing towards the other storage room through the wall, the one with the giant pipe leading in from the vast glass water tanks in the room they were standing in. "Your little helpers were keen to keep me away from it, so that's what I'm betting."

Fisher laughed. A small laugh at first, then breaking bigger and bigger.

"Is that what you think? All the hassle you've been causing me, and you think that's what's going on? You really are a total helmet, aren't you?"

"I wasn't sure at first. About the scientists, not the total helmet thing. But I eventually pieced it together. There's been something wrong from the start, and I don't claim to have worked out even ten percent of it, but I'm as sure as I can be about Jules and Mike. So, what – you saying you don't have them here? Why don't we just go through there and see?"

Fisher laughed again, shaking his head in wonder.

"Yes, why not? Let's all go in there and have a look, shall we? See if Mr Burns' missing geeks are all shackled up."

"Boss?" Banjo said to him, keeping it low. "We can't go in there."

"It's fine, my little inbred friend. They want to see in there? Let's show them. We're beyond the stage where it matters anymore, anyway. Go on, open it up."

Banjo used his pass to open the large double doors. Easter kept his gun trained on the pack of five do-gooders. At a nod from Banjo, he motioned them in with the barrel. They trooped in, single file, followed by Easter and then Fisher.

Once inside the room Banjo hit some light switches on the wall by the door. To Zander's surprise the room was just as vast as they one they'd just come from. But it was emptier. Only two of the massive glass-sided tanks in this room, sitting in semi-darkness by the wall, with several oversize oxygen canisters around the edge of the room feeding into the tanks through thin pipes. Lots of concrete floorspace, what looked like uncon-structed lifting equipment, but no obvious places to store two scientists.

"So, Mr Burns. What was it you said you were looking for? People, was it? See any people around here?"

Zander walked slowly around the room, peering into corners, looking back to Catriona for moral support. She had a half-hearted look around too. There was clearly nothing to see.

Except those big glass tanks.

Zander walked closer to one. He put his face up to the glass at one end, trying to see through the murk. Was there something in there? Was that a shape he could make out?

A big face bumped the glass from inside.

"Jesus fucking fuck!"

He leapt back, losing his footing and falling on his arse.

"What the fuck...?"

Catriona and Hector both rushed to help him up. Fisher was in a giggling fit as he walked over to the tank, flicked a switch at the side, lighting it up from within.

It was a giant. At least eight metres long, a long, curved back, thick middle, an almost shark-like nose, a small dorsal fin down near its pointed tail. The biggest fish Zander had ever seen.

They all stared at it, utterly transfixed. The fish stared back, swaying gently in the tank.

Zander looked over at Fisher, his face begging an explanation. Fisher was still having outbreaks of giggles.

"I shouldn't laugh," he said. "I think I must be delirious or something. Or the painkillers. This fucking thing has caused me no end of bother."

"What is it?" Zander said when he'd managed to pull himself together.

"Sturgeon," Hector said, moving nearer to the tank for a closer inspection. "Beluga sturgeon. Well over a hundred years old, going by the size."

"Thank you, David fucking Attenborough," Fisher said. "Yes, a sturgeon, according to what I read on Google. More importantly, this is what is commonly referred to as the Loch Ness Monster. Ladies and gentlemen, meet Nessie!"

And then Fisher started laughing again. He was the only one.

"You mean...." Zander said, pointing at it.

"Yes! It's just a big fish! And who's going to pay a fortune to come and see a big fish? No bastard with any sense, that's who. All the mystery of it flushed down the crapper. Almost a hundred years of sightings and this almost mystical being, maybe the last dinosaur, millions of people all over the world fascinated by it. And look at it – it's just a big ugly fucking fish. What an absolute horror. Can you imagine that gruesome coupon on a t-shirt or a hat? Can you imagine wee Tyler or Kylie-Jade cuddling a furry version of that spiny bastard? The nightmares that'd trigger? Parents would be suing me for therapy bills from now until the twelfth of fucking infinity."

"Tried to tell you," Hector said to Zander.

"When? How did you know?"

"A few nights ago. Sneaked in here, had a nose around. Saw it then."

"And when did you try to tell me?"

"Mentioned it a couple of times. Something important to tell you. You were busy, though. Understandable. Been a busy time. But that's when I changed my sign."

"To what?"

"'It's Just a Big Fish'. Sort of a message, if you like."

"But you didn't think of maybe pressing the point to me? Making sure I listened?"

"Wasn't sure it was relevant. Still not sure."

"Oh, it's relevant. Isn't it Mr Fisher?" Zander said. "You said it yourself – who's going to shell out to come and see a big fish?

Bit of a let-down. Not exactly a star attraction for a multi-million-pound theme park. So who discovered it?"

"I think you've worked out the answer to that yourself."

"Jules and Mike. They weren't looking for it, but somehow they ended up finding it."

"Correct. And do you know what? It's all my fault. I was the one insisted on putting motion sensors in the water to make the big gates open into the loch, so that if Nessie was outside, they'd open up, and Nessie would swim in, and be our centrepiece in that big pool we've got. All utter shite, of course. All just for publicity, so we could say we were secretly serious about catching Nessie. Until about a week ago when this ugly bastard shows up. Your two boys phone me up saying this is incredible, this is going to shake the world, proof that a monster exists, except it's a monster fish. Triumph of science over myth. Total fucking beardy-weirdy, pointy-head, sandal-wearing shite, completely out of touch with the real world. They're thinking this is brilliant. Can you imagine? How thick do you have to be not to realise that a discovery like that makes the sky fall in for so many people? Including the person paying their wages. No offence, but they clearly weren't the sharpest. Anyone normal would've clicked right away. But no, they had ethics, they had morals, they had a duty to science, a duty to the world, they had to tell everyone. Fuck that! What about their real duty, the duty to the millions of dreamers and believers out there who don't particularly want their fantasies smashed on the ground and rubbed in their faces? But no, your boys had stars in their eyes, saw themselves as superstar scientists, the men who caught Nessie. Put me in a really uncomfortable situation, really uncomfortable. I didn't appreciate it, not after all I'd done for them."

"So where are they now?"

"Sorry to disappoint you, but they're sleeping with the fishes. Not that one, obviously," Fisher said, nodding at the sturgeon. "Anyway, I don't get involved in all the details of how my associates deal with a problem – I leave that sort of thing to them. As far as I'm concerned, there was a problem, and the problem went away. And that would've been that, if it hadn't been for a certain person going all Miss cocking Marple and getting his nose stuck right into it all, making folk nervous. You've caused an absolute fuckload of grief for me this week."

"Just trying to get to the truth."

"Oh, the truth, is it? So, you're another of these brown-ricers, are you? Hold up the carcass of truth for everyone to see, no matter how much it smells and what it does to people? Where do you stop? Maybe the yeti's just a big white rabbit. Bigfoot - just a pissed guy in a hairy suit doing it for a laugh. How does you telling your 'truth' actually help anybody, by taking that mystery and magic away from them? By making everything ordinary?"

"But it's not worth murdering people for."

"Well, that was more to do with the money, to be honest. Sorry, but that's the way it is. A lot of people have a lot at stake here. I don't think you fully appreciate the pressure I've been under over all of this," Fisher said, his two hands curling into crushing claws before he realised what he was doing. "Big decisions had to be made. Yeah, ok - your two pointy-head mates are somewhere at the bottom of that loch out there. If they'd seen sense, they'd be wealthy men. Not rich, but they'd have a good wad in their pockets – I offered it to them. But they had different ideas. They knew better. And a little knowledge can be a devastatingly dangerous thing. For them, anyway."

Zander felt sick to the depths of his soul.

"What was the point in that? Why kill them? Why not just put the fish back in the loch, tell them to shut up, sack them, discredit them, whatever."

"I'll tell you why – because it's fucking stuck. Those two id-
iots thought it was a great idea to transfer it from the pool
through to the holding tank, then in here. In advance of putting
it into the big aquarium. I don't know how to get it back out into
the pool and out into the loch. And the only person who does is
the bloke who designed it, and he's currently sunning himself
in Florida while he runs down his contract and isn't exactly
available for telephone consultations on how to rid your facility
of massive fucking mythical monster fish. So we can't get it out
of there, we can't kill it and eat it, we can't dissolve it and make
three thousand barrels of fish fucking sauce. We're stuck with
it for the moment, until we come up with a plan which doesn't
ruin me and everything I've worked for. And believe me, I've
tried to come up with something. Safe to say the last week has
involved a lot of improvisation – this isn't exactly how I'd im-
agined the week panning out. You might say it's all escalated a
little."

"Okay then, so where do we go from here?" Zander said.

There was a loud chiming sound. Fisher grabbed his phone
from his pocket. A text.

"Whoop-de-fucking-do," he said, scrolling through the message. "It's through. It's all through," Fisher said to everyone and
no-one in particular, smiling wide. "Every fucking penny is in
the pot. Frank Fisher is the king of the world! Fuck, yes!"

He started off on a celebratory dance around the room, little
shuffling steps and punching the air.

"I'm simply the best! Better than all the rest!" he sang to
them, Tina Turner reborn as a middle-aged man from Glasgow
with a voice better at shouting than singing. "Better than any
cunt! Any cunt you've ever met!"

He stopped his song and dance and checked his phone again.

"You absolute beauty," he said, still grinning like a maniac as he came back to stand next to Banjo and Easter. "You might not appreciate it, you lot," he said, pointing to the five of them standing there. "But you've just witnessed history. Twenty years from now, some insightful bastard will probably rename this Frank Fisher Day, because today is the day that Frank Fisher took this godforsaken country out of the dark ages and into a bright and glittering future. All systems are go." He rubbed his hands. "Right, ok, where was I before I was so delightfully interrupted? Ah, yes, where do we go from here, what's the grand plan. Glad you asked. Banjo? Kill them. Kill them all."

CHAPTER THIRTY SEVEN

The very deepest kind

Banjo raised his high-powered rifle. Easter copied with his shot-gun. Banjo had decided. Smarmy English Uni boy first, then the rest – didn't matter what order.

An animal roar filled the cavernous room as Bruce launched himself at Banjo, knocking the barrel down but failing to rip it out of his grip. Easter was confused, not sure whether to shoot the others or help Banjo, who was rolling on the floor with Bruce, both grappling with the gun. Catriona rushed forward, helping her dad by landing kicks on Banjo's ribs.

Zander used the big man's confusion to grab whatever he could – a foot-long metal winch handle – and whacked it on the side of Easter's head.

"Ya bastard!" Easter said, hand rubbing at his temple. It wasn't quite the knock-out blow Zander had been after, but at least it made Easter lower the shotgun. Hector grabbed Easter's gun hand while Zander thumped him in the stomach, which didn't seem to bother him at all. A leg-like arm swatted at both Zander and Hector.

Mary kept her eye on Fisher as she reached for her phone. Time to call in the cavalry.

And then the shot.

It's not clear whose finger was on the trigger, Banjo's or Bruce's. But the shot, so loud in the room, stopped everyone dead.

They only had half a second to see if anyone was hit. Because that was when the world exploded.

Not the world, exactly. Just the big oxygen tank behind the monster fish tank. The force of the oxygen tank blowing knocked another couple of them over, valves breaking, sending them like rockets around the room as everybody hit the floor. One of the flying tanks smacked into a steel girder in the wall. The sparks set it off, lighting the escaped oxygen and causing a secondary boom in the room.

Pandemonium. The walls cracked, the glass tanks splintered, water beginning to seep out, everyone lying stunned on the floor. Zander and Mary were among the first to shake themselves out of it. Zander reached for Catriona to help her up, then they both grabbed Hector to get him away from flames creeping up a wall next to him. Easter stumbled away, and Bruce ran after him. In all the smoke, fire and confusion, Mary noticed something of crucial importance.

Fisher was gone.

Not 'dead' gone. But not in the room. He'd been furthest away from the first explosion, perhaps protected from the blast by some loading equipment. Maybe Banjo had recovered first and dragged him away. Either way, neither of them were there.

Mary looked around for her phone, which had been blown from her hand. She spotted it on the floor, in a pool of water coming from a leak in the tank holding the giant sturgeon. As soon as she picked it up, she saw it was useless, screen smashed beyond hope.

"Damn it!" she said, throwing it away. She turned to Catriona, Hector and Zander. "You three get out of here now."

"Where are you going?"

"The control room. Got to get back-up in here, pick up Fisher and his men. Use the CCTV to see if we can spot them. Right – get out."

She dashed off. Zander turned to Catriona, nodding over to

the fish tank. The sturgeon was agitated. Zander could have sworn it looked worried, although he'd very little expertise in deciphering fish facial expressions.

"We've got to save it," he said. "It'll die if we just leave it here. I hate to say it, but Fisher's right – about one thing at least. We leave this here to be found, it destroys everything about Loch Ness. It's just a deep pool of water without the monster. We can't let that happen."

"Whatever happened to Zander Burns and his pursuit of the truth? I thought you'd want people to know."

Zander shook his head.

"There are lots of different versions of the truth. Let's stick with the version that people like. One that doesn't have a massive gloomy fish spoiling everything."

Catriona smiled.

"Okay," she said. "But how?"

"It got in here somehow, so there must be a way to get it out. If we can get it through the pipes and out into the big pool, we just open the gates to the loch and let it swim out. Maybe Mary can call up one of her IT geniuses to talk us through how to work the system."

"I could give it a go," said Hector. "I'll get into the system, find a way. Up in the control room."

"Good idea, Hector. I'll stay here, see if it works, talk you through it," Catriona said, grabbing an internal phone handset from the wall. "Remember this extension, Hector – 167 – call me when you get to the control room."

Hector set off in a shuffling jog in the same direction as Mary.

"We can't stay here," Zander said, looking at the flames. They'd spread already, and he was worried about the smoke and the remaining gas cannisters.

"We can't, but I can. Look, I know how to get out from here.

But someone needs to talk it through with Hector, let him know it's working. And I need you to go and help my dad. I don't fancy his chances up against that big bastard."

Zander gave her a tight smile.

"Don't risk leaving it too late," he said. "This place could fall apart any second. I don't want you at the bottom of all of it."

"Help my dad," she said. "For me. Now, go."

She gave him a gentle shove. Zander raced to the corridor he'd seen Bruce and Easter go down. Catriona looked around her, at the flames creeping up the walls, the smoke, the broken tanks. The fire alarm was blaring out and the sprinklers sprayed water from the high ceiling, but it was all a bit tame to deal with the chaos going on. Please, Hector, get there soon.

She grabbed the wall-phone as soon as it trilled.

"I'm here," said Hector. "Need a moment to get inside the system. Keep the line open."

Catriona looked over at the fish. There was a loud screech, and a crack in the thick glass lengthened by a couple of feet.

"No pressure, Hector. But if you could make something happen now, that'd be good."

Frank Fisher managed to build up a faster pace than anyone could reasonably expect from a man with trussed testicles. He was ahead of Banjo all the way. When they got to the big glass doors at the entrance to Nessie's Lair, Fisher stopped.

"You go back," he said to Banjo. "Finish the job. I don't care if you have to burn the whole building down to do it, none of those little shits can be allowed out of here. Get me?"

"But boss, I need to stick with you, to protect you."

"Protect me from what? All the problems are back that way."

Which is when he heard sirens and the high growl of powerful vehicles, the noise brought in on the breeze.

"Fuck-a-dog!" Fisher said, trying to see if there were any flashing blue lights and where they were coming from. It wasn't necessarily anything to do with what was happening in the theme park, but he couldn't take any risks, not now. "Right. You – back in there, fuck up anyone you find, get rid of the evidence, and while you're doing it, get onto whoever's on security at the main gate and stop them letting in any bastard in a uniform. Keep those gates closed."

"What are you going to do, boss?"

"What any great leader would do in this situation. Hide until it's all over."

Mary dropped the phone down onto the console after three quick calls to mobilise the teams. One team was heading up the hill above Drumnadrochit, ready to hit Fisher's house and impound anything and everything. Two teams were on their way to the theme park, one to take control of Fisher's office, the other to grab Fisher and his men.

Police colleagues in several different places were part of the operation too, in Glasgow, London, Manchester, raiding properties, grabbing evidence, impounding cars, houses, offices. Others were slapping financial handcuffs on bank accounts and suspect investments.

She didn't know half of what was going on, but she knew what her job was now. Find Fisher and his men, guide her colleagues to them.

"Don't know what you're doing here," she said over her shoulder to Hector, who'd come into the control room when she was on the phone, "but I want you to get out. Now. That is an order."

"Just a mo," Hector said. "Think I've got it." He started scanning something on his monitor.

Mary didn't have the energy to deal with him. She focused

on the task in hand. She had CCTV on three big screens in front of her in the control room, each screen split into nine feeds from different cameras around the site, each location identified with a few letters in the corner of each picture.

Nothing so far. The screens refreshed every few seconds as she hit buttons on a keyboard, showing new angles to the site.

There. Movement in the foyer of Nessie's Lair. Zander. He was looking around, then ran through the doors outside.

Mary switched to the outside camera. Zander was turning around, scanning the park. Who or what was he looking for? He started jogging up the road a little, up nearer a couple of the rides. And then Mary caught other movement in the foyer. The unmistakable figure of Banjo. And he still had his gun. He crept towards the doors, stood for a few moments staring through the glass, up to where Zander was moving. And then he slipped through the door, rifle held in readiness.

"Shit," Mary said. "The very deepest kind." She willed her colleagues to get there sooner. She changed the screens to show cameras near the main entrance. The site gates were closed, locked. She couldn't afford the reinforcements to be held back for a moment. She grabbed the phone, stabbing at the numbers.

"Who's that? Malcolm?..... Oh, hi, Pete. Mary here. Look, I need you to open the gates...... I know it's after hours..... Yes, I know that, but we've got some urgent business and we need the gates open.....Says who?......Well, you don't work for Mr McKenzie, you work for me....Well, even if that was coming from Mr Fisher, I'm head of operations, and that means if I tell you to open the gates, you open the gates.....What exactly did he threaten to do to you?......Well, that's pretty much constructive dismissal right there, even if it's probably not physically possible.....Look, Pete – you've got to decide if it's really in your best interests to follow orders from someone who threatens to cut your cock off and shove it so far down your throat it fucks your lungs, or.....Well, I'm telling you, it's not. Open the gates or in about five minutes you'll be looking at gaol time for obstructing the police."

In the background, Hector thought he was onto something. With the phone cradled in his neck, he hit a few buttons on a likely-looking programme he'd found.

"Anything moving?" he said to Catriona on the other end of the line.

It was close, but not close enough. Instead of moving something in the holding tank zone, Hector's efforts woke up the animatronic ten metre Yeti outside the Yeti Mountain vertical drop ride. The Yeti's great hairy arms swung back as the beast's head tipped back and a dreadful noise somewhere between a scream and a wail filled the evening air.

"Fuckorama!" Fisher said, rolling out from under the curtain of white hair covering the bottom of the Yeti's legs. "The fuck was that?!" So much for the hiding place.

He glanced around. Yes, sirens still in the distance, but getting closer. And the fire alarms and the fucking Yeti mating call or whatever it was. And there he was, the annoying young bastard who'd made his life a nerve-shredding misery these last few days.

"Time's up, Fisher," Zander said, dropping from a jog to a walk as he reached him. "Your only hope now is to give up as gracefully as you can. Call off your thugs, agree to go quietly."

"I'm going nowhere, sonny-boy. So, a few sheep-shagger cops get a bit excited about some noises out at NessieWorld? Fuck all to do with them. They can fuck right off back to whichever sheep farm they've been hanging out in."

"You don't get it, do you? This is over. Mary – she's not who you think she is. You've got the National Crime Agency coming down on your arse like a ton of arse-seeking bricks. So, I'm saying to you again, stop all this. There's no need for anyone else to get hurt."

"Does Frank Fisher look like the sort of person who just gives up? Frank Fisher didn't get where he is today by giving up. You seriously think I'm just going to put up my hands and surrender?" Fisher laughed. "What do *you* think, Banjo?" he said over Zander's shoulder. "Do I look like the surrendering type?"

Zander swung round fast. Banjo was ten paces away from him, his rifle at his shoulder, pointed at Zander's head.

"No, boss. I don't believe you do."

The Yeti screamed again. Banjo's eye's flicked up at it. Zander dashed to his right, putting an empty hotdog hut between him and the men. A shot slammed into the side of the hut, punching a hole through it.

He looked around for other cover. Over the other side of the road, the building housing the entrance to the Nessie's Revenge ride. If he could get over there, he could maybe barricade himself in until the police arrived, keep Fisher and Banjo where they were, trying to get at him, keep them away from the others. It was a plan. A quick plan full of holes he didn't have time to think about. He could sense Banjo coming for him.

Three deep breaths and he broke cover, running a zig-zag across open ground towards the ride, dodging and feinting this way and that as if he was trying to avoid being tackled by invisible rugby players. He'd read it somewhere or seen it in a film. He had no clue whether it would work.

Behind him, Banjo dropped to his knee, raised the rifle, squinted down the sight, and squeezed off a powerful round which shattered the trunk of a young, thin tree Zander had passed a split second beforehand.

Zander got to the entrance door of the Nessie's Revenge ride with a moment to spare, another powerful round blowing out the glass in the window next to him.

Play for time, keep them busy, keep them focused on you, Zander said to himself, running past the ticket booths and into the body of the long building.

He found himself on a platform with low fences and metal gates, presumably where thousands and thousands of people would queue up every day to get on the ride.

Parked at the edge of the platform, four ride carts with spaces for eight people each. On the other side of them, the exit platform. If he could get through there and hide somewhere.

Clattering behind him. He risked a look. Banjo, sprinting through the building, gun in hand.

Zander had nowhere to go but onto the ride cart, slipping between the seats to try to get to the other side. And then a hand was at the back of his neck.

Hector was struggling under the pressure. This wasn't a part of the computer system he'd had a look at before, so he was having to learn quickly.

"Ok," he said down the phone to Catriona. "How about this?"

He pressed a few buttons.

"Nope, nothing, Hector. Hurry, please. It's getting a bit nasty down here," she said, as another crack appeared in the giant fish tank with a piercing shriek.

But the buttons Hector pressed did something. Something quite important. They started Nessie's Revenge, the looping, hanging, swirling ride that was supposed to help make the park world famous. The same Nessie's Revenge that Zander was hanging onto when it jerked into life, pulling him out of Banjo's grasp.

Zander hauled himself up on the padded chest guard which

had moved down into position, nearly crushing him, as the cart moved off. Banjo was thrown to the side but recovered quickly, grabbing onto the rear of the cart as it left the building and began to follow the route, sliding along a track above their heads.

It was slow at first, going along flat, then up a steep incline, the gears grinding as Zander scrabbled around for a better grip, realising he was too high in the air to risk jumping, looking behind him and seeing Banjo pull himself up the back of the cart. At least there was no sign of his gun. Small victories.

The cart reached the top of the incline, seemed to stop for a moment, then plunged down at sixty degrees.

This was not good. This was not good at all. Zander's stomach sank and his arm slipped from the grip he'd thought was secure, his legs flailing beneath him. The cart swung to one side, then the other, a lurching swaying motion which threatened to make Zander lose hold altogether.

He grabbed at a metal bar, trying to curl his arm around it. Just when he thought he was secure again, the ride went into a loop. Zander felt his sinews being stretched to the limit as he swung underneath the cart, flashes of the park and the loch in front of his eyes. He tried to pull his legs up, managing to get one of them up around a backrest on the row of harnesses in front of him. As he tried to pull the other leg up the cart swooped down fast, and he was swinging free again, both arms screaming at him, holding on with his legs dangling down as cart sped on.

Zander tried to twist around, managing only a half glance over his shoulder towards the back of the hurtling cart. It was enough.

Banjo was coming for him.

CHAPTER THIRTY EIGHT

Nessie's revenge

"How about this one?" Hector said, trying a different section of the control programme on the screen in front of him.

"Something's happening," Catriona said into the phone as a loud hum filled the room. It was coming from the tank with the big fish in it, which was in turn connected to a two-metre-wide plastic pipe which went through the wall into the main room next to the pool arena.

It was a turbine of some kind, drawing the water – and the fish – into the pipe.

"It's working, it's working!" Catriona shouted into the hand-set. "You beautiful man, Hector. Hold on, I'm going through to the next room."

Catriona got Hector's extension number, hung up, and ran through the connecting doors to the cavernous room next door, leaving the smoke and flames behind her. As she reached another wall-mounted phone and punched in Hector's extension, a ripping, yawning, cracking nightmare of noise came from behind her. A section of the wall from the room she'd just left fell in, a girder from the roof bashing through it. The fire was spreading, weakening the building.

She checked the pipe. Yes, the fish was there, moving towards the bigger tank, the holding tank next to the pool at the centre of the arena.

"Hector, it's nearly into the next tank. Whatever you're doing, just keep doing it."

Then another loud explosion in the next room. Flames leapt through the large hole in the wall. Time was running out.

It was all Zander's nightmares come true. Hanging on for dear life on an out-of-control theme park ride, no safety harness on, feeling like spewing any second, while being pursued by a violent psychopath.

He tried to squeeze through to the row in front of him, grabbing onto a u-shaped padded shoulder harness. His hands, slick with sweat, slipped. Only hooking one leg around a metal pole stopped him from falling out. As it was, he was now upside down, hurtling through the air, being swung around, no sense of up or down.

He jack-knifed his body, crunching his abs like they'd never been crunched before, stretching his arms as far as he could. On the third crunch he got a grip on the padded harness again with his left hand and pulled himself up as best he could. He was almost safe when the knife flashed by his face.

"What's happening, Hector? The big fish is in the holding tank. We need to get it into the pool somehow."

"Trying," said Hector, trying to see the links between the codes on the screen. An instruction manual would be nice.

He tutted at himself, opening a tab at the side of the terminal. Not quite an instruction manual, but a better guide than guesswork.

"Give me a second," he said.

"How about half a second?" Catriona said, looking at the flaming wall about to fall on half of the room. "Things getting a bit toasty down here."

"Got it," Hector said. Two clicks, and the contents of the holding tank were discharged into the main pool in the amphitheatre.

"Brilliant! You still ok up there, Hector. You might want to think about getting out of here now."

"One last thing," Hector said, examining the terminal. "The gates out into the loch. Got to open them."

"I'm going through to the arena," Catriona said. "Going to see I can open the gates myself. You get out."

"Wait, I'll just...." Hector said, before being yanked out of his seat by Mary.

"You're coming with me," she said, trying to find the sweet spot between keeping his arm secure behind his back and not snapping a pensioner's fragile bones. "Our teams are in. Nothing more for us to do here - not safely, anyway."

"But I've got to..."

A loud noise between a snap and a crack stopped them both as all the lights and electrics in the control room clicked off. Then one wall buckled and burned, flames darting into the room.

"Looks like that decision's been made for you," she said, forced him towards the door, pushing him through, then marching him down the corridor in the vague direction of safety.

Catriona sprinted down an aisle of plastic seats, down to the side of the big glass-sided pool in the middle of the arena. If only the thousands of people who'd cram these seats in six months' time could see the show now. An ancient fish which had lived through two world wars and countless attempts to catch it or capture evidence about its existence. What would the people think if they could see it? Would they hate it?

But it was something magnificent to Catriona. And there she was, the only spectator in a hall built for thousands, seeing a performance you couldn't put a price on.

She watched as the sturgeon checked out the pool, moving slowly around the edge by the glass, drifting off to the middle, investigating the edges again. It didn't seem damaged by its time in captivity. What an absolutely incredible beast. A monster, yes. A beautiful, ugly, wonderful monster.

Up some metal stairs halfway along the pool, then along the narrow walkway at the pool's edge. Finally, she got to the open-air end of the cavernous arena, the evening glow outside on the loch and a slight chill blowing in. She ran along the gangway towards the two gates sunk into the water. Yes, there were control pads beside the gates. But when she got there, she saw there was no power – the screens were blank. She looked for a switch. Nothing.

So, it would need to be the old-fashioned way. She eyed the cogs, gears and handle of the mechanism to the side of the gates. She hoped someone had oiled it recently.

The boom of a shotgun echoed around the chamber. A spray of shot hit the metal gangway by Catriona's feet, two or three pellets stinging into her. She cried out and dived for cover behind a low wall. The last thing she saw before hiding was the figure of Easter, high above her on the overhead walkway near the roof. Shotgun in hand, rope coiled around his torso, murder on his mind.

She prayed. Prayed to a God she didn't believe in. Prayed hard.

The knife slashed down again. Zander was able to shift enough at the last moment to avoid a full stabbing, but the blade nicked his left shoulder. Pain shot through him, and he instinctively let go of the metal bar he'd been holding. He scrabbled for a grip again, then swung his right fist at Banjo's leering face. It connected, but didn't affect Banjo, who pulled himself higher up on the cart and kicked out at Zander. A foot caught him on the side of the head, but he held on. It was such a cramped space. No room to move, and plenty of ways to fall. The ride was at the top of a long incline and was ready for another stomach-churning plummet.

Banjo sliced his knife down at Zander's hand but missed. The knife hit the metal bar and got jarred out of his grip as the cart shot downwards, the blade catching the side of Banjo's eyebrow as it passed him.

He reached up a hand to cover his eye. Zander wrapped his arms around the padded harness once more, almost out of energy, willing it all to end. He swung a kick at Banjo as hard as he could, giving it everything he had left. It caught Banjo in the midriff just as he was adjusting his position. He slipped through the gap between the hanging seats, but just managed to hang on to the bottom rung of the cart with one hand.

Zander looked down at him. He could see every fibre in Banjo's ropy arm straining against gravity as the ride forced them down and down. Down towards the loch, Zander realised. Down and down, faster and faster.

Banjo was in trouble – Zander could see that. And no-one would have blamed him if he'd left the thug to fall. But he was a better man than that. He started shifting down the cart, keeping his legs wrapped around the harness but reaching down to grab Banjo's hand in both of his.

Frank Fisher had found a better hiding place. Just as well, given that he could hear the invasion of police further up the park. He knew how he'd escape, though. He'd worked it out.

But for now, he was watching from behind a storage shed as his pride and joy, Nessie's Revenge, was in full, glorious flow, winding and swirling around its record-breaking track.

Who the fuck had started it up? Fuck knows. But there it was. And if it caused a diversion, so much the better.

But when he looked closer – what the fuck? A couple of people on it, fighting. Banjo, and that Burns bastard. And then one of them hanging right down, nearly losing it as it came up to the loch. Banjo hanging there. And Burns gripping his hand, not letting him fall as the ride reached its finale.

Ah. The finale.

Fisher watched as the cart swung down towards the loch, Banjo's feet almost skimming the water, then rising up quickly.

I wonder if they fixed it, Fisher said to himself, as the huge animatronic Nessie head burst from the loch and twisted up to meet the ride car. The monster's metal head locked in place at just the right angle for the sharp line of teeth to sheer Banjo's body in half just above the waist.

No. No, they didn't.

Zander screamed in shock, letting go of Banjo's dead hand, letting the top half of the man's body fly far out into the loch where it landed with a dull splash.

"Fuck on a bike!" Fisher said. "That's going to sting in the morning."

Time to leave. This had gone far beyond saving. Get away now and he could trigger his emergency escape plan, get far from Loch Ness, Scotland, the Jimmies, Tommy Gallagher, all of it. A life of well-funded anonymity in the sunshine by the Black Sea.

Ok. Time to put Project Saving Frank Fisher's Arse into action.

The ride slid back into the platforms with a hydraulic hiss. Zander staggered off, arms and legs strained, in agony, like he'd just been on a medieval rack. Head spinning with all the disorientating twists and turns, and feeling a bit queasy about Banjo's game of two halves.

But amidst the confusion and horror of it all, one thought stood out clearly. Find Catriona. Get her and Hector out of there. Her dad too, if he was still around.

He hobbled off towards the Nessie's Lair complex, grabbing a nearby golf buggy to get him there quicker. He was aware of sirens and flashing lights behind him, but he was more concerned with the smoke and flames coming from the complex itself. If Catriona was in there...

Catriona risked a look over the top of the wall. Almost instantly, a boom followed by a spray of shot spattering against the wall.

He was up there, just waiting to pick her off.

And there was nowhere to go. She was trapped at the far side of the walkway, the loch to one side of the barrier, an open target on the walkway on the other side of the wall.

If there worst came to the worst, she'd have to swim for it. But it was a long way around the edge of the building in open water. She'd be a sitting duck. Or a drowning one, riddled with holes.

"Catriona!" Zander shouted, over and over, as he ran through corridors, up and down stairs. He was forced back twice, the corridors blocked by flames or rubble.

"Catriona!" he called again, bursting into the pool arena by a door at the back of a high bank of seats.

"Zander! Watch out for..."

Her next words were blocked by a loud blast from Easter's gun. Zander threw himself down between a row of seats, pain jolting through every part of him.

"Zander! You okay?!"

"Absolutely peachy, thank you," he said back. "Couple of minor flesh-wounds. Fractures, maybe. You?"

"Fine, but I can't go anywhere. He's got me totally pinned down. And we need to open these gates. The fish is in the pool. Got to get it out into the loch. But as long as he's up there,

there's no chance."

Zander thought for a moment.

"Easter!" he shouted. "Can you hear me up there?"

Another boom, and a couple of the plastic seats to Zander's left disintegrated with the force from the shot.

"Easter, listen to me. It's over. Fisher has surrendered. He's handed himself over to the police. He's probably dropping you right in the shit as we speak. Best that you give up, make a deal."

"Never!"

Another shot, this time down towards Catriona's hiding place.

Zander peeked between a narrow gap in the seats. He could see Easter high above them on the walkway suspended above the pool, reloading his gun. A clear line of sight anywhere in the vast room. But he had his back to the other end of the walkway. And that's where Bruce Mackie was standing, face set in grim determination.

If there was one thing Zander could do for him, it was to buy time.

"Easter, listen! Banjo's gone. He's dead."

"Liar!"

Another blast, hitting the wall behind the seats, no-where near him.

"It's true. I was there when it happened. I held his hand as he died. And after he died. For a little bit. It's over, you know it is." Zander could see Bruce edging along the walkway, getting nearer to Easter's broad back. "If you give yourself up now, I promise I'll..."

Zander didn't get the chance to make his promise, as Bruce chose that moment to launch himself at Easter, rugby-tackling him around the legs. The big man topped over, shaking the walkway with the force of his fall, spilling the shotgun over the side. It dropped forty feet into the pool.

He twisted around and stamped at Bruce, trying to free his legs, but Bruce held tight.

Zander got up and ran over to the pool, over to where Catriona was huddled behind the low wall. He reached down to her, boiling with a million emotions, so many things he wanted to say.

"Grab that handle over there," she said to him. The old romantic.

They both strained and shoved, gripping the metal handle of the gate's opening mechanism. It gave with a jolt, and they turned the wheel again and again, the gates opening inwards. The gap grew. From a foot to a metre to a few metres, until the gates were fully open.

"What do we do now?"

"Whistle? Not really sure how you wrangle a fish. Maybe just wait for it to swim out when it feels like it?"

Up above them, Easter had got to his knees. He swung a sledgehammer of a fist at Bruce, catching him a glancing blow. Bruce went down in pain, holding his head. Easter kicked out, knocking him over. He stood, helping himself up by holding on to the railings. Bruce lay still before him on the walkway.

"Dad!" Catriona shouted. "Dad, get up! Get up!" She looked at Zander, fear all over her face. "Well, don't just stand there. Help him!"

Before Zander could work out if that was even possible, Bruce sprang to his feet and thumped his shoulder into Easter's stomach, forcing him back against the handrail. His back bent over the rail as he flailed his hands, searching for a grip, and for a second it looked like he was going to regain his balance. Then he tipped backwards, tumbling down towards the pool with a roar, the coiled rope over his shoulder unspooling as he hit the water with an almighty slap.

He broke the surface a few seconds later, fixing Zander with a furious stare, and began to swim to the side.

The fish, spooked by the splash, set off towards the loch at a fast lick. Its hanging jaws got caught up in Easter's coiled rope, but that didn't stop it. It was heading home, back to the loch, and if that meant dragging some roped up monster of a man down to the murky depths, well, that was just fine with the fish.

Easter tried to grab hold of the gate as the fish dragged him through, but there was nothing to cling on to but the slimy metal surface. Zander, Catriona and Bruce watched as Easter was first pulled out into the loch, and then down beneath the surface, his screams silenced as his huge head disappeared into the gloom.

Zander and Catriona ran for the exit. Masonry and metal fell from the roof and the wall, blocking their way. Fire was raging through the wall to their left. No way out. All exits were blocked.

Just a few steps and he'd be home and dry. Fisher knew about the weak point in the fence – his security team had mentioned it to him, but he'd been too busy to tell them to do something about it. Just as well. The cops had the front entrance under their control from what he could tell. Officers were swarming the place now. All he needed to do was slip through the gap, steal a car from the car park at the Dores Inn, and then head south. Pick up his escape plan pack - cash, passports, false identities, offshore bank details - all stashed at a safe house in Glasgow, and then he was gone for good.

The only slight problem was that the security lights were quite bright. He had to squint to make out where he was supposed to go, the sharp glare from the lamps creating deep shadows.

But he was pretty sure it was over in that corner. He moved

out from behind the cover of a shipping crate, edged slowly towards the fence.

The light was blocked for a moment, and Fisher strained to see what was happening, shading his eyes with his hand.

A silhouette, the bright light behind it. The silhouette of a man, a tall, thin man. He stepped forward, and Fisher could see him more clearly. A tall, thin, old man. In tweeds.

"Who the fuck are you?" Fisher said.

"My name is Donald MacDonald. I have a dog called Shep, and a friend called Hector. And this is from them."

Donald swung his heavy, gnarly walking stick in a fast arc, slamming it neatly and forcefully into Fisher's crotch.

"Holy mother of fuck!" Fisher said, collapsing down on his knees, hands clasped to his groin yet again.

"And this is from me," Donald said, raising the walking stick high above his head.

"Stop!"

Donald stopped. He brought the stick down slowly to his side, not sure he could believe his own ears. That voice.

Hector stepped forward, followed quickly by Mary who pinned Fisher's hands behind his back, told him he was under arrest and rattled off his rights.

The two men stood and looked at each other. The slightest hint of a smile beneath Donald's moustache, the faintest twinkle in Hector's eye. They gave each other a curt nod.

"Hector."

"Donald."

There was nothing more to say. Until Donald reached into his jacket pocket and took out a folded piece of cloth. He handed it to Hector, and it unfurled as he took it. His cap, the one he'd lost in the loch that night escaping from Banjo and Easter.

"Had it dry cleaned," Donald said. "Needed quite a going

over, apparently. You owe me three pounds and forty nine pence. You can give it to me later if you like."

Hector fitted the cap on his bare head. Everything felt right again. He reached out his hand. Donald looked at it for a second, surprised, and then the men shook hands. Not too long, not too short. Just right.

"The boat," Bruce shouted down to them, pointing to the far side of the gate, out in the loch. "Take the boat. I can still get out this way. Meet you outside."

Catriona insisted on waiting to make sure her father got clear of the overhead walkway and out the door. Only then would she agree to get in the rowing boat tied to a small jetty to the side of the building.

Zander cast them off and they pushed out into the loch, an oar each, getting away from the blazing complex. Dark smoke billowed up into the evening sky, and violent flames attacked the domed roof now, half of the vast building leaking orange light through cracks and fissures. Windows burst in the heat, sending shards of glass flying into the evening air. Burning sections of wall fell into the loch, fizzing and hissing as the embers met the water's chill.

They heaved on the oars, straining through the choppy water. Zander's left shoulder howled at him, begging him to stop. But he fought against it with the last scraps of strength and grit that he had left. They matched each other stroke for stroke, side by side on a bench seat, dragging the boat out further into the loch. They intended to travel in a wide arc, landing over at the shore by the Dores Inn, but that would have to wait. When their arms couldn't take it anymore, they stopped rowing, raising the oars out of the water, letting themselves drift. They were both bent over, trying to get enough oxygen into their lungs. Booms and rattles sounded from inside the dome as it crumbled in the heat.

Zander and Catriona drifted near enough to the shore to be able to make out the police cars and vans by the fence. Donald, Hector and Bruce looked on as Mary bundled Fisher into the back of one of the cars.

"Now that is a beautiful sight," Zander said as the police car took off at speed, heading for the cells in Inverness. "Well worth the entrance fee."

They collapsed into one another, Catriona's head on Zander's shoulder. They just sat for a while, holding one another, drifting.

"Is that it? Is it really over?" Catriona said eventually.

"Yeah. I think so. If anything like this can ever really be over, yes, I think it is. As long as Fisher gets put away for a long, long time. Justice for Jules and Mike. And for poor Nigel, whatever they did to him."

"What about you? What happens to you now?"

"What do you mean?"

Catriona lifted her head up, moving around on the bench so that she could look directly at Zander. He turned to face her too. Flickers of flame reflected in his eyes.

"Does this mean you're heading back South?" she said. "Now that it's over?"

Zander looked off towards the warm glow of NessieWorld. It was quite pretty, as burning theme parks went.

"Dunno," he said. "There's no job for me there. No reason for me to go back. Thought I might stick around here."

Catriona's eyebrow raised.

"And what exactly would you do around here?"

"I heard there's a theme park going cheap. Slightly fire damaged. Might try my hand at being in the Nessie business. Mind you, I could do with some help."

Catriona's mouth softened into a smile, and she moved closer to him, their faces now just inches apart.

"By the way, did you mean what you said back there?" she said.

"A little more specific?"

"About me being a friend. A friend you could rely on."

"Of course. Absolutely."

"Oh."

"Why 'oh'?"

"A friend. That's fine with me. Friends are good. That's totally okay."

"I don't know why, but I'm sensing that's not totally okay?"

"Well, it's just that friendship rights don't usually include pressing ourselves up against one another in wet clothes. Which would be a shame."

They moved even closer, their lips almost touching, eyes locked.

"I see your point. Do you want me to...?"

"Just shut up and kiss me."

As flames danced behind them, turning the NessieWorld dream to ashes, and as blue police lights strobed the darkening sky, they moved the final millimetres together. And as their lips brushed, a monstrous thump from under the boat launched them up in the air and over the side.

The truth. It's out there.

Or in there.

Or under there.

It's somewhere.

Probably.

Printed in Great Britain
by Amazon

21539837R00192